Piping Her TUNE

By

MAGGIE BROWN

Bella
BOOKS

2015

Bella Books, Inc.
P.O. Box 10543
Tallahassee, FL 32302

First Bella Books Edition 2015

Editor: Shelly Rafferty
Cover Designer: Judith Fellows

ISBN: 978-1-59493-460-5

About the Author

Maggie is an Australian, born in Queensland. She looks upon situations with a humorous eye and likes a good joke. Her love of books led her to become an author in her own right. *Piping Her Tune* is her third novel published by Bella Books.

Dedication

To my readers. May this book give you some exciting hours to escape into another world. Enjoy!

Acknowledgments

A big thank you to my editor, Shelly Rafferty. With a firm hand, she lifted the quality of my writing to another level. Her insight and expertise was invaluable, and inspired me with a new confidence. She also bridged the geographical gap between us, and made me feel not so isolated living so far away from my publishing company. Thanks too to the Bella team for their production of this book.

I had fun writing this novel. The characters are a product of my imagination, as is the mining company. However, the downturn in the mining industry is a very real situation in Australia today.

Every portrait that is painted with feeling is a portrait of the artist, not the sitter.

-Oscar Wilde

CHAPTER ONE

Abby Benton dipped her brush into the oils on the palette. Colours swirled onto the bristles, the ochres and flesh tints ready to be added to the portrait. As she layered the paint on the tightly stretched canvas, she struggled with the need to hurry. The whole business had turned into the worst nightmare—time wasn't just running out; it was bolting away.

"Do you mind moving to the left slightly, Ms Myers?"

"How many times do I have to tell you to call me Victoria?" Victoria Myers set her shoulders in a stiff line and shuffled a little. "Is this the right pose?"

"I'm painting your lips so I would appreciate if you closed them," ordered Abby with more authority. Teeth always ruined a portrait—they invariably looked like tombstones.

When the mouth jammed shut, Victoria looked like she'd sucked a lemon. "Relax. Just be natural," Abby called soothingly.

When she'd first met the businesswoman, Abby had been intrigued. Photographs hadn't done her justice; Victoria was much more vibrant in the flesh—an artist's dream. Her skin was smooth and flawless; the contours of her cheekbones delicately enhanced the dark eyes which simmered under arched brows and long lashes; her black glossy hair cascaded to her shoulders, and her body was tall and slender. To Abby she was the epitome of elegance, and it was no wonder she'd hit the tabloid pages as one of Australia's most eligible women. Not only was Victoria a natural beauty, she was also extremely wealthy, one of the major shareholders of the giant coal and iron ore company, Orianis Minerals. Abby hadn't felt a hint of envy. To be allowed to paint her was a reward in itself.

But after three weeks, Abby's esteem—or rather hero worship if she was honest with herself—had deteriorated into frustration. Victoria had proven an exasperating subject, constantly on her iPhone. Although Abby was prepared to make some concessions, it seemed hardly fair for Victoria not to give the full posing time. Why she had consented to be the subject of her Archibald entry was beyond Abby's comprehension.

The guidelines of the Archibald, the most prestigious portraiture competition in Australia, stipulated that the subject had to be someone in the public eye. Three months earlier, Abby had written a letter to the mining magnate to ask if she would sit for a portrait, though she hadn't really expected a reply. When Victoria agreed, Abby thought she'd won gold lotto. Now she wholeheartedly regretted asking. She'd be lucky to get the damn thing finished.

She glanced at her watch—five minutes before the session was over. Out the window, the light was declining as fast as her mood. She took out her camera and adjusted the settings. "I'll take some photos, Ms…um…Victoria, so I can continue until the next session."

Another ring from Victoria's phone stabbed the air. Abby felt like screaming as the pose again disintegrated. *Crap! It'll take me ages to get it right again.*

She tapped her foot on the old sheet protecting the floor; the cover was so stained it could almost be mistaken for an extension of the work. She looked round the room, trying to ignore the phone conversation. The studio was el cheapo, but the dearest rent she could afford. Not an inspiring room for creativity; it was pokey, there was no air-con and the dull green wallpaper had a shitty, tight, geometrical pattern. With a shake of her head, she turned her attention back to the painting. *Six sittings and it's only half finished. Panic stations, girl!* At the rate Victoria's calls appeared, she had been lucky to get ten minutes out of the two-hour sessions, not nearly enough for a canvas so big. And with her new style, she needed all the time she could get. But as much as she preferred to paint from life, it had become abundantly clear she would have to complete the work from photos.

While she waited for Victoria to finish, Abby cleaned the brushes, her temper fraying as the seconds frittered by. "Please, can you ring back later? I have to be somewhere in an hour." To enforce the words she waved her hands. Oil-tinged turps flicked off the bristles like shrapnel and peppered the Armani dress with coloured blobs.

Victoria said a hurried goodbye into the phone as she lurched backwards. "What the hell!" She quickly surveyed the damage and glared back at Abby. "Have you any idea what this dress cost?" Then with deliberation, she eyed her up and down. "No, I guess you don't."

Those words were the last straw. "Excuse me? That remark was insulting."

Victoria flushed. "Sorry. I'm a bit frazzled. Work has been extra busy lately."

"*Sorry* doesn't cut it, Victoria. You're not the only one under a great deal of pressure."

"I said I was out of line. Let it go. Please."

Abby ignored the begrudging apology—it didn't salve any of her hurt. The woman obviously looked upon her as a poor relation. She didn't know why Victoria's judgmental opinion upset her so much, but it did. "You should think before you speak," she snapped testily.

"I beg your pardon. Who do you think you're talking to?" said Victoria, her voice equally as forceful as Abby's.

Abby swatted irritably at a fly hovering close to the wet paint. The insect deftly avoided the swipe and landed with a splat into the oil. "You're someone who doesn't give a damn about other people's feelings."

"For heaven's sake, I apologised, didn't I? What bee's in your bonnet? Or maybe I should say fly..." Victoria made a tiny sound through her teeth which Abby took to be a snicker.

She untied the strings of her apron and jerked it off. "It's no joke. I would have ignored the remark if that was the only thing you've done. I've had to put up with you denying me my allotted time ever since we started. You're obviously not prepared to set aside your work for the portrait. You've been the most difficult subject I've ever had."

Victoria folded her hands in her lap and her eyes narrowed. "Oh, am I indeed? Well, I've got responsibilities which I can't ignore. You must have known that when you asked me to pose."

"Then why the heck did you agree? I could have invited someone else who would have been more accommodating," retorted Abby.

"What a pity you didn't. We would have both been far less stressed. You make pissing people off an art form."

"And you don't? Pleaseeee!"

"Maybe we should quit this before we go too far," said Victoria, turning her head to look out the window. "How many more sittings will you be requiring?"

"You'll be happy to know I'll make this the last one," said Abby as she attached her camera and pushed the tripod in front of Victoria. "I'll take some shots to finish the painting and you can get back to your precious office. If you're prepared to keep still, I won't keep you any longer than necessary."

"Good," said Victoria, freezing in her pose.

Abby manipulated the camera quickly, zeroing in on Victoria's face, neck, shoulders. *Victoria might be a bitch, but she has flawless skin.*

"We're done here," Abby muttered.

Victoria abruptly rose, imparted a perfunctory word of thanks and hurried to the door.

As she watched her walk off, Abby uttered a parting shot: "If you're so worried about your damn dress, send me the bill for the dry cleaning."

Victoria didn't bother to turn around as she replied, "If you insist."

As the door slammed behind her difficult subject, Abby was already planning what the finished portrait would look like. She quickly tidied up. In ten minutes she was expected at the Legal Aid building for her evening shift in their translating and interpreting department.

A struggling artist had to eat.

* * *

The next day in her office, Victoria was unsettled as she mulled over the tiff. She knew she should never have personally attacked the artist, but Abby Benton had a knack of annoying her. Victoria's agreement to pose for the portrait would have to go down as one of the worst decisions of her life. She was aware the tension between the two of them was mostly her fault with her work calls, but Abby had to take some responsibility. Her reaction had been over the top, as far as Victoria was concerned.

When Abby's letter of invitation to pose arrived, she had been flattered, so she immediately Googled the artist's profile. Abby's gallery, though not large, was impressive—the kind of paintings Victoria admired: contemporary with vivid colours. Although the thought of having her own portrait painted was tempting, she had to decline, not having time in her schedule.

However, Victoria unwisely produced the letter as a talking point at a party late one night. "Have a look at this. This woman wants to paint me," she announced. Her mother's words of wisdom, 'when the wine is in, the wit is out' were the last things on her mind.

"You're kidding me," said her friend Annabelle. "Are you going to let her?"

"No way. I'm far too busy."

"Come on, Vic, it'll be a blast," said Annabelle. Her entreaty was enthusiastically applauded amid raucous laughter.

Victoria brushed at a trickle of chardonnay that had escaped the corner of her mouth. "What the hell. Why not?"

"I'll send her an email now." Annabelle disappeared in a flash to the study.

In the days that followed, Victoria hadn't given Annabelle's enthusiasm another thought; the last couple of hours at the party had been quite hazy. A week later, Abby's reply turned up. Victoria went into a cold sweat. The company was extra busy with the downturn in exports, which made her time too valuable to squander. On the horizon loomed an overseas trip to personally negotiate new sales. Before she went, she had so much to organize, but she was committed to the painting.

The whole business had ended up a disaster. Not only had it taken up too much of her time, but the offhanded way Abby ordered her about like a piece of meat to be eaten by the canvas had been demoralizing.

* * *

Abby, completely focused in the artistic zone, painted day and night when she wasn't at Legal Aid. Her determination to exhibit the *real* Victoria was reinforced by the bill she received from the dry-cleaning service: the total cost of damage and repair was more than she normally paid for a new dress.

Layer upon layer of oils brought the huge portrait to life, surpassing anything she had ever produced. The portrait was more adventurous than her previous works, with its impressionistic, slightly abstract style, the colours reminiscent of Fauvian art with its bold undisguised brush strokes in high-keyed, vibrant hues. She used the palette knife as well to emphasis the structure and form, and elongated the face and upper torso to a small degree. And without a qualm, for once in her life Abby let her emotions rule her talent. Victoria's confrontational words echoed in her head as she worked. Ever so subtly, she incorporated all the undesirable traits she imagined the businesswoman possessed, not really aware she was doing so.

Finally, she stood back to study the finished canvas. The colour and composition were exactly the effect she had striven for. But as she assessed her work, Abby's mind moved from critiquing its artistic merit, to the overall likeness. Even though it was more an intricate coalescence of colour rather than a distinct form, Victoria was still instantly recognizable. Abby swallowed as she stared at the canvas, and comprehension of what she had produced sank in. And the entry was due—she couldn't change anything, the oil would never dry. In the painting Victoria was no longer a child of Aphrodite. Encapsulated in a background of fiery reds and oranges, she looked rather like the devil...

CHAPTER TWO

In early July, Abby received the news that her portrait of Victoria had been chosen as a finalist. She gulped, proud of her achievement though worried. Her anger gone, she realized the enormity of what she had done. Victoria Myers was going to murder her, or worst-case scenario, sue the pants off her.

Not that she could blame her. Abby should have been more understanding about Victoria's work. She was, after all, the CEO of a very large organization, one that required her full attention. After she bundled the canvas off for the Archibald judging, Abby had gone about her daily life in trepidation. Whether she won the competition or not, the painting would be viewed in the Art Gallery of New South Wales for a lengthy period, as well as being posted on the Internet to flit merrily around the world in cyberspace.

After a phone call informed her that she had won the coveted Packing Room Prize, she seesawed between exhilaration and apprehension. Congratulations poured in all day, reporters wanted interviews, and her portrait of the mining magnate flashed on the screens in nearly every home over the vast country. Reduced to television-size, the painting made Victoria look even more stark and forbidding.

As much as she was proud of her work, Abby was besieged by guilt. She had admired Victoria for years for having reached a top executive position in a male-dominated profession, and now she had set her up for public ridicule. Why had she let the woman get to her like that? Abby fervently prayed Victoria wouldn't come to the awards ceremony.

* * *

Just as Victoria strolled out the boardroom, her phone rang. She checked the ID: Annabelle. With some relief, Victoria reminded herself she'd had enough business for one day. The shareholders' meeting had been particularly gruelling; everyone wanted huge dividends which were not possible in the current fiscal climate. The shareholders should have been darn grateful the company's share price was holding its own.

"Hi Annabelle. What's up, chick?"

"Did you watch the news tonight?"

Victoria frowned as she caught the quaver in Annabelle's voice. "I've been in a meeting all day. You sound strange. What's happened?"

"You better get on the Internet and look at the headlines."

"What am I supposed to be looking for?"

"The Archibald Packing Room Prize."

Victoria felt a flush of pride for Abby. Though they had parted so acrimoniously, Victoria hadn't been able to fully discard the image of the artist from her mind. There had been something about her…"Did she win?"

"Yes, but…just ring me when you've seen it."

"Okay. I'm about ready to go home so I'll look when I get there."

"Do it now, Vic." The words came out as a loud screech.

Victoria stared hard at her phone and hurried to her office. Her fingers drummed impatiently on the polished desk as she waited for the site to pop up. The photo of the portrait morphed onto the screen; all she could do was stare. The painting was brilliant; there was no question of that. The style was arresting, the colours superb as they melted together in harmony. But as the full extent of how she had been depicted sank in, hurt and betrayal rushed through her.

She hit the Print Screen button on her keyboard, and settled in her sturdy leather chair to study the image. A mass of vibrant colours was her first impression. Abby had incorporated in her usual impressionistic style a slightly abstract variation. She'd captured Victoria's likeness to a T (her imperious cheekbones were hard not to recognize), but her elongated form, in a stern, unsmiling mien did not make Victoria attractive. Far from it. She looked rigid and unforgiving. And added to that, the fiery background smacked of an apocalyptic battlefield.

Was that how Abby saw her? *Hell!*

Victoria heaped a double shot of coffee into a cup to boost her flagging spirits. She swallowed a mouthful—its bitterness matched her mood.

The phone jangled; she composed herself before she answered. "Hi, chick."

"Did you see it?"

"Yep."

"Well? Aren't you fuming?" Annabelle paused. "That was perhaps a poor choice of words…"

Anger now replaced the hurt and Victoria spat out the words, "She's going to be very sorry she did *that* to me."

"What are you going to do? Sue her?"

"Nothing so crass. Get your best outfit ready. We're going to the awards ceremony next week."

* * *

Abby slipped on her dress and peered in the long mirror in the hallway. Her eyes widened—the person reflected in the glass was a stranger. The hairdresser had done wonders with her hair; the blond curls had been arranged high on her head to accentuate the length of her neck. The visit to the salon afterwards for a makeup application had completed the transformation. Her freckles had vanished, her eyes were luminous and her lips: plump cherries. The long white dress with its scalloped neckline was worth every penny. The frock draped stylishly over her body. Abby swivelled round to study herself from every angle. Even though she remained naturally curvy, judo classes had certainly whipped off any excess fat. For once in her life she felt attractive.

Her mother patted her arm. "You look very nice, dear. Put in your contacts tonight."

Abby smiled. A fussbudget, her mum seemed oblivious to the fact that Abby was in her thirties, quite capable of looking after herself. But, not able to fully discard the role of dutiful daughter, Abby put aside her glasses and slid the slippery discs over her eyeballs. "Shall we be off, Mum? The taxi should be here any moment."

Judy Benton, her plump face creased in a smile, wove their arms together. "I'm so proud of you, dear."

Abby tried to smile, though failed miserably. She had nothing to be proud about. In spite of the praise she'd received from the press and positive reviews from prominent art critics, she had made Victoria Myers the laughingstock of the nation.

As she passed through the imposing columns of the NSW Art Gallery, Abby felt humble. Over the years, some of Australia's most prominent artists had walked this walk on such an afternoon. The exhibition rooms were already crowded with the elite of the country's artistic community when they entered. Expensively dressed patrons mingled with artists, who compensated for their limited budgets by wearing creative outfits. Abby chuckled at some of the getups.

Jittery as she moved through, she heaved a relieved sigh to see that Victoria was nowhere in sight. For the next hour, she and her mother studied the portraits and grazed from the assortment of bite-sized nibbles, canapés and tasty little savoury tarts.

Abby was beginning to tire of accolades she continuously received by the time she spied a lawyer friend from Legal Aid.

"There's Adam," she muttered to her mother. She waved and gave him her first genuine smile of the night. "Do you mind?" Her mother smiled. "I'm happy to browse alone."

Adam was nursing a beer. "I thought you might need some moral support," he offered. "You look ravishing, by the way." Abby looked at him fondly. His support was welcome. They had an uncomplicated friendship, for not only did they share the same sense of humour and basic values, they were the only two gays in the office. She gave him a quick hug. "It's all a bit daunting being thrust into the limelight. Thank goodness Victoria Myers didn't turn up."

He set his face into a haughty look and poked a devilish finger from each side of his head. Abby burst into giggles. Trust Adam to see the funny side of a disastrous situation. A waiter appeared with a tray of drinks, and she took another glass of Riesling, savouring its acidic, fruity taste as it washed over her tongue. Things looked brighter; time to appreciate her achievement.

Adam was pleasant company. He had just started a joke involving an Irishman and a leprechaun, but stopped mid-sentence, his mouth agape. "She's here," he stammered.

Abby followed his gaze across the room. Victoria stood in the doorway, appearing totally at ease as she swept her eyes over the gallery floor. Abby tried not to stare. Victoria was breathtaking, and the dress—heavens knows what it cost. She looked like she had been poured into it, every curve of her magnificent body accentuated.

Abby glanced at Adam. His mouth had formed into an O— even her gay friend appreciated the beauty of the woman. He raised his eyebrows. "How could you make *that* apparition into a Jezebel?"

She slapped his arm. "I found her completely self-centred and very difficult to work with."

Victoria threaded her way through the crowd. Her face held a saintly quality as she greeted people, her smile benevolent. She fairly glided from one gallery guest to the next. The auburn-haired woman by her side was movie queen material as well, though she didn't radiate Victoria's charisma. Abby forced herself to turn away as a warning bell pealed in her ear. After watching Victoria's performance, Abby would end up being the she-devil tonight: a cynical, jealous, bitch of an artist.

* * *

The artist was nowhere to be seen. Victoria fixed an angelic countenance on her face as she moved into the crowd. After a while she tired of the pretence. *As soon as the presentation ceremony is finished, I'm out of here.* Annabelle must have been feeling the same way, for she whispered in her ear, "Stuff the art. I've just seen a delectable morsel in the corner on the right and I've gotta have a taste of it."

Victoria growled her disapproval. She hated that her friend had no morals regarding casual seduction. Whatever vices Victoria had, they definitely weren't in the sexual department; if anything, she was straitlaced, the product of a strict religious upbringing. Sex without knowing and liking a partner had no appeal whatsoever. She cast a cursory glance over at her friend's objet de desire. The blonde looked pleasant enough and even a little familiar, though, after she grappled with her memory, she couldn't quite place her. Then it hit. *Far out! It's Abby Benton.*

Victoria had only seen Abby with her hair pulled back in a ponytail, her face smeared with paint and dressed in an apron nearly to her ankles, with a pair of black-rimmed glasses perched on her nose. But here she had been transformed into an attractive woman, with a curvy athletic body which filled out her simple white dress. Out of nowhere, a small stab of concern hit—Annabelle had her sights set on her.

"Don't be an idiot. That's Abby Benton."

"So? She's available, isn't she?"

The little muscles around Victoria's mouth twitched. "You haven't got a dog's hope there. She would have seen you come in with me."

"Wanna bet?"

"Don't be so sure. She's with a man anyhow, so she's straight."

"Bullshit," whispered Annabelle. "He's got 'I'm gay' stamped all over his forehead. Really, Vic, you should get out more. See you later."

Victoria squared her shoulders as she watched her friend join the pair in the corner. It was time. She eased her way through the throng of people to her portrait. The crowd parted like the Red Sea.

The gallery curator, a dapper man with a paisley pocket square and a pinched mouth, hurried to her side and sniffed cautiously. "It's an excellent portrait, Ms Myers. We're so delighted to have you here."

A soft laugh purred out before Victoria raised her voice. She crossed her arms over her chest and cocked her head to one side. "It's very good. The colours are amazing, though I'd say Ms Benton is probably one hell of a dissatisfied shareholder."

The quiet that had fallen over the room was broken by titters.

He shuffled from one foot to the other. "She's very talented."

"I suppose you could say that. What a pity though her perspective on life is so negative. She obviously sees the Mr Hyde in people. Not a good trait for a portrait artist, is it? I doubt anyone would like to be her next customer if she made *me* look like this."

"An artist's perception of the subject is always unique, which makes the good ones stand out from the crowd."

Her eyes glinted. "Ah, yes. Beauty is in the eye of the beholder, as they say. Benton may perhaps be more suited as a war artist. There's plenty of death and destruction on the battlefield without having to imagine it." She reached in her purse and held out an envelope. "Nevertheless, one must be above all that. She's been her own worst enemy. Now I digress. The reason I came was to give the gallery a donation."

He slid open the envelope and his eyes widened. "Very generous indeed."

"My pleasure. I try to support the arts."

He smiled and fussily tucked the envelope into his suit coat. "I'm sure the trustees will be most appreciative. Now it's time to announce the winners."

* * *

Abby looked away from Adam as she grew aware someone approached. She blew out a nervous breath as she recognized Victoria's companion.

The woman touched her arm and smiled. "Hi there, I'm Annabelle. Excuse me for interrupting but I thought I should meet the artist…"

"You came in with Victoria, right?" Abby waved her hand at Adam. "This is my friend Adam and I am…"

"Yes, I know…Abby Benton. Victoria Myers is a friend," interrupted Annabelle. "In spite of that fact, I wanted to tell you how much *I* enjoyed your work." She plucked a snippet of fluff off Abby's shoulder strap. "Have you been painting long?"

For a moment Abby was taken aback by Annabelle's disloyalty to Victoria. Out of the corner of her eye, she caught Adam's wink. "I'll leave you two to talk," he said before he sidled away into the crowd.

Conscious of Annabelle's scrutiny, Abby made an effort to be pleasant. She resisted the impulse to cross her arms over her breasts and continued the small talk. "I've been painting for many years. Are you an artist?"

Annabelle raised an eyebrow. "Hardly, though I can appreciate beauty if I see it."

Despite the fact Abby had little inexperience at flirting, these advances seemed childish. She ignored the innuendo. "What's your favourite portrait here?"

"I prefer my subjects in the flesh."

Really annoyed now, Abby stared at her. Was the woman for real? She guessed she probably should be flattered, but Annabelle had fast become a nuisance and all Abby wanted was to see what Victoria was doing. She craned her head to search the room, and spied Victoria chatting with the curator. She hissed. Annabelle turned to look. "Hell," muttered Abby. "What's she going to say? She doesn't look upset at all."

"Believe you me, she's cranky as hell."

"How can you tell? She's looks composed to me."

"By the way she's standing; she's wound up tight as a spring. I wouldn't like to be in your shoes."

The room fell quiet and the conversation floated over as clear as a rustle of wind on a fine summer's day. Abby winced and tears prickled behind her lids as she listened to the words. She imagined her career disappearing down the plug hole. As Victoria handed over the cheque, she snarled and anger replaced the desire to cry. "The goddamn woman is throwing money at him."

Annabelle laughed. "Oh, yes. She's making him aware she's more important than you."

"You don't have to be a rocket scientist to work that one out. She's denigrated my work in front of all these people and doesn't give a damn."

"She's hurt. Victoria is a lot of things, but not cruel."

Though sceptical, Abby held her tongue. Clapping resounded through the room, ceasing further conversation. The official party had moved to circle the microphone. "The presentations have started. Let's watch."

The ceremony began with the Wynne and Sulman prizes first. When it came to her turn, Abby walked forward; she kept her head high as she accepted her award with a gracious smile and then joined her mother. "Come on, Mum, let's go."

"Don't you want to see if you've won the major prize?"

"I just want to get out of here," muttered Abby.

Judy Benton rose, looking formidable, though she wasn't any taller than her daughter. Her plump body was set in a firm stance, her knobbed, twisted fingers clutched around Abby's wrist. "Abby Charlotte Benton. You will not let that nasty Myers woman ruin your evening. We came here to see the ceremony and stay we shall until it's over."

Abby merely nodded; it was useless to argue when her mother spoke in that tone of voice. The winner was announced and when it wasn't her, she pushed back the feeling of disappointment. "Okay. Let's go, Mum. Please."

"Just one minute then, dear."

Abby watched in horror as her mother went over to Victoria. She came back to join Abby with a smile. "I'm right to go."

"What did you say to her?"

"Just a few pertinent words to show my displeasure. She got the message."

* * *

Victoria strode to the back of the room to watch the awards ceremony. It came to the Packing Room prize; she leaned forward to watch Abby walk forward to receive it. Abby didn't return to Annabelle's side and Victoria felt a twinge of relief. Whatever else Abby had done, she didn't deserve to be one of Annabelle's conquests, most likely to be discarded like a used dishcloth in the morning.

After the major Archibald winner was announced, a white-haired woman who was a heavier, older version of Abby, moved directly towards Victoria.

"Abby forgot to include two important things in your portrait," the woman began with a whisper.

Victoria frowned. "Oh? And what's that?"

"Your horns and pitchfork."

"And who are you?"

"Her mother." Without another word she rejoined her daughter and they disappeared into the night.

Victoria bit her lip as a dull headache crept into her skull. Annabelle appeared at her side, apparently miffed that Abby had rebuffed her advances.

"Not the friendliest sort," Annabelle offered.

"I told you she wouldn't be susceptible to your charms."

"No, she wasn't. Pity you put her in such bad mood. You've been holding out on me, Vic. If I remember correctly, you said she was plain. You must need glasses. I wouldn't mind having another go at breaching that particular fortress. She's a cutie and has a sort of charming innocence about her."

"Does everything have to revolve around a conquest with you?" snapped Victoria.

"Oh, my, aren't we touchy tonight? I would have thought that casting aspersions on someone's work would have put you in a good mood."

"She sullied my reputation."

"Oh come now, that's rather dramatic, isn't it? With all your money, it doesn't matter what people think. Your pride's hurt, that's all. But she has real talent and you ground your heel into it. Except for the fact she made you look like the Whore of Babylon, the painting's fabulous. Sometimes you can be a real turd, Vic. Now, I'm going for a drink with the girls. Do you want to come?"

Victoria shook her head. "I'm going home to bed." She began to feel nauseous as she went out into the cheerless street. As she walked to the parking lot, she scuffed her shoe on the concrete pavement. Why had she said those things to the curator? She should have swallowed her pride and laughed it off.

CHAPTER THREE

Victoria smiled as Malcolm Hardy entered the room. The Chairman of the Board of Directors was not only an old friend but a father figure as well. Even in his midsixties he was handsome, though the years were winning. His thick dark hair was shot through with silver, his once angular features padded out with age. He was gazing at her as though he wished he were somewhere else. She felt a niggling feeling of concern—it wasn't a social call. "You look like you've something important to tell me, Malcolm."

Malcolm fidgeted, seemingly of two minds about where to start. "You're probably not going to like what I've got to say."

Her smile faded. It wasn't like him not to be forthright. "Well, out with it. What am I not going to like?"

"It's about your trip to negotiate the contracts. The board has agreed you're the one who has to go and you'll be gone for six months. As a single woman, you may be hassled."

"So what? I'm used to it. I'll have two support staff and can take care of myself."

Malcolm shook his head. "Only Fiona can go. That's our dilemma. We can't spare anyone else for that length of time. The board would like you to take a person—a partner—with you for your protection."

"A partner?"

"Not an employee, but someone who can act not only as your assistant, but also will serve as your personal—shall we say—companion. Six months on the road is a long time. Though you're no stranger to the demands of negotiating in a high-powered man's world, we'd feel more comfortable if you were...ah...taken. In a foreign country, it can be difficult for a woman alone, and you're going to look at factories and mines. We feel that, if you present yourself as though you were 'in a relationship', it will make things safer for you overall."

Annoyance fizzled through Victoria. "You know I'm gay. I've no intention of hooking up with a man for the business, even if it's purely platonic."

Malcolm's hands fluttered up in the air. "Whoa, we weren't suggesting that. A woman would be better—if it was a male, most negotiators might expect to deal with him." He cast her an embarrassed look. "Are you seeing anyone?"

"When do I get any time off to date? I'm married to this goddamn office for god sake. So, what do you want me to do, pluck someone off the street?"

"Would any of your friends be willing to go?"

"They're all professionals with careers of their own. It would be asking too much."

Malcolm formed his fingers into a steeple. "I presumed that such would be the case. I've been giving the situation a lot of thought. The alliance would be simply one of convenience, so she would only be a consultant and a binding contract would ensure that."

Victoria shrugged. Fiona, a dour Scotswoman, while being an excellent administrative assistant and good friend, poorly lacked in the social department and retired to bed early. "Okay. It'll be someone else to talk to. If Fiona were my only company, I'd definitely need someone else for more conversation."

The chairman patted her hand. "Good. I'm glad you've agreed. It'll take a load off my mind to see you have another person with you for safety reasons."

"So how are we going to find someone?"

"I'll set up some interviews. Let's make a list of what her accomplishments should be, shall we?" said Malcolm.

Victoria rapped her fingers on the arm of the chair. "I don't want anyone too young. I'm thirty-seven, so I would expect her—whoever she is—to converse with intelligence and maturity."

"Point taken. Naturally she must have another language other than English. It'll help if she's multilingual, but Mandarin or Japanese would certainly be necessary."

"We'll have to have another requirement as well to narrow the field down or Fiona will be days trying to sort it out."

Malcolm nodded. "Okay. What about speaking two other languages and being proficient in some form of martial art? It'll be handy in some places you're going."

"And single. I don't want a jealous lover chasing me."

"Good point," Malcolm chuckled. "Reasonably attractive, do you think?"

"Sounds fine." Victoria forced a laugh. "So where are we going to find such a paragon? With these added attributes, such a woman is not going to be out there hanging on a tree."

"Since it's a partnership of convenience, it won't matter if she's straight or gay. Most women would be willing to go if we offer enough money."

"She'll have to be well compensated to give up a career for that length of time."

"We'll work the wage out later, just as long as it's enough to attract good applicants. Let me place an ad in the Saturday paper and Fiona can whittle the list down to four. I'll invite them to a dinner party and you can choose which one would suit. It'll be an opportunity as well to set down the ground rules; you're the one who has to live with her. Bring a friend with you for support if you like." He got up, then hesitated. "Do try to make sure you relax and treat some of the trip as a holiday. You haven't been your usual self the last couple of months, so it's time to reduce your stress."

Back in her office, Victoria gave some thought to suitable women she knew but rejected them almost immediately. Living together in close proximity could lead to unwanted familiarity. A stranger would have no expectations. Annabelle perhaps? They were best friends—not lovers. *Heavens no, Annabelle's too much of a loose cannon, too indiscreet. Not good for diplomatic relations.* The thought of a complete stranger as her partner, roiled Victoria's stomach into knots. Chantal was in town. Maybe she would consent to come along to the dinner to help vet the applicants. She was planning to see the Frenchwoman now that she was in Sydney.

Victoria shook her head, despondent. What a washout she was, in her late thirties and they had to pay someone to be with her. Where had all the years gone? Why hadn't she ever met anyone special enough to want to settle down? Her few relationships in the last ten years had fizzled out in a matter of weeks. She tried to think about the last time she'd had a date. One—maybe one and a half years ago. Marge or Meg someone.

God help me. I'm married to my vibrator. But at least it can be turned off while I answer the phone.

* * *

The advertisement in the Saturday paper immediately got Abby's attention:

Wanted: Personal Assistant for a six-month assignment overseas. Must be energetic, multilingual, diplomatic, flexible and competent in some form of martial art. Generous compensation and benefits. This position offers an exciting opportunity for travel and to be a part of a progressive organization. Please remit a letter on interest, vita: M Hardy, Esq, P/O Box 1756, Vaucluse 2030.

Excited, Abby reread it—the position seemed made for her. If she could possibly score such a post, it would solve all her pressing financial worries. With her mother's constant medical bills and no commissions following the Archibald fiasco, she was struggling to keep her head above water. The Packing Room prize, although prestigious, only netted her fifteen hundred dollars. A pittance for all the work she put into the painting. Her job with Legal Aid was only part-time and not well paid, which left her to live from one pay packet to the next. As much as she hated to do it, it was time to abandon her art and seek well-paid employment. The ad signalled perhaps the start of a promising future.

She typed out a required letter and composed her résumé with no mention of her artistic experience. The position was solely related to her linguistic skills and judo training.

Two weeks had elapsed before an email informed Abby that she had been successful in gaining an interview. She was over the moon. The news that the interview was to be held at a dinner party, she found rather odd, but accepted it pragmatically. As it seemed to be something of a diplomatic appointment, the employer probably wanted to view her social skills.

Two days before the event, Abby took a shopping trip to find something to wear. As her budget was limited, it took all morning to find a suitable dress. As luck would have it, she found a stunning one at a small boutique, reduced to half price because of a small stain on the hem. The low-cut red dress fit her snugly, making her look quite sophisticated.

On the day of the dinner, her work at the office was particularly busy. She had no time to waste. As she flew home to get ready with only an hour to spare, a nagging thought persisted. Maybe she should have done more research before she jumped in boots and all. There had been only a Vaucluse house address on the letterhead, which probably meant she'd be paid by a private person. *But hey—what the heck—at the very worst, I'm getting a free meal. Better than vegging out with a take-away in front of the telly.*

With the final touches to her outfit completed, Abby put on her glasses reserved for social functions. At six she dialled for a taxi. Half an hour later, it reached an avenue of luxurious homes overlooking an expanse of parkland. The cab slowed.

Abby gazed in awe. While her street smelt of mortgage, this one reeked of money. She was pleased she'd opted to take a taxi rather than drive her minivan. After ten years, the van had settled comfortably into a rent-a-bomb look. Not an appropriate vehicle for the occasion.

The driver nosed the cab through an iron gate, and followed a silver Jag up the tree-lined driveway to a stately Italian-style house surrounded by tailored shrubs and manicured lawns. Abby alighted from the cab, blinking through the bifocals, rather shell-shocked at the opulence of the marble portico. As she walked up the path, one of her heels, which she knew were ridiculously high, caught in a crack between the pavers. She stumbled and two hands reached out to steady her. A voice, smooth like a good malt whiskey, purred in her ear, "Are you all right, *mon ami?*"

Her reply, *Je vais bien, merci*, brought a wide smile from the woman who clutched her arm. "Ah, you speak French. *Très bon.*"

Abby stared, enchanted by the vivacious creature holding her. She was of average height like herself, but the aura radiating from her exquisite features made her seem much taller. She dominated the space around her.

"Did you come alone?" asked Abby shyly.

"*Oui.*" With a dimpled grin, she twined her arm through Abby's. "Come. You would do me a great honour if we went in together."

The butterflies in Abby's stomach vanished immediately. She leaned into the body beside her, mesmerized by the warmth spreading into her skin. "I'd be delighted. I'm Abby."

"And I'm Chantal. 'Tis a pleasure to meet you, *chérie*. So, let us go in."

The door opened after their first knock, the tuxedoed man who showed them inside as imposing as the house. Abby quashed down a moment of panic, but Chantal strolled down the hallway as if a butler answering the door was as common as breathing. Abby, humming "Money, Money, Money," trotted along behind. The butler led them through the house to an outside patio where people stood socializing, while a waiter moved through offering drinks and nibbles. The house was on top of a hill; the view over the harbour was breathtaking. The last rays of sun shimmered on the water dotted with white sails. The garden setting was cosy, with clusters of flowers and a hint of sweet perfume in the air.

Chantal and Abby stepped through the patio doors, and a woman hurried forward to greet them. A harassed expression clouded her face. "You must be Chantal and Abby. You're the last to arrive. I'm Fiona McPherson."

Abby smiled, happy to see someone who looked more out of place than she felt. Fiona was short and dumpy, somewhere in her fifties, with grey hair tied severely back in a bun. A Scottish burr rolled off her tongue.

"Come and meet your hosts, Malcolm and Jan Hardy," she said as she led them to an older couple who chatted with a dark-haired woman. Malcolm flashed a broad toothpaste smile when he was introduced to Chantal, obviously charmed by the Frenchwoman. Then Abby shook his hand; his eyes widened and the smile faltered. He glared at Fiona. Thrown off balance, Abby squared her shoulders, and then relaxed as his wife stepped forward quickly to circle her arm in hers. "So you're Abby Benton, the artist. How very nice to meet you. This is Emily Hawkins, another of our guests."

Emily was a tall, striking brunette, sporting an *I've-just-been-to-a-tropical-island* tan. She smiled shyly at Abby. "I'm a great fan. You painted a portrait of a friend of mine, Colin Harris. We all loved it."

"Ah, yes. Professor Harris. He was a good subject with quite distinctive features."

"We're both marine biologists and work together a lot." From the way his name spun off her lips, Abby had the impression Emily wished the professor were more than a colleague.

Chantal lit up. "So you're an artist, Abby. I'm impressed. Me, I'm hopeless when it comes to art. What about you, Fiona?"

A soft laugh from Jan interrupted. "I'm afraid Fiona is a workaholic. I realize now she doesn't follow the artistic scene."

Fiona eyed the chairman's scowl, her accent more pronounced in her answer. "Nay, I'm far too busy."

Malcolm inclined his head in agreement. "Fiona's got tunnel vision, all work and no play. It'll do her good to get away for a while." He tugged the secretary's arm and pulled her out into the lawn. "Come, we've got a few things to discuss so we can leave my wife to do the introductions."

Abby relaxed as the two moved off, though perturbed by his reaction to her. She had no idea what it was all about. She could see him cast looks over her way and mop his brow as he talked to the Scottish woman.

She returned her attention to her immediate companions. Her hostess introduced the two other women, Grace Newport and Karen Young. Grace was part Chinese with straight jet-black hair, cut short, layered around flat androgynous features. Her muscular build signalled she could kick some serious butt if pressured. Karen was small and dainty; her darkish skin suggested Mediterranean origins, although her accent was all Australian.

Jan smiled as the five women looked at her expectantly. "I imagine you're all wondering what the invitation is all about. We'll fill you in over dinner, but suffice it to say that to whom the assignment will be offered, she will be well paid, as promised. You have all been handpicked as suitable applicants; those not successful will be awarded a two-week fully paid holiday in Australia to a destination of your choice. Your presence is most appreciated, especially those who have travelled so far to attend. The cost of your travel will be reimbursed, of course. Get to know each other while I organize the meal. The guest of honour will be arriving any minute."

"Let me give you a hand, Jan," Chantal offered.

"No, I'm fine. Stay here and relax and talk to the girls. I want you to get to know them."

After she moved off inside, Karen remarked. "Well, that was cryptic. Has anyone any idea what it's all about?"

Emily shrugged her shoulders. "I haven't a clue. Maybe we can work it out, my friends. What do you all do?"

"I'm a computer analyst," said Karen.

"A mining engineer," offered Grace.

"A marine biologist," said Emily. "And Abby's an artist. None of us have anything in common."

"Actually, my main job is an interpreter for Legal Aid. My art doesn't exactly pay the bills yet," said Abby.

"And I am an event organizer. I own my own business. I'm here as a friend of our hosts," said Chantal.

Grace tossed her hands in the air. "So let's just enjoy the party. All will be revealed."

Abby sipped her wine and plucked a caviar nibble from the waiter's tray. Happy, she revelled in the intimacy among the women as they exchanged stories. She turned to the door when she heard it open.

Victoria Meyers stood on the patio, elegantly dressed in a dark blue pantsuit, the yellow silk shirt underneath open enough to expose the soft swell of her breasts. Her hair hung loose over her collar, her makeup was understated and flawless. The overall impression was of a sleek jungle cat ready to pounce. By her side, Annabelle stood laughing. Flustered, Abby spun back around to look for an escape. As she ducked past the waiter to hide behind the potted palm, she fought to stifle rising panic. "Hell! Hell! Hell!"

Immediately Chantal came to her side, concerned. "What's wrong, *chérie?*"

She clutched the Frenchwoman's hands as a life line and said in a low voice, "I've got to get out of here. I don't want to see her."

"Ah, *mon ami*, how can you not be seen? Stay for a little while and compose yourself."

Abby straightened her shoulders, her chin jutted in defiance. "You're right. I'm made of sterner stuff."

The older woman reached over and stroked her finger down Abby's cheek. "Come, give yourself time to calm down and put your arm through mine and we will beard the lion in his den together."

CHAPTER FOUR

Victoria knew something wrong when she spied Malcolm. His hands were clenched at his side while Fiona jiggled from one foot to the other. She quickly cut to the chase. "What the hell's happened?"

Malcolm swallowed and made an obvious effort to keep his voice even. "Everything's fine. What makes you think there's something wrong?"

"So why do you both look like you're at a funeral?"

"It's been a long day. We're just tired. I'll…I'll have to go to my study to do a few things so Fiona can do the introductions. Have a half an hour chat with the girls before you come in to dine."

Victoria eyed him with suspicion and whipped her gaze to the Scot. The older woman wouldn't meet her eye. Quickly Malcolm pulled free of Fiona's clawing hands and hurried off.

"Come on, Fiona. I'm interested to meet whom you've chosen," Victoria said sternly.

With a resigned slump of her shoulders, Victoria's assistant led the way from the lawn to the patio. Annabelle appeared at her side with a scotch and dry and murmured, "You might need this."

Victoria took the glass as she sized up the applicants. She didn't take long to form an opinion. Grace didn't appeal at all. Although from the mining industry, which was a big plus, the engineer spent most of her time furtively looking down Vic's front. Victoria had no wish to fight off advances the whole six months. Karen had a distinct charm. She was quiet, knowledgeable and definitely worth getting to know. Emily, too, had potential. She seemed astute, caring and interested in what everyone had to say. From her conversation, she was a seasoned traveller keen to see more of the world.

"I think there were four applicants, right? Where's the other one?"

On cue, two figures emerged from behind the palm. Victoria's eyes widened. "Is this a damn joke, Fiona?"

As Fiona began to stutter, Abby poked a finger in the air, her tone caustic. "I'm an invited guest, Victoria, so you'd better be civil to me."

"You've got the hide of an elephant turning up here."

"If I'd been aware of what it was all about, I certainly wouldn't have come."

Victoria forced herself to calm down. She shot a look at the entwined arms, and only then noticed Chantal. Surprise and delight flushed through her. "I knew you were coming, but I hardly expected you to…"

"Oh, Vic, the night is turning out to be so entertaining," Chantal offered with a soft laugh. "Come, be nice to my friend Abby and give me a hug. Tell me what you've been up to all these years. It has been a long time."

Victoria relaxed and anger dimmed in her eyes as she clasped the Frenchwoman. "Too long. It's so good to see you."

Fiona seized the opportunity in the unexpected calm and suggested they adjourn to the dining room. Victoria felt Annabelle tug on her sleeve and heard the whisper in her ear. "It's time to be a good hostess."

Victoria stifled the cutting retort that hovered on her lips.

She's right. Tonight, diplomacy will have to be the better part of discretion. If I continue the confrontation with Abby, it'll only alienate the others. I'll just have to damn well ignore her the rest of the night.

She inclined her head in agreement; Fiona's face registered heartfelt relief. Without any more ceremony, Victoria took Karen's arm with one hand and Emily's with the other. She walked them into the house and the others followed in their wake. Jan Hardy greeted them at the door of the dining room and cast a look of trepidation at the CEO. Victoria regarded her, poker-faced, so she smiled. "Come in. You might like to organize the seating arrangements."

"I'd like to sit at the head of the table between Karen and Emily. Grace can sit next to Emily and Fiona, Annabelle next to Chantal." She eyed the far end of the table. "Abby can sit between you and Malcolm."

As they filed in to take their seats, Chantal patted the chair next to her. "I think Abby can sit here, if that's not a problem."

"Of course not," murmured Jan when Victoria didn't answer.

Annabelle quickly slid into the seat on the other side of Abby. "This one will do me." She looked at her friend with a hint of a challenge in her green eyes. "Is that all right, sugar?"

Victoria gritted her teeth, acutely aware of the others' stares. A muscle clenched in her jaw as she nodded.

With a satisfied smile, Annabelle moved her chair closer to the artist.

* * *

Abby felt the pressure of Annabelle's thigh pressed against her leg with disquiet. Damn the woman. How could anyone be so hormonal all the time? Was she was just promiscuous or acting out some sort of role? Well, it was a game she was definitely not going to play. Abby regarded her blandly before she cleared her throat. "Perhaps you could move your chair a bit more to the right. It'll give us room to eat."

Annabelle stiffened. She had just been rebuked, subtly but very definitely. Abby knew rejection from a woman was probably a new and very unwelcome experience. To make matters worse, Abby looked up to catch Victoria's gleam of interest.

Annabelle smiled though it didn't reach her eyes. "Of course," she said and quickly shuffled her plate and flatware slightly to the right. Abby had no doubt she was planning her next move. Conversation ceased as the soup arrived, which gave Abby time to gather her thoughts. Victoria left her edgy and disturbed. Abby stole a peep at her with fascination. The intensity about the businesswoman struck a chord. She recognized that familiar look—Victoria had had it when she was being painted, a barely contained throb under the skin. And it was hard to ignore how fetching Victoria was. Abby frowned at the thought, annoyed by the involuntary twitch of arousal. Trust her libido not to recognize the enemy. The old adage was true. Love is akin to hate, and she certainly disliked Victoria Myers.

Abby tilted her head to the side to study Chantal. The Frenchwoman was sweet, gorgeous and no doubt a fantastic lover. She tried to visualize them in bed together making love, but the thoughts provoked no reflex arousal, no erotic cravings.

"I am intrigued. You and Vic seem to have a rocky history," said Chantal, catching her gaze. "Did you have a bitter parting?"

Abby's eyes widened. "Goodness, no, she's far too sophisticated to be interested in anyone like me. She's way out of my league."

Surprise flitted across Chantal's face. "Oh, I have completely misconstrued the situation. But you do yourself an injustice. What's the story with the two of you?"

Annabelle, who finally extricated herself from her conversation with Malcolm, caught the last question. "Abby painted Vic's portrait for the Archibald," she said a little smugly.

Chantal raised her eyebrows. "A portrait? Wasn't it any good?"

Annabelle chuckled. "I've got it on my iPhone. Want to have a look?"

The picture flashed up, and Chantal drew in a sharp breath. She turned to peer closer at Abby. "It's spectacular; you are very talented. I can see though why Vic dislikes it. So, what have you against her?"

"She and I clashed badly at the studio. I found her quite rude. Then at the Archibald presentations, she denigrated my work."

"But perhaps she didn't like to be represented that way?"

Abby spooned some soup into her mouth to avoid answering. The Frenchwoman didn't continue with the questions, and gave Abby's hand a comforting squeeze. After the soup plates were taken away, Annabelle draped her arm over the back of Abby's chair. Chantal must have noticed Abby lean slightly forward to avoid contact, for she whispered in Abby's ear, "Don't worry. I'll protect you from her." Thankfully the main course appeared, which forced Annabelle to take away her arm.

* * *

Once the plates were removed, Victoria placed her hands on the table, ready to commence her speech. As every eye in the room centred on her, she felt suddenly nervous, dubious about the whole affair. Quiet interviews at the office would have been better. Competing with each other wouldn't bring out the best in the women.

She gazed round the room and kept her voice steady. "I understand you've been waiting to hear the nitty-gritty of the position. In a week I leave for a six-month tour to negotiate new contracts for Orianis Minerals. The position for which each of you has applied is a private appointment. My assistant, Fiona, will be accompanying me. However, for my protection in some foreign countries, the board members in their wisdom have decided I need a partner to accompany me on the journey. To be more specific, a partner means a personal mate, not a work employee. The woman will actually be an employee, but to the outside world for all intents and purposes, she will be someone who shares my life."

"You mean like a wife?" called out Grace, excitement in her voice.

"It'll be for appearances only when we're overseas. The arrangement will be purely platonic. Your sexual orientation is of no concern. In Australia you will be just another administrative assistant, so you won't have to suffer embarrassment if you meet people you know."

"Do you mean they actually have to pay someone to be with you?" murmured Abby, though loud enough to drift through the room.

Victoria tingled with anger. "The person chosen has to have particular attributes."

"Oh, I bet. The mind boggles," said Abby.

Victoria gripped the edge of the table harder. "This...um... partner needs to speak more languages other than English. All of you have that ability."

"Any particular ones?" asked Emily.

"We don't expect you to be fluent in them all, but suffice to say each one of you can converse in two other languages."

The marine biologist nodded. "I speak Arabic and Japanese."

"Good for you," called out Abby in Japanese. "Did you work in Japan?"

Emily slid with no effort into that native tongue. "Three years in the Okinawa region where we did a study on improving the fishing grounds."

Victoria rapped the table and hissed through her teeth. "Please speak English."

"What languages do you speak, Karen?" Abby ignored her, on a roll.

The petite computer analyst looked with hesitation at her host before she replied. "I lived in China until I was twenty-five. My father worked for Travel Company there. I speak Greek too of course—that was my parents' homeland. I can also manage some Japanese."

As Abby rattled off a few phrases in Mandarin, Victoria let out a harsh growl. The woman was making her look like a fool. The presentation was disintegrating into a farce; Malcolm looked uncomfortable and Fiona appeared agitated. Only Annabelle and Chantal seemed to be enjoying themselves. "Let's get back to business."

"What about my turn?" said Grace peevishly.

Abby raised her glass to peer at her over the rim. "And what are your specialties?"

"Mandarin and Russian."

With some effort, Abby called out a basic Russian greeting. Grace slumped back in her chair and glared sullenly.

"All right, you've proved your point. You're the best here. How many do you actually speak?" asked Victoria.

"I can speak Japanese and Mandarin fluently. French too. But rest assured, Victoria, I can manage to say 'Up yours' in a few more languages. I work for Legal Aid."

* * *

Victoria reined in her temper. A swift assessment of the situation made her realize that she needed to reassert her authority, but instinct told her it would be better done with charm. "We had to narrow down the field of applicants so we made another requirement: some experience in the martial arts. It was considered a necessity in the event you were called upon to cope in sticky situations."

Grace flexed an arm muscle. "No trouble there. You can rely on me."

"I bet she can," murmured Abby.

Karen looked a little perturbed. "Are you expecting trouble?"

"Not at all." Victoria smiled her reassurance.

"So, you expect us to be an expert in self-defence. How good do we have to be? Like James Bond or just able to kick a bloke in the crown jewels if he comes on to you?" asked Abby.

"I'm not expecting you to protect me. We'll simply be happy if you can look after yourselves."

Abby shot a fierce look back. "Okay. We have to be GI Jane and speak in many tongues, so what else is necessary for the fabulous job?"

"You have to be able to conduct yourself with propriety." The words were shouted out.

Chantal quickly covered Abby's hand resting on the table and whispered, "Let it go, *chérie*."

Abby pursed her lips but sank back into her chair without replying.

"What will be our duties?" asked Emily.

"It'll be mostly routine work, helping Fiona with computer data and the organization of bookings, etc. When there's a function, you will accompany me as my partner," said Victoria with a grin. "It won't be all work and no play. I expect there'll be plenty of time for sightseeing and night entertainment. All at our expense, of course."

"You will be paid one hundred and fifty thousand dollars for the time you will be away. Payment in two equal lumps sums, the first at the beginning and the remainder at the end of the contract. Any questions?"

"I'm sure we all agree that's an extremely generous wage," said Karen.

"Is that tax free?" called out Abby. "The taxation department will take forty-five cents on the dollar if you pay that way."

Malcolm intervened quickly. "Let me answer that one. I'm sure we can manage some creative accounting to reduce the tax, although some will have to be paid. We will be notifying the successful applicant on Sunday. Now I believe dessert will be here in a moment."

* * *

Abby pushed back her chair; claustrophobia weighed heavily on her heightened emotions. She needed to get out of the room to get herself under control. Victoria brought out the worst of her. She turned to Annabelle. "Which way's the powder room?"

"It's down the hallway to the left. Come on, I'll take you."

"There's no need. I can…"

Annabelle took her arm with a firm grasp. "Nonsense. I have to go too."

Abby stiffened. The last thing she wanted was to be alone with the woman, though she was reluctant to make a scene as she was propelled from the room. Out of sight from the others, she tried to maintain a facade of nonchalance as the redhead's hand moved from her arm to stroke her back.

"I was captivated by you at the gallery," Annabelle whispered. Abby swallowed and didn't answer. The hands slid downwards to her backside and she jerked away. "I'd appreciate if you didn't touch me."

Breathy words whispered in her ear. "But I think you're really hot. Your bickering with Vic turned me on. Would you like to go out next week?"

"Sorry. I'm too busy," said Abby, taking a step backwards.

"Come on. I can promise you'll have a very good time."

"What don't you understand? I'm not interested—full stop!" Abby let her dislike show as she stared her in the eye.

Annabelle, her displeasure visible on her face at the rebuff, snapped. "You think you're going to get a better offer? In your dreams. Vic's never..." Abby's ears pricked at the mention of Victoria's name and she waited for her finish the sentence. But Annabelle abruptly pivoted on her heels and stalked back down the corridor.

* * *

Victoria drummed her fingers on the table as she tried to concentrate on her conversation with Emily. Try as she might, she couldn't help her eyes from drifting to the door to the hallway. Abby and Annabelle should have come back by now. She'd recognized what reflected in her friend's eye as they passed. She'd seen it too many times before. Lust. Conceit. Triumph. With an effort to keep her voice even, Victoria answered a question while she cast another furtive glance towards the door. She caught Chantal staring at her intently, concern on her face.

The door burst open and Annabelle hurried over. "I'm heading home, Vic. I'm not feeling well. Give my apologies to Malcolm and Jan, will you? Don't get up, I'll just slip out and get the butler to call me a cab." And without another word she was gone.

Victoria sat back, stunned. If Annabelle's body language was any indication, she wasn't sick—more like furious. She watched the door but Abby didn't appear. A chair scraped and Chantal disappeared into the corridor.

* * *

Abby was staring into space as Chantal approached. "Are you all right, *chérie?*"

Abby turned at the sound of her voice. "I guess."

The Frenchwoman took her hands and stroked the knuckles. "Did she hurt you?"

"No."

"What then, my dear?"

Abby pulled her gaze away; again she stared into the distance. "It was...oh, I don't know...I guess I've never met anyone quite so...well...so predatory. I made it quite clear that I wasn't interested, yet she persisted. And she certainly didn't take too kindly to the knock-back."

"She wouldn't have," said Chantal with a wry smile. "She's used to getting everything she wants. A typical spoiled socialite. I've met plenty like her in my profession."

"The only thing was, though, I had the impression it wasn't really about me at all. I've had plenty of experience at Legal Aid to recognize when someone is fabricating a lie. It was as if she was playing out some sort of power role. I've no idea why she'd do that." Then Abby blinked as a thought popped into her head. "Maybe...maybe she's..."

"In love with Victoria?"

"That could be the reason. I've seen the way Annabelle looks at her. Not the average *just friends* regard."

"*Oui,* I've noticed it too. Annabelle wants Vic and I suspect she's been seducing any woman she thinks might be a threat for years. Hell hath no fury like a woman scorned, as they say."

"But why would Annabelle hassle me? Victoria and I don't get on."

Chantal twined their fingers together. "But you still have a relationship with her, even if it's a fighting one. No one likes to share a sparring partner. Come, let us go back. We have been away too long. They might think we've indulged in—what do you say here—some hanky-panky."

Jan announced coffee was being served in the drawing room. Annabelle was nowhere in sight. As the guests rose to vacate the dining table, Jan came over to Abby and linked her arm through hers. "Can I interest you in a walk round the back garden, my dear?"

Abby looked at her in surprise. "I'd be delighted. I was admiring the flowers earlier. A gorgeous array of blooms."

Chantal waved an elegant hand at them. "I will leave you and talk with my good friend, Victoria. We haven't had a chance to catch up yet."

They reached the patio; Abby cleared her throat. "I owe you an apology for my behaviour earlier, Mrs Hardy. I'm afraid I was rather rude during Victoria's presentation."

"We don't stand on ceremony here so please call me Jan." She nodded her head. "I think perhaps you do, though knowing the history between the two of you, it was probably a fait accompli you two would clash. You both have such strong personalities. I haven't seen Vic so rattled—ever. Poor Fiona's been like a cat on hot bricks and I fear Malcolm has gained more grey hairs, though it's entirely his own fault for not checking the list. Fiona obviously never listens to gossip." Her hostess chuckled. "Actually, and don't tell them I said this, I haven't been so entertained in years. Our dinner parties are usually so dreadfully boring."

A moan escaped from Abby. "Did you see the painting?"

"Goodness me, my girl, everybody flocked to see it." She gave a small laugh. "Excluding Fiona, of course. She told Malcolm you only put in your profile as an interpreter in the application letter. The gallery probably hasn't done so well in years."

"I shouldn't have done it but Victoria made me so mad. She's...she's so..."

"Infuriating?"

"And self-centred."

"I'm aware she comes across like that, though to be honest, she has no conception how beautiful she is. She's brilliant and a keen mind is all she cares about. She's worked very hard to get where she is. She started out as a geologist, becoming a multi-millionaire by the age of thirty."

Abby snorted. "I still can't admire her. Not after the way she went on at the gallery."

A laugh exploded from Jan. "On the contrary, Vic's made your career for you, my dear. The painting and her capricious reaction was the talking point for weeks in our circle. Everyone is waiting for the furore to die down before they order a portrait. You're on the cusp of hitting the big time."

"You think so?"

Jan toyed with the stem of a rose. "That's what I wanted to talk to you about. I'd like to commission you to paint a portrait of Malcolm. I adore your vibrant style—you're an excellent artist, though I'd like something more traditional. Would you be interested?"

Abby's step faltered. "Of course, I'd be delighted. I'll contact you during the week to discuss the appropriate size and my price." She peeped sideways at the older woman. "Aren't you worried how Victoria's going to take it?"

"Let me handle her. Besides, she's off on her trip next week."

For some reason she couldn't explain, the words gave Abby a sense of loss. She shook her head. What did she care that the aggravating woman was about to leave the country? "Who do you think she will choose to go with her?"

Jan's voice had a puzzled tone. "I've absolutely no idea. I usually can read her but I've been watching her all night and still haven't a clue. The only one she won't want is Grace. Vic likes to be the one in charge."

Abby laughed. "Grace is way too butch. Victoria wouldn't cop her for a day. And there's one other she won't choose as well. Me."

"Yes, definitely not. She couldn't handle you. Who do you think she'll pick?"

"Maybe she'll try to persuade Chantal to go."

"Perhaps," said Jan, "though I imagine they'll have to offer her more money."

"If Victoria wants her enough, she will. Money doesn't seem an object to her."

"Yes, Vic's extremely wealthy; if she prefers her, she'll pay the extra herself. Six months is a long time if you don't get on with your companion. Now I must get back to my hostess duties."

* * *

Life stopped being a game for Victoria after her fledgling exploration company found the iron ore deposit in Western Australia. Business accelerated at a rapid rate, and by the time their first coal mine in the Bowen Basin was developed, the company had already gone public. The share price climbed steadily. Victoria's personal wealth continued to accumulate—not even she had a good idea of what she was worth, but to the average person it would be substantial wealth. The business took a hit in the global economic crisis, though firm contracts minimized the effect. She sighed. With the downturn in China's economy, things were tight again. She was getting tired of the constant pressure.

As Chantal approached, Victoria was filled with nostalgia. How good it would be to go back to those carefree days, with no pressure, no commitments. The Frenchwoman had matured into an alluring creature and wore an air of worldliness like a soft mantle. Victoria smiled her welcome. "Let's go out onto the patio, Chantal, for some privacy."

"Of course, and perhaps I can have a cigarette out there." She laughed. "It's my little wicked indulgence after a meal. Frowned upon in many countries I know, but nevertheless, I enjoy one occasionally. Now tell me all about yourself, *mon ami*. You are very wealthy now, I see."

"With a bit of luck and lots of hard work."

"But still single. Have you never found anyone to share your life? You have so very much to offer. Beautiful. Successful. Why is it, Vic?"

The question put Victoria off balance. She struggled for an answer. "I...I honestly don't know. I work all the time, though that's a feeble excuse. It's just—well—as soon as I think I'm interested in someone I get disillusioned. Maybe I'm looking in the wrong places."

"Perhaps you can't see the forest for the trees. She could be standing right in front of you and you can't see her."

"Like you?"

A laugh tinkled. "Not me. We've had our time together. We have gone our separate ways. One thing I've learnt in life, you move on and seldom can go back."

Pensive, Victoria twirled her glass. "You were my first love, Chan."

"And you, mine. We loved, yes, but were we ever *in* love? I think not. If we had been, we would never have left each other."

"And did you ever find that kind of love?"

"I thought I did. Vivienne and I were together five years."

"What happened?"

Chantal breathed out a long sigh. "Like you, I let my work rule my life. My business took me away from home too much, so in the end, she left. It was six years ago."

Victoria glanced at her in surprise. "Six years...that's a long time to be alone."

"Ah, it's the pot calling the kettle black, no?"

"Come on, I've already bared my pathetic love life. This is about you. Wouldn't you like to settle down again?"

"*Mais oui.* I really would like to find a partner. I miss the closeness of having someone of my own, someone who will adore me for what I am, warts and all."

Victoria chuckled. "You sound like you think you're over the hill. By the look of you, you're in your prime. I'd bet women are falling all over themselves to attract your attention."

The lightness in Chantal's voice faded. "I turned forty this year, Vic, and the grey hairs are beginning to appear at regular intervals. And my body, *mon dieu*, it has started to sag."

"I know how you feel. So if you've been looking, what's the problem?"

"Ah...it becomes harder, and I've become a little jaded. The posturing beauties in my social circles do not appeal anymore." She snapped her fingers. "I would not give *this* for them. But the keepers are mostly all taken at my age," she hesitated, "though..."

"Sooo," said Victoria, leaning forward with interest, "You have met someone."

A gleam appeared in Chantal's eyes. "Oh, yes. Very recently. She's...she's rather interesting. I only hope I'm not too late. We shall see what happens."

Curious, Victoria studied her. "That's very cryptic. I can't imagine any woman able to resist you."

"It depends on what my competition does."

"You've got a rival?"

"Maybe."

"God, Chantal, you haven't changed. Always mysterious." Victoria reached over and touched her hand. "I'm so glad you came to this dinner. I trust your intuition about women."

Chantal tipped forward in the chair. "I suppose we should get on to the business of choosing your companion. They all seem quite lovely, though there is one who wouldn't suit you."

Victoria went rigid. "You mean Abby?"

"*Oui*. The resourceful Mademoiselle Fiona made a gaffe there."

"Yes, she damn well did."

"She painted your portrait, I hear."

"She made me look like a damn harpy."

Sadness appeared in the Frenchwoman's eyes. "Annabelle had great pleasure in showing me the picture. A Dorian Grey— is that who you've become, Vic? The face flawless, but the character—not so much?"

Victoria slid her eyes away. "That was only her interpretation,"

"Yes, but I have come to know her over the last few hours. She has an innocence about her that is rather rare. She also seems to be able to read people."

Victoria stared pensively into her glass. "We didn't get on when I was posing for the portrait. It was mostly my fault, I guess—I was always on the phone. Then I said something without thinking, something I shouldn't have. She burred up and it escalated from there." She raised her eyes to Chantal. "How she depicted me in the painting wasn't fair. There was no excuse for being so hurtful."

"Perhaps you both should, how do you Australians put it, bury the hatchet."

Victoria's head shake was emphatic. "That won't happen. She's not going to get away with it so easily. As far as I'm concerned, she went too far."

"Come now. Surely you can be magnanimous; she only wounded your pride. Go in and make up with her."

"No way." Victoria peered at Chantal, keeping her voice even. "What happened between Annabelle and her? I haven't seen Annabelle so angry in years."

"Annabelle didn't seem to have the wit to realize Abby wasn't interested in going out and became a little too persistent in her attentions. Abby brushed her off, which didn't sit too well. She's used to getting what she wants. Is that not so?"

"She's a desirable woman and seems to be able to get anyone she pleases."

"If I were you, I would review your friendship with the woman. I don't like her, Vic. She's so...so bourgeoisie."

"She'd hate you for saying that," said Victoria with a laugh. "Perhaps it is time, though, that she and I had a talk."

Chantal patted her arm. "Come, my friend, let's discuss more pleasant things. Who would you like to go with you on the trip, Karen or Emily?"

"Not Grace?"

A red-nailed finger waggled. "She can kick butt."

"Yeah, probably mine before we even get out of the country."

Chantal studied her intently. "You haven't answered my question?"

"Um...I haven't decided."

"You're being very evasive. You're not one to procrastinate over decisions. I think Karen would be the ideal companion. She's bright and very personable."

"Well...oh, here's Jan back. I think most people are ready to head home. I must say my goodbyes," said Victoria and rose quickly.

* * *

Abby collected her purse to join the queue out the door and Chantal appeared at her side. "You have a lift home, *chérie?*"

"I'll ask the butler to ring for a cab. I didn't bring my car."

"I would be most happy to drive you. Where do you live?"

"Neutral Bay. It's sure to be out of your way so I won't put you out."

Chantal smiled. "I am not far away so it will be no trouble at all. Besides, I am not ready to part with your company. We will have more time to get to know each other."

Abby squeezed her arm. "I'd like that."

Their hosts and Victoria waited at the door to bid them goodbye. Jan winked as she slipped a piece of paper into Abby's hand. "My mobile phone number. Give me a ring on Tuesday," she murmured.

Malcolm shook her hand with a mumble of farewell. He looked embarrassed. Victoria awkwardly thrust out her hand. Abby gazed at it for a long moment and instead of clasping it, leant forward to mutter in her ear. "Not everybody can be bought."

The dark eyes glinted and a whisper floated back, "Everyone's got a price."

As Chantal helped her into the car, Abby looked back to see Victoria staring at them, a frown on her face. She resisted the urge to thrust a finger in the air before she clipped on the seat belt.

"Well, that was an interesting night," said Chantal as she manoeuvred the Jag into the traffic.

"You can say that again," said Abby. She snuggled back in the seat and savoured the scent of perfume mixed with new leather. "Nice car."

Chantal chuckled. "One of my vices. I adore fast cars."

"Me too. One day I'm going to get one like this. I may just be able to afford it now in a few years."

"Ah, you sound happy about something."

"Oh, yes. Jan's commissioned me to do a portrait of Malcolm. My Archibald entry created quite a stir in a positive way. My art may just take off after all. It'll be so good to be able to paint for a living."

"That's simply wonderful news. Then Victoria didn't ruin your reputation after all? She did in fact, do you a good turn."

Abby hesitated, tempted not to comment on the assertion, but was compelled to answer when Chantal added, "Is that not so?"

"I guess," she said with reluctance. "But that doesn't excuse her behaviour."

"I think perhaps she regrets what she said."

"You can think that, but I'm more of a realist. Victoria considers me beneath her."

Chantal leaned gently on the brake to stop at the red light and turned to face Abby. "Ah, so that is the problem. You imagine Vic considers she's better than you."

"She does look down on me."

"She may be arrogant in some ways, but she definitely isn't a snob. Now, I have a question. You are passionate about your art, yes?"

"It's my life. I would wither away without it."

Chantal looked wistful. "I envy you. It has been a long time since I have felt such enthusiasm. I would like very much to see some of your canvases."

"You should come by my studio," said Abby shyly.

"You would perhaps allow me to take you to dinner next Friday night? Afterwards you can give me a private showing. Is it a date?"

"*Mais oui*. I'd be delighted."

"I will look forward to it," Chantal replied as she pressed down on the accelerator again.

Abby leaned closer and voiced what she had wanted to all night, "Can I ask you a personal question?"

"You want to hear about Victoria and me, of course."

"Um…I am a little curious. You seem more than friends. Were you ever lovers?"

"We knew each other many years ago. In London, when we were both developing our careers. We had a short affair, *oui*, but were we ever in love? *Non*, only in lust. We were young and our hormones raged. The affair was fun while it lasted and we parted as friends. She is more complicated now, I think. And so in control!" A soft rain had begun to patter the windshield and Chantal clicked on the wipers. "It would be fascinating to see my friend tied up in knots by love, though it would take an extraordinary woman to do that. Now it is my turn to be personal. You prefer women?"

Abby gave a little hop in her seat at the directness of the question. "Yes. I knew I liked girls when I was in high school, but...well, it was difficult."

"How so?"

"The friends I knocked around with never mentioned anything like that. Then I had a giant crush on a year twelve girl when I was in year ten. It was huge deal to me. I used to go out of my way just to be near her. I think she liked me too, because she was always staring at me."

"You never spoke to her about it?"

Abby gave a little sigh. "No. The end of the year came and I never saw her again. I still think about her occasionally."

Chantal turned her head from the road momentarily to look at Abby. "You haven't been with a woman?"

Abby shook her head, conscious the sophisticated woman must be finding her pitiful. "No, I never met anyone who was a lesbian when I left school, though I wouldn't have recognized one if I fell over them. No one ever approached me and so I did what every other girl was doing, I dated boys. When I was twenty-three, I met Damian and we went out for two years, but eventually I couldn't stand him touching me. It was a nightmare."

Chantal gave a murmur of sympathy. "Not a good situation to be in."

"Definitely not. I enjoyed the sex well enough at first, but I knew something wasn't right, that there should be more to it than just a quick orgasm." Abby gave a sniff, "When I was lucky enough to have one, that is."

"So what happened?"

Abby shuddered in remembrance. "I eventually told him I wanted to break up, though I didn't exactly pick a good time. It was while he was driving me home from the movies. He didn't take it very well and carried on like a pork chop, so I got out of the car and walked the rest of the way."

"So...did you date much after that?"

"Nope. I knew by then I'd never be happy with a man. The trouble was, Mum needed me more and more, and I was flat-out trying to paint and work as well. And where we lived, people didn't exactly embrace gay people. There are lots of bigoted dickheads around, Chantal, and it's certainly a deterrent to come out of the closet."

The older woman tapped her hand on the wheel briefly. "You poor love. You are comfortable with liking women now?"

"Oh, yes. We moved to Sydney and I met a gay man at work. He taught me it was nothing to be ashamed of. Then I plucked up the courage and told Mum. She was great about it." She gave a wry smile. "I started downloading lesbian books; I've accumulated quite a library. At least I know what to do—some authors certainly don't hold back with the titillating bits. Not that it's done me much good. I'm too busy, and shy, to go out and meet anyone."

Chantal laughed. "I suspect you will catch up soon enough. Now tell me more about your family."

Conversation flowed easily the rest of the way as they shared details of their lives. Abby loved the process of discovery in a fledgling friendship. They had formed a definite connection when, all too soon, they reached her house.

"The drive was rather short, I'm afraid," said Chantal with regret. "I will walk you to the door."

"Do you want to come in for coffee?"

"Not tonight. It is very late." She stroked her finger down Abby's face before she kissed her, first on one cheek, then the other, letting her lips linger. "Goodbye, *chérie*. Until Friday."

Abby watched the car disappear down the road. The Frenchwoman's lips had been soft like silk on her skin, and she had really enjoyed her company. But questions spun through her mind that she couldn't ignore. Shouldn't she have felt something a little more, for why did her body tingle when all Victoria did was whisper in her ear as they were leaving? Despondent, Abby went inside.

Sleep took a long time coming. She lay staring at a black moth pressed up against the windowpane, silhouetted starkly in the glow from the streetlight outside.

CHAPTER FIVE

"Have you gone stark raving mad?" The chairman flashed a dark frown; his anger formed a palpable barrier between them. "Why Abby Benton?"

Victoria's gaze was hard, her answer was uncompromising. "She's the one I want. You said it was entirely my decision."

"Oh, for heaven's sake, Vic. Don't be so stupid. You'll kill each other in a week."

"She'll have to toe the line. I'll be her employer and she *will* do what I say."

Malcolm ran his hand through his hair. "Is that was this is all about? A power thing with you? Grow up, my girl."

After a deep breath as if she tasted the air, Victoria leaned closer over the desk and lowered her voice. "Don't you dare patronize me. I want her with me because she's the only one who won't bore me to tears."

"Rubbish! Karen and Emily are bright, intelligent women."

"Emily is a marine biologist who's just completed a study to help save coral growth on the reef. Where do you think we stand on that, pray tell? We ship coal out through the reef if you haven't forgotten. I'm not spending months with an environmentalist who despises what I do."

"What about Karen? She's a computer expert, which will be a definite asset. Instead of the data having to be sent back, she can record and analyse it onsite. It'll save weeks of work here."

Victoria's face set in a stubborn mask. "She's too serious. No sense of humour."

The chairman opened his eyes wide in disbelief. "When have you been a laugh-a-minute? I spoke at length to the woman and found her quite charming."

No reply; he threw up his hands in defeat. "All right, have Abby. That is if she'll go, which I doubt."

"She'll accept. She won't be able to refuse. I'll throw in another one hundred thousand of my own money." Her eyes took on a glint. "Make sure you tell her it'll be tax-free."

"I'll email her on Sunday," said Malcolm suddenly looking weary. "That'll give you twenty-four hours to reconsider your decision. But remember this, Vic. For all your excuses, I'm not stupid. The personal vendetta had better be worth it, so don't come whining back to me if she makes your life hell. You'll have to live by your decision, so make the partnership work. Now I'd better break the news to Fiona. She's not going to be happy."

Victoria leaned back in her chair, satisfied. It was going to be fun having Abby at her beck and call. *She's going to have to do exactly what she's told, like it or not.* No special effort had been required to find out her financial status. Abby couldn't afford to pass up the offer, especially since she battled to support her mother's household as well as her own. She barely had her head above water.

But a niggling thought persisted. Abby had gone home with Chantal. The Frenchwoman might persuade her to stay. Desire was a powerful emotion and they may already have formed an attachment. Maybe it was Abby that Chantal had referred to as interesting. She wondered why that last thought twisted her mind into panic.

* * *

Abby read the email, at first flabbergasted, and then angry. How dare the damn woman assume she could be bought? All day she stewed as she focused on every undesirable trait in the mining magnate. By six p.m., she had worked herself up into such a state she could no longer focus on something as mundane as preparing the evening meal. She burnt the carrots and overcooked the steak. Not that she could eat anyhow—each mouthful seemed to swell up in her mouth, making swallowing impossible. Abby was tempted to ring her mother but resisted. It would only worry her mum, who already disliked Victoria enough as it was.

When eight o'clock arrived, Abby knew she was beaten. With all her financial commitments, it was impossible to pass up the position. But stuff her, she was going down fighting. By her calculations, to pay off some of the mortgage on her house and her mother's six months of living expenses added up to one hundred and twenty-five thousand dollars. Victoria would have to cough up more cash if she wanted her. No way would she budge on that.

Abby sat down at the computer and composed the email.

Dear Mr Hardy,
Thank you for your kind offer. I will be happy to accept the position as Ms Meyers' _platonic_ partner. However, on calculating my mortgage residual and my mother's living expenses while I will be away, I estimate the sum comes to $125,000. Could you please inform the CEO her contribution must rise by the amount of $25,000. (I presume _she_ will be supplying the _tax-free_ monies. Please correct me if I'm wrong.) If she is agreeable, I would expect _her_ contribution be paid up front as a gesture of goodwill.
Yours sincerely,
Abby Benton

Satisfied, she hit the Send button.

* * *

At home, Malcolm sat down heavily on the sofa after pouring himself a large slug of scotch. Too early in the day he knew, but his nerves were completely shot by the confrontation with Victoria. The way she acted was distinctly out of character; she was usually so levelheaded to the point of being stodgy. He'd never seen her so consumed, so off-kilter. Jan entered and noticed the drink. She raised her eyebrows, "Bad day, dear? Want to talk about it?"

Malcolm shook his head. Vic might change her mind by tomorrow and if she did, he didn't want to break her confidence. He waited the rest of the day on tenterhooks, but finally realized by nightfall that she wasn't going to budge. With reluctance, he sent off the email on Sunday morning.

Every hour he checked for a reply, relieved there was no answer from Abby. Thankfully, the woman wasn't interested. Vic would have to come to her senses and choose a more appropriate partner. Before retiring to bed, Malcolm had one last look. His incoming mail flashed one from the artist. He shuddered. After he read the reply he shook his head in disbelief and called out plaintively, and in some desperation, to his wife. "Have a look at this, will you?"

Jan chuckled with amusement. "So, she chose Abby. Of course, that explains why I couldn't read Vic. I was looking in the wrong direction. Isn't it delightful?"

"Delightful? Have you gone completely mad?"

"Oh, Malcolm, you are obtuse. It's a courtship between two tigers, although they both aren't aware of it yet. Abby raked Vic with her claws at the dinner party, so Vic's taken her by the tail and the girl's snapping back."

"But they dislike each other."

"Of course they don't."

"Then why doesn't Vic date her and give her flowers and chocolates like every other bastard in the country?" he asked, annoyed.

"Because both are such passionate women. They didn't start off well and now they're fighting for dominance in their relationship."

Malcolm rolled his eyes. "You've been reading too many of those damn romance novels."

"We shall wait and see," Jan said smugly. "And if I were you, my dear, I would give poor Fiona a suit of armour. She's going to need one. Thank goodness she's the one going with them. Anyone else would run a mile away. Now I'm off to bed. Make sure you forward me the rest of the emails when they come."

"Vic won't quibble about more money. It's a drop in the ocean to her."

Malcolm arrived Monday morning to find Victoria already waiting at his desk. She looked at him expectantly, so without a word he handed her a printout of Abby's email. After she skimmed through it, she raised her eyes and his skin prickled. Giving a gulp, he forced himself to ask in a pleasant tone, "Are you happy with her terms, Vic?"

"No, I'm not. I will draft a reply for you to send."

Half an hour later she swept into his office and tossed a piece of paper on the desk. "Send it immediately."

Malcolm read it with trepidation, groaned and typed the words. Four more emails shot back and forth until he decided enough was enough. He'd put in the shortfall himself. They would never agree—they'd be haggling over cents soon.

When Victoria appeared five minutes later, he said, "She's accepted the price."

Her mouth curved into a satisfied smile. "Good. Tell her to come in and sign the contract."

"I've emailed it to her. She wants to look at it first."

Victoria's eyes narrowed. "She'd better not change one word." She disappeared out the door.

The chairman went back to his work and forced himself to concentrate. He ignored the urge to access his mail, but in the end, his curiosity won out. Malcolm jabbed the key of the mailbox. In spite of his determination to remain calm, emotion closed his throat.

Dear Mr Hardy
I have studied the document in detail and wish to make the following amendments:
Page 2 – paragraph 4. The employee is to have time off at the discretion of her employer. I wish to delete <u>at the discretion of her employer</u> *and replace it with* <u>in lieu of time owing</u>.
Page 3 – paragraph 2. The company will provide the cost of suitable clothing approved by her employer for social occasions. I wish to delete <u>suitable</u> *and* <u>approved by her employer</u>. *I am confident I have the intelligence and flair to choose what I wear.*
Page 5 – paragraph 1. The employee promises to fulfil the length of her contract. Could you include the clause, <u>unless irreconcilable circumstances require the termination of her agreement</u>?
Thank you for your consideration.
Yours sincerely,
Abby Benton

The atmosphere in the office was tense. Silence swelled to fill all the spaces as Victoria raised her eyes from the page and Malcolm felt like a beast being led to the slaughterhouse. He could see by the set of her face that there would be no compromise. "Well?" he snapped.

"No!"

"I'd like to remind you she will be an employee of the board. She ultimately will answer to us, not you."

"I said no. Don't even try pulling rank on me."

He looked at her beseechingly. "Come on, Vic. They're only words. Surely you can agree to some of her terms."

Victoria spread her hands on the polished wood as if ready to eat him. "All right, I'll agree to two and three but one stays. Make it quite clear I don't intend to change my mind and tell her to sign it before five or the deal is off."

Malcolm felt himself floundering. "For heaven's sake, it's already two o'clock. If she argues, there's no way it can be done by that time."

"Yes, I'm aware of that," said Victoria with sly grin.

Malcolm slammed the flat of his hand on his desk. The picture of his wife shot off with a crash. "I'll take my time or you'll have to find someone else to go with you."

"I won't be going then," she yelled back.

With a shake of his head, he turned away from her with disgust and began punching the keys.

Ten minutes later the reply came.

Dear Mr Hardy,

Thank the CEO for agreeing to two of my amendments. However, since number 2–paragraph 4 is the most important, I find I have to insist that Victoria reconsider. As for signing the contract by five o'clock, I have a date for drinks with a friend at 5 p.m., so I shall be there at half past four. Please have the document ready.

Abby Benton

As Malcolm studied Victoria while she read the email, his face betrayed his astonishment. She turned pale and her shoulders slumped in defeat.

"Get the damn thing ready. She can have what she's asking for," she muttered. He stared as she left the room—why she'd conceded he had no idea.

CHAPTER SIX

When Malcolm arrived home after work, Jan was in the living room and passed over a scotch without being asked. "Well, dear, out with it. What happened? I'm betting you need a drink."

He took the glass without a blink. "The whole business was horrendous. Vic was completely out of control and that damn Abby wasn't any better. Come into my office and read the correspondence. It'll explain the whole frustrating business better than I ever could."

As Jan scrolled through the emails, she let out periodic puffs of laugher. "Oh, isn't it simply delicious."

His look was withering. "You're choice of words astounds me."

"It's far better than any of my romantic novels."

"More like a Stephen King horror," Malcolm snapped.

"Sooo—You're putting in some money," she said with a wink.

"How did you guess?"

"Oh, come on. They were on a roll. Vic wouldn't have given in that easily."

"They were inching their way down. It would have gone on all day. Now it's a stalemate. They both think they've won."

With a secret smile, Jan patted his hand. "You did very well, dear. Brilliant move."

"God, love, you should have seen Vic. I've never seen her so worked up over anything. She was downright scary. It was just as you said; she looked like a big Bengal tiger when she snarled. But all of a sudden she caved in after she read the last email. I thought the contract business would take the rest of the day. She'd given Abby the ultimatum to sign by five and then—whoosh—without any more argument, she backs down."

Jan's mouth twitched. "Ah, our Ms Benton is a formidable opponent. She's subtly informed Vic of another interested party, that she isn't the only fish in the sea."

Malcolm glared at her. "Speak English. I don't understand what you're talking about."

"She's having drinks with Chantal, of course. The woman made it obvious at the dinner party that she liked Abby. Vic knew the contract had to be signed before Chantal could talk her out of it."

"Do you mean to tell me that girl has two of the most eligible women in the country chasing after her? She's pleasant enough looking but not that special."

"Looks can be deceiving. She has an innocent quality about her that's very appealing. And she's extremely smart. Passionate and talented as well. Her emails show that. Both Vic and Chantal are used to women throwing themselves at them. I can see why Abby would pique their interest. She doesn't fawn all over them."

"Well, Chantal's missed out. Abby's going with Vic. The contract's been signed."

* * *

Abby left the Orianis building with a few misgivings. Like it or not, she was committed. After her decision to accept the position, she invited Chantal to meet for drinks. To blurt out the news over the phone would insult the woman. Abby owed her the courtesy—she was fond of the Frenchwoman.

Chantal waited inside the foyer of The Criterion, dressed in soft brown pants with a cream blouse which subtly showed the contours of her figure. The faint, tantalizing scent of exotic perfume shimmered over Abby in the Frenchwoman's embrace. *Wow, she's even more gorgeous than I remember.* "I'm glad you could come, Chantal. I've got something to tell you and I wanted to do it in person."

The older woman led her into the lounge bar. "Let me get us a drink first. I think I'm not going to like the news, no?"

Abby shrugged weakly. "I'll have a glass of chardonnay, thanks."

They were settled down with their drinks, Abby broached the subject. Face-to-face, the words were more difficult to say than she had imagined. She *cared* what the woman thought of her.

"Um…Malcolm Hardy contacted me yesterday. Believe it or not, it seems Victoria has chosen me to go with her."

Chantal eyed her thoughtfully over the rim of her glass. "And have you accepted?"

"Yes," Abby said in a small voice.

"Why? You made it obvious you don't like her."

"I…I can't afford not to. It's an opportunity to become financially secure. I'm supporting my mother as well as myself. Mum's debilitated with rheumatoid arthritis and has to live on an invalid pension. The money is never enough for her to have a decent lifestyle, so I chip in part of my wage. I can't work full-time because I need some hours for my painting, which makes it a constant struggle to make ends meet."

"But you are starting to take off with your art. Can't you hang on a few more months until money comes in?"

Frustrated, Abby ran her fingers through her hair. "If only. I've been going over and over the figures for the last twenty-four hours. When I start getting enough commissions, I'll have to give up my job with Legal Aid. We won't have anything to live on for at least a month. Victoria's putting in another one hundred thousand, so it'll set us up."

Chantal narrowed her eyes. "Oh, she is, is she? I could help you set up a bank loan to tide you over."

Abby felt overwhelmed by the gesture. "That's very kind of you, Chantal. It's nice to have your friendship, but this way is the best. Besides, I signed the contract the afternoon."

"There are ways to get out of a contract."

"I can't break my word. I signed it in good faith and I couldn't live with myself if I did that."

"Again I must apologise. It was stupid of me to think you would." She leaned forward to take Abby's hand. "It's just desperation on my part. I've become fond of you and would like time to know you better."

"I want that too."

"But the clock has run out for me," said Chantal, a disappointed edge in her words.

"It's only for six months. I'd like to see you again after I get back, if that's okay with you," said Abby shyly.

"May I take you to dinner tonight?"

"I'm so sorry to have to refuse, but I'm going over to see my mum. I haven't told her yet." She ruefully twitched her mouth. "God, she's going to have an absolute fit."

"Wouldn't she be pleased about the money?"

"Not if Victoria's giving it. She doesn't like her. She'll be concerned that Vic will make me her slave and I'll be sacrificing myself so we can have a better life."

Chantal put her glass on the table and eyed her keenly. "And do you think that will be the case?"

Abby suddenly arched forward until she poised like a coiled spring on the edge of the chair. She bared her teeth and tossed her head back in defiance. Her blond curls bounced round her head. She uttered a low growl. "She'll try. And what a surprise Ms Myers is going to get. She won't have a clue what's hit her."

Chantal's mouth formed into an O. "Abby, you look like a glorious snow tiger ready to pounce. *Merde*! Victoria's in for the shock of her life."

Abby laughed. "She's not going to get things as easy as she thinks."

"Will I see you again before you go?" Chantal asked.

"I don't think that's possible. We leave on Friday, so I'll be too busy. I'll have to buy clothes tomorrow and get my hair trimmed. Then say goodbye to my friends, and pack and organize Mum's finances as well. It's going to be a hectic three days."

"Then I shall ring you constantly so you don't forget me while you're away."

Abby enveloped her in a hug. "I couldn't do that. This is *au revoir*, not goodbye."

* * *

Abby couldn't remember being so nervous at the prospect of seeing her mother. It was as if something was caught in her throat. She hesitated for a moment at the door, set her shoulders and she pushed it open.

"Is that you, Abby?" her mother sang out from the kitchen.

"Yes, Mum."

"I'll be with you in a minute, dear. Dinner is nearly ready."

Abby debated the time to tell her. She'd be too anxious to eat if she didn't get it over with. "Could you come into the lounge before you serve? I've got something to tell you."

As her mother sat down on the chair opposite, Abby's tight smile bunched her cheeks like a pair of apricots. "I…I've got some news."

Judy Benton gazed at her quizzically. "What is it? There's nothing wrong, is there?"

Abby shook her head as she struggled with her composure. "You might say it's great news, but maybe you won't."

Judy looked a little bewildered. "For heaven's sake, Abby, what are you going on about? Just tell me and I'll work it out for myself."

"Um...I've been offered a job. The good news, it pays very well. The bad news, I have to go overseas for six months."

"That's not an insurmountable problem. Joyce next door can keep an eye on me. I'm not helpless. What the position?" She narrowed her eyes. "There's more to this, isn't there? You're not going to be doing something illegal, are you?"

Abby couldn't stop fidgeting—it felt like ants were dancing a tango down her spine. She waved her hands. "No—no, of course not."

"Well?"

Abby slid her gaze away. "It's who my employer will be that you may find upsetting."

"Go on."

"It's Victoria Myers." The words shot out in a gush.

"That woman! How could you work for *her*?"

"The company has offered me two hundred and fifty thousand dollars to accompany her to negotiate contracts. We'll be gone for six months."

"What do you have to do for that sort of money? It doesn't sound right," said her mother.

"Well, actually the wage was originally one hundred and fifty thousand but Victoria threw in the extra 'cause she knew I wouldn't be able to refuse. I would have, refused that is, but I had to accept 'cause it'll get us out of financial trouble. But I didn't go down without a fight. I told..." Abby stopped babbling at the confused look on her mother's face.

Judy straightened up and delivered a hard stare. Abby knew the look—it was time to be worried. "Do you mean to say that Myers woman is giving you an enormous amount of money over and above the wage? What exactly are you expected to do?"

Abby fluttered her hands, suitably vague. "This and that. Mostly secretarial work and some data analysis. Be her support at functions—you understand—that kind of thing."

"You may work for the wage offered but you are definitely not going to accept her personal contribution."

Abby snarled and sprung to her feet. "Oh, yes I am. She can afford it."

Judy blinked at her daughter as if she were a complete stranger. "When have you been so blasé about other people's money? That's not like you."

"Tush. It's only Victoria. She doesn't count."

"Why doesn't she count?"

"Because she hates me and I hate her," said Abby with a satisfied smirk.

The logic seemed lost on Judy, who tried a different tack. "You'll be less than a servant if you accept it. She'll own you."

A sneer appeared on Abby's face. "Huh! She wishes. She's going to be in for one big fat surprise."

"Perhaps you should reconsider, dear."

"I'm going and that's that."

Judy slowly got up and looked down at her. "I haven't a clue what's going on. We were on different wavelengths the entire conversation. I don't understand what the true extent of your relationship with Victoria Myers exactly is, and I'm beginning to doubt if you have any idea either. I just pray you understand what you're doing." She took her hand. "Remember, dear. Be careful what you accept. There is an old saying, 'He who pays the piper calls the tune.' If you take her money then she will have full control over you, on a personal as well as a business level. You'll be the piper, bought and paid for, and you'll have to play whatever tune she wishes."

CHAPTER SEVEN

Victoria gave Fiona a friendly wave as she exited her office. The Scot had been taciturn all day, showing her displeasure at her boss's choice of travelling companion by limiting their interaction to a bare minimum of words. Victoria decided to ignore her ill humour, trusting it would run its course by the next day. If not, she would say something, for there was too much work to do before they left.

"Get me the drafts on the new mine site at Glenreagh, please, and have our itinerary ready so I can go over it tomorrow. I'm off now," Victoria said.

Fiona grunted.

"I hope that meant yes," called out Victoria as she walked to the lift. She looked at her watch. Just enough time to pick up some Thai takeaway and get home to change before Annabelle was due to arrive. She wasn't looking forward to tonight's encounter. Her friend had inundated her with text messages for two days to find out who was going on the trip. Fobbing her off hadn't been easy, as each subsequent text became more demanding. In the end, Victoria invited her over. She knew Chantal was right. A heart-to-heart was long overdue. No use putting it off any longer.

Victoria slipped into the shower; the cool water refreshed her physically, though did little to erase the feeling of disquiet. After changing into jeans and a T-shirt, she padded downstairs to the lounge. She didn't have long to wait. She opened the door at the chime of the bell and motioned Annabelle inside. "Go into the lounge and I'll get you a drink."

The redhead tucked her legs as she curled with grace into the cushions. Victoria handed her a glass and walked to the window to stare down at the traffic in the street below.

"Well, I'm waiting, sugar. Which one did you choose?" Annabelle asked with a hint of impatience.

Victoria turned back and tried to appear casual as she eyed her friend. "Relax for a minute. There's plenty of time to talk."

She remembered the first time she'd met Annabelle. Orianis had just opened its office in Sydney and the attractive lawyer was hired to negotiate the contracts. For the next two years, Annabelle continued as a consultant until they employed their own in-house legal staff. The two of them had remained friends ever since. Annabelle became an invaluable part of her life. With Victoria's workload, she let the lawyer organize their outings, choose their friends.

Not that they were ever lovers, although in the beginning Annabelle had tried very hard to bed her. But Vic knew to shy away from that final intimacy. She had seen her friend with women, her love-them-and-leave-them attitude too cruel and calculating. Victoria often wondered, with the myriad women Annabelle had had sex with, why she'd never found someone for a steady relationship.

With an irritated shake of her head, Annabelle said, "Out with it. You've been ignoring me for two days."

Victoria stroked the textured back of the lounge chair before she sat down. "Who do you think I picked?"

"What's this? Twenty questions? I suppose it's Karen, but Emily wasn't out of the running."

"I'll leave you guessing. Come and see us off Friday at the airport, it'll give you something to think about the rest of the week." Victoria's voice was off-handed but she intently appraised her friend's reaction.

The lawyer stared at her, undisguised anger in her eyes. "Why the hell are you taking such an attitude? I'm your best friend. I'm entitled to be told."

"Why, so you can screw her before we go?"

Annabelle's eyes widened, her mouth tightened. "Excuse me? What did you just damn well say?"

"You heard me."

Annabelle's laugh exploded in the air like a bark. "You're kidding me, right?"

Victoria shrugged. "Maybe, maybe not. Anyhow, both Emily and Karen are straight."

"Well, what's your problem?"

"I've got no worries. Want another drink or would you prefer to eat?"

"What's wrong with you tonight? I demand to know who is going."

Victoria's voice held a challenge and for an instant, bitterness. "It's entirely my business. I'm taking control of my life from here on in. But I can tell you it's not one of those two."

Annabelle flinched. "You're taking Chantal? Why, so you can get back together after all these years? Rekindle your lost youth. Is that your plan?" Her voice changed into a pleading tone. "It won't work, Vic. She's not the one for you."

"What a load of crap. Who are you to think you're an authority on relationships? You've never had one. Why is that? You've had sex with enough women."

Annabelle leapt up and paced around the room. "Why didn't you ask me to go? I would have. What's wrong with me, Vic?"

Victoria narrowed her eyes. They were at the real issue. "Because no matter whom you meet, you can't seem to keep your hands out of her pants! You've got a problem, Annabelle, so do something about it. Get some therapy. I'm serious."

Annabelle strode over until their faces were inches apart. "How dare you judge me, you bitch."

"Shouting at me won't help. Go to a professional to sort out your problem."

The lawyer looked at her; resentment hardened her face. "I'm going home so don't bother seeing me out. Have a good time with Chantal."

Victoria hadn't intended to tell her, but the words popped out without thought. She regretted them immediately. "It's not Chantal I'm taking. It's Abby."

Annabelle whirled, her face contorted. "Are you out of your fucking mind? You prefer that frigid shit to me?" She raised her hand.

A warning was growled. "That's enough. Back off."

The arm dropped. "On second thought, you two will suit each other just fine. You're both such cold fish."

And, without another word, Annabelle strode out of the room. The door slammed behind her.

Victoria sank back in the lounge chair and took deep breaths. It had been worse than she anticipated. She hoped Annabelle would do something about her problem.

* * *

The rest of the week flew as the travellers gathered the documentation needed for the trip. Fiona regained a portion of her good humour, enough to avoid a reprimand from her boss. But she still went into a huff at the mention of Abby's name. Victoria would have to ensure that her attitude changed; it'd be an uncomfortable trip if her two assistants were at loggerheads.

"Is the itinerary ready, Fiona?" asked Victoria on Thursday morning.

"Aye, here it is."

With the papers in hand, Victoria made her way to Malcolm's office for the final briefing. He smiled as she entered.

"Not long before you go, Vic. How's the preparation going?"

Victoria handed over the portfolio. "Nearly there. I want you to have a look at the dates. Barring anything unforseen, they should be okay. Fiona's given us a few days leeway between countries. I thought we could take two weeks off at the end to do a tour of the Continent and the UK. Maybe spend a few days in Paris. We're going to need it, judging by all the appointments she's pencilled in. Work will be pretty full on in Asia."

He skimmed through the itinerary. "It looks fine. It'll give Fiona time with her folks in Scotland as well."

"That's the idea."

"Will you be ready to fly out in the morning?"

Victoria shook her head. "I haven't had time to pack. I've told Bruce we won't be leaving until two in the afternoon. Fiona's booked rooms in the town overnight and contacted Bill about our change of plans."

Malcolm pulled her into a hug. "I won't see you tomorrow. Say hello to Bill and Ellen for me. They're going to make sure you take the weekend off to relax before looking at the site. Keep in touch and have a good trip. Stormy days are ahead for you and Abby, so try to get on."

CHAPTER EIGHT

Abby fiddled with her hair. The style was much shorter and, with the length gone, the strands floated in a mass of riotous curls around her face. Even though she didn't want to admit it, she was keyed up about the trip. Excitement built all week at the prospect of travel; it had been years since she'd had the opportunity. When he was alive, her father, a cross-cultural business specialist, had taken his wife and daughter to live in Japan and China, plus a two-year stint in France. And now she was going overseas again. With Victoria.

At the thought of Victoria, Abby resorted to bolstering up her dislike of the woman by conjuring up all her undesirable traits. Despite the defence mechanism, she actually looked forward to bandying words with her. Not that she liked Victoria any better. That would never change, but she'd be disappointed if she never saw her again.

Friday afternoon finally arrived. Heavy clouds hung low with a promise of a late afternoon storm. Abby donned a flannelette shirt over the tank top and jeans. A limousine pulled up outside her house, and the driver shuffled her luggage into the boot. She climbed into the back to join her boss. Victoria frowned when she sank into the seat opposite. "Couldn't you find anything better to wear?"

Abby yanked at her seat belt, stabbed it into its slot and swept her eyes down the full length of the CEO's body. "You could have put on a more sensible pair of shoes. They're way too high for plane travel."

Victoria didn't deign to answer; her stony expression indicated her elegant shoes were not up for discussion.

Five minutes later a jingle sounded in the cab, and both women reached in their pockets. Abby, aware it was petty thing, still felt a stab of satisfaction to find it was her phone.

"Hello, *chérie*. I'm just ringing to wish you bon voyage."

"Hi, Chantal. We're in the limo heading for the airport." She quietly chatted with the Frenchwoman as they sped through the suburbs. After she finally punched the off button, Abby said with a disarming inflection in her voice, "That was Chantal."

The muscles of Victoria's face bunched. She stared out the window and ignored Abby for the rest of the journey.

Fiona waited for them outside the General Aviation terminal; her grey worsted overcoat and sensible black shoes merged in with the leaden sky. Abby studied her. Her features were regular enough and she had pretty eyes. A bit overweight, though better fitted clothes would help. Perhaps it was time someone jazzed her up. Maybe when they went shopping Abby could persuade Fiona to buy some new gear and get her hair cut into a more fashionable style.

"Aren't we flying commercial?" asked Abby.

"We'll be taking the company plane while we're in Australia," said Victoria and strode out to a sleek Gulfstream jet on the tarmac. Abby and Fiona followed in her wake.

Adrenaline pumped through Abby's veins; the adventure had begun and a corporate jet made it even better. She turned to Fiona, who carried a bulging briefcase as well as an oversized square handbag. "Let me take something for you."

The Scot eyed her with surprise. "Why, thank you, lass."

"No probs." Abby flashed a complicit grin. "I'm here to help."

Two men and a tall blond woman, with Orianis logos embossed on their uniform pockets, stood beside the aircraft. Victoria introduced them as Bruce, the pilot, Marv, the co-pilot and Marcia, the in-flight attendant. The inside of the cabin left Abby gaping. The luxurious space was designed for comfort, with eight plush leather seats lining the aisle in twos. In front of the cockpit door was a well-stocked bar with three cushy stools. With some hesitation, Abby approached Fiona. "Do you mind if I sit here?"

"Please do. I don't enjoy flying, so I shall be pleased with the company."

"Very classy," murmured Abby as she wriggled into the soft upholstery.

"It is indeed. Let me show you how things work." Fiona pointed to a feature on the armrest. "This control panel has a touch screen for the temperature, lighting, window shades and the entertainment screen. The plane has a wireless network and there's a room at the back where there's additional Internet service, printer and phone service." She reached forward and pulled down the tray. "See, it's wide enough to hold a laptop and papers."

"A flying business office—wow! So, where are we headed? Nobody's told me a thing."

The secretary made a clicking sound with her tongue. "I canna understand Victoria sometimes. She should have told you. We're flying into a Central Queensland city and then driving from there. The small town, Wilga Plains, hasn't an airstrip long enough for the jet. We left much later than planned, which means an overnight stay at a hotel to avoid driving at night. Apparently the gravel road to Glenreagh hasn't been graded for quite a while and is rough in patches. Bill and Ellen Norman, friends of Malcolm's, own the cattle property. The company is negotiating to buy a section of their land for a new coal mine, hence the reason for the visit. They've invited us to spend the weekend to relax before the business discussions."

"Sounds exciting. I've never been so far north." As they sped down the runway, Abby looked across at the rows of commercial planes at their loading bays in the distance. The aircraft shuddered as it climbed through the layer of dark clouds hovering over the airport and Fiona uttered an audible gulp at the turbulence. Abby instinctively reached out a hand to reassure her. "We'll be right once we get higher. It won't be long."

Once at cruising height, the Scot began to relax and rubbed her stomach. "Ma baggie won't be able to take much of that. Thank you, lass, I think I have misjudged you."

"I know we're going to become good friends. What part of Scotland are you from?"

"Thornhill. My mother still lives there."

"That must be hard for both of you. How long have you been in Australia?"

"Over twenty-five years." Fiona took off her glasses and wiped the lenses. "I came out to help my Aunt Moira when Uncle Angus died. By the time she passed away, Australia had become my home and I had made good friends here. Aunt left me everything she had, and I had an excellent position with Orianis, so I stayed."

Abby felt a wave of compassion for the woman, aware how difficult it must be to have divided loyalties. "Do you get back to see your mum often?"

"I try to fly over every eighteen months. She's getting old, so I'm pleased I've the opportunity to stay a month with her after this trip."

"So tell me about Thornhill."

Fiona's face lit up. "I'd like to very much, lass." She chuckled. "It's not often I have a captive audience. It's a pretty wee village south of Glasgow, and Drumlanrig Castle is nearby, one of Scotland's grandest buildings. The town used to be an old stage post in the eighteenth century; a number of the coaching inns are still in business..." She chatted on happily, animated now that she was talking about somewhere she loved. As Abby listened, any anxiety she harboured melted away. She had an ally on the trip.

* * *

Victoria unclipped her seat belt after the pilot advised over the speakers they were free to move about the cabin. Perched on a barstool, she poured a Diet Coke. As much as she tried to relax, she couldn't resist stealing looks at Abby and Fiona deep in conversation. *Well, well—thick as thieves already. And Chantal's continuing to creep after Abby. She'd better back off. Abby's at my disposal for six months.*

Victoria furtively studied the younger woman. The dimples that appeared with Abby's smile were cute, and the blond curls looked soft as silk. Abby wasn't a classic beauty or dollishly pretty, but there was something out of the ordinary about her, something appealing. Her face was one you'd look twice at. It had character, and her body had real curves—she was all woman. Victoria's eyes dropped downwards to fix on the outline of the full breasts that strained against the tank top. Mesmerized by their swell and hint of nipples, she allowed her thoughts to wander off into the realms of fantasy. They blossomed into visions of Abby on her knees as she grovelled for forgiveness. The image turned into Abby *naked* as she grovelled. Perspiration glistened on her back and trickled...

"Are you ready for something to eat?" Guilt and confusion swept through Victoria. What had just happened? She straightened and turned to the flight attendant. "Afternoon tea will be great, Marcia."

Upset by her traitorous libido and not having the remotest idea why it suddenly kicked in after so many years of hiding in the wilderness, Victoria returned to her seat. She opened the paper to continue the crossword, but her thoughts arrowed straight back to Abby. What was it about the artist that pushed Vic's emotions so out of whack? Chantal's phone call to Abby in the limo had provoked a wave of something that Vic had never felt before. She struggled to put a name to it. Not anger exactly—something deeper, more unsettling and complex. Exasperated, she shook off her reflections and tried to focus on the next cryptic clue. Eventually it registered she didn't have a hope in hell of concentrating, so she gave up, put on earphones and stared out the window.

Two hours later they landed and confronted a wall of hot air as they exited the plane. Summer was in full force, the air clear, though oppressive with the heat shimmering off the tarmac. There were no traces here of the storm clouds that had blanketed Sydney. The atmosphere was dry as chips, and the surrounding countryside was coloured a light brown with barely a tinge of green. At the door of the terminal, Victoria stumbled as the heel of a shoe caught in a crack in the concrete. She gritted her teeth when she heard Abby snicker. Without a backward glance, she swept inside the building to pick up the keys for the hire car. Once their suitcases were loaded, they said goodbye to the crew who were returning to Sydney.

Bruce tipped his cap. "See you Tuesday morning at eleven, Vic. Have a safe trip."

Fiona struggled out of her coat as they walked out the airport door. She sweated freely in the heat; the beads of dripping perspiration imprinted more of a hang-dog look on her face than normal.

Abby, who looked comfortable in the tank top (she'd divested herself of her fleecy shirt in the plane), patted her arm. "Don't worry. We'll be in an air-conditioned car soon."

As the vehicle cruised along, Victoria only chipped in a word occasionally; the other two chatted like comfortable old friends. She took in the country as she drove. The monotony of the interminable scrub had a charm of its own—subdued but also peculiar—so foreign from the urban landscape that had been her home for many years. It was different too from the endless expanse of red dust of the Pilbara Region in Western Australia where her first mining venture had begun. Over 400,000 square kilometres, the Pilbara was known as the engine room of Australia—home to massive mining industry ventures. It also had some of the remotest places on the planet. Orianis Minerals owned two iron ore mines in the area.

Half an hour into the drive, the road began to climb over the spur of the Great Divide. It levelled out again as they reached the plains beyond; there would be no more hills left to navigate, Victoria knew the road forward was straight and flat. Her mind turned to the coming weekend. She actually looked forward to the break. A few years ago, horse riding had been her main outlet from work. For two hours every Friday afternoon, she'd taken her neat little thoroughbred, Bella, for a trot round the track where she was stabled. After Bella died, Victoria hadn't purchased another horse, and instead took up swimming as her exercise. She did miss being in the saddle, though. Now relief was in sight: the Normans had promised her some riding time across their expansive property.

An hour and a quarter later, they reached the town, Wilga Plains. Victoria eased the speed down to a crawl as she drove down the street to find the hotel.

"There it is," called out Fiona.

Victoria parked across the street and stared at wooden two-storied building. Not only did it need of a coat of paint, its overhanging veranda seemed to lean forward a little, though that might have been her imagination. She scrutinized it with a disappointed eye. Victoria frowned at her secretary. "Is this the best you could do, Fiona?"

The Scot stuck her chin out. "There are two hotels in town and the only motel is closed for renovations. The travel agent advised me to book here. He described the other one as 'not fit for ladies.'"

"My god," said Abby, "it must be a doozey if this one is the better of the two."

The proprietor, a squat man with a jolly smile, showed them to a room at the top of the stairs. It was situated directly above the public bar. Three single beds, a large wardrobe, and a stand with an ornate porcelain jug with two glasses perched on top, provided the only décor in the room. Threadbare white towels, plus small cakes of soap, sat on the end of each of the beds. Directions to the bathroom were tacked to the back of the door and a faded print of the Sydney Opera House hung on the wall. Victoria sank like a deflated balloon onto the bed. She gave a groan. No personal bathroom. No room service.

Abby, much to Victoria's annoyance, seemed in her element as she hummed cheerfully. She tested the bed, looked in the cupboard and walked out onto the balcony to gaze out over the street. "Isn't it fun? Reminds me of the backpacking holidays my friends and I used to go on. No frills and fuss. You can see the real country this way."

"You call it fun? More like slumming to me," groaned Victoria as she poked the thin mattress rigidly supported by a heavy board. "The bed's hard as a rock and I've got a touchy back."

"Oh, it's fine. You'll sleep like a log."

"After we have showers, we'll go down to eat," said Victoria.

By the time they arrived in the lounge, it was full, and the clientele spilled out into the beer garden. The dining area was separated from the public bar by a laminated wall. The room was decorated with all sorts of local sporting memorabilia, mounted bulls' horns and cartoon sketches of odd-looking people. The air smelt of beer and fried food and the barmaid, a blowsy blonde in a low-cut top, expertly served drinks at a rate only to be admired. A tired jukebox huddled in the corner, grinding out country music. Victoria sighed with relief when the song finished and nobody rose to feed it another coin.

Abby volunteered to get the drinks. "What'll you have?"

"A chardonnay will be nice," said Victoria. "See if they have a wine list."

"I doubt they do, but if not I'll get you a glass of the best on offer. What about you, Fiona?"

"I always say, when in Rome. I'll have a beer."

"Good for you. I'll get you a pot and I'll have one too. I see we have to order meals at the bar." Abby looked up to the sign above the counter. "There's steak, chicken or pork chops."

Victoria shrugged. "Steak will do. Since we're in cattle country, it should be tender."

Their meals arrived; the slab of meat overlapped the plate with a pile of chips beside it. "It's enormous," said Abby.

Victoria pushed the chips onto her bread and butter plate before she sliced the meat. She glanced with disapproval at

Fiona; the Scot had forsaken her diet. Fiona munched her way through the chips and Victoria could nearly see the fat cells pounce onto her already ample rear end.

They lingered after the meal over a glass of brandy before retiring for the night; Victoria ordered an extra one for fortification to face the bed. Much to her annoyance, Abby and Fiona seemed to go off to sleep immediately. As much as she tried, she couldn't find a comfortable spot on the hard mattress. Her back was killing her after an hour. She drifted off at last due to overwhelming exhaustion, but then a crash erupted from the bar underneath. Her eyes snapped open. It sounded like someone had thrown something. Loud voices rang out, followed by electric guitar music. Victoria wrapped her ears in the pillow and cursed. A few hours later the noise downstairs miraculously vanished and she wriggled into the hard bed with the hope she still could get enough sleep. She didn't have a chance. With no competition, Fiona's snores dominated the room. Vic jammed a pillow on top of her head again. She itched to strangle the life out of her assistant.

Victoria had barely dozed off when a cheery voice floated through the room. "Rise and shine, sleepyhead." She opened her bloodshot eyes to see Abby fling back the curtains. The bright sunlight brought a wave of nausea. "Give me another half an hour," she begged.

Abby made a noise that Victoria's sleep-deprived brain interpreted as a contemptuous snort. "It's seven—time to get up. Fiona's already gone for her morning walk."

"I said I want more time. She kept me awake all night with her snoring."

"Nonsense, I didn't hear anything. Get up. Bill rang to say he expects us by nine for a late breakfast. Apparently it'll take us over an hour to get there."

Victoria hauled herself out of bed, rifled in her suitcase for clothes and ripped off her PJs. As she reached for her underwear, she caught Abby staring, her face a rosy pink. Victoria realized she was naked.

The younger woman turned abruptly to hurry out the door.

CHAPTER NINE

Abby stood in the corridor, her emotions in turmoil. The sight of Victoria's nude body left her breathless. The aftermath still tingled and her thighs twitched. *Cripes, I've got to get on top of this.* Abby fought to calm down, to suppress the unfamiliar longing that seemed to permeate every nerve ending. Her arousal was as unexpected as it was bewildering. She tried to push the surprisingly strong feeling aside, though she had little hope of that. She hurried down to the communal bathroom and bathed her face in cold water. *Snap out of it, you idiot. Just because you haven't had a date for umpteen years, you can't go gaga over that woman.* Ten minutes later, more composed, she slipped back into the room to collect her case. A subdued Victoria sat on the bed, jiggling the car keys in her hand. "Let's go. We can take down Fiona's stuff between us."

By the time they loaded up the Landcruiser, Fiona appeared, looking cheery and refreshed.

"We better make a start," said Victoria as she stretched her back and cricked her neck.

Two kilometres out of town the bitumen ended and the wheels hit the gravel surface with a thud. From then on, the road was an obstacle course. The vehicle bounced over corrugations and Victoria had to use all her skill to dodge potholes etched into the bulldust like miniature moon craters.

"It's a road from hell," moaned Fiona.

Abby privately agreed and wished she'd worn a firmer bra. Then, when a calf darted out from the grassy fringe, barely missing the vehicle, Fiona began to backseat drive. Abby could see Victoria's knuckles whiten as she clutched the wheel. Tension hung like a storm cloud in the car by the time they reached the turnoff to the homestead.

Ellen Norman waited at the gate to welcome them. With a scathing look at Fiona, Victoria pushed open the door.

Ellen hugged her with affection. "Welcome, Vic. It's so nice to see you again." After the introductions, she waved a hand towards the door. "Come in and meet Bill. He'll show you to your rooms where you can freshen up while I put on the jug. I've put Fiona and Abby together in the two-bed room and you in the other."

Abby liked the couple immediately. Ellen was a short, matronly woman, with a face scored with fine lines and hair the colour of light chocolate streaked with grey. Her eyes were a washed-out blue and a perpetual smile hovered over her mouth. Bill towered over his wife, his rugged face long and angular, his skin burnt brown by the sun, his eyes bright and watchful.

As Bill led them up the inner staircase, Abby gazed with approval at the polished cypress pines walls that stretched to high ceilings. The old house was grand. Their room had its own en-suite, with two queen beds and ample space for them not to be falling over each other. She had a peek into Victoria's room next door. A huge four-poster bed sat in the middle of the room and bay windows led to a small balcony. The room was as big as half her apartment at home.

The day passed quickly. After breakfast, Bill took them for a tour of the property. They looked at the proposed mine site and Abby took snapshots of the surrounding vegetation. She had offered to be the official shutterbug on the trip, for photography was a particular hobby. Not only was it a fascinating pastime, but the activity proved essential for accumulating subjects for her portraits. Whilst commissions would pay the bills, she really wanted to capture intriguing people for an exhibition one day.

Back at the homestead, they had barely enough time for a rest before dinner. After her shower, Abby went out onto the balcony. The bush had changed its mood. It no longer looked harsh as it had in the middle of the day. Now it exuded a mythic quality, a sensual glow in the light of the setting sun. On the crimson dusk, a flock of grey and pink galahs wheeled above the garden, and then disappeared over the trees in the distance. The intense heat had diminished into a warm, friendly night and the countryside had come alive. Birdsongs mingled with the buzz of insects, and the croaks of frogs echoed from the house-dam nearby. The gentle sounds were so soothing it took an effort to go back inside.

At six thirty, Abby, with Fiona in tow, went downstairs to join the others. She sat back, content to listen to the conversation, conscious she had little to contribute as they talked about people far removed from her own limited world. After a while, a melancholy sadness swept over her—as much as she would have liked it to be true, she didn't have anything in common with these people. Hers was a life of struggle, mortgage and personal sacrifice. Suddenly she felt like crying; she should have stayed home where she belonged. She forced herself to perk up when she caught Victoria's gaze of concern.

Her hostess must have caught the interchange of glances, for Ellen turned to her with a smile. "I'm sorry, Abby. You must think us rather rude, but it's been such a long time since we've seen Vic. Have you seen much of Queensland?"

"I've only been to Brisbane. It's been a real treat to see your property."

"Good," said Bill, "then you should enjoy the itinerary tomorrow. Come into the dining room and I'll tell you what we've got lined up." Once they were seated around the long cedar table, he continued. "We'll muster the back paddock to brand the calves. I believe you're keen on having a ride, Victoria?"

"I'll be pleased to get in the saddle again. I miss riding."

"Then you'll be handy to have along. I realize it's no use asking Fiona. What about you, Abby?"

She shook her head. "Sorry, I don't ride." *Just another damn thing I can't do. When did we ever have the money to buy a horse? Of course it was a sure thing that superwoman Myers would be at home astride a horse.*

"No worries," said Ellen. "I'll be driving out with lunch so you can see them work in the yards. We'll have an early night, for it'll be a big day."

By the time Abby finished her shower, she discovered Fiona in bed already asleep. Abby's mood had lightened a little as she settled under the blanket. Time she put aside her feelings of inadequacy to enjoy the rest of the visit. It might be a road less travelled, but that didn't mean she couldn't fit in. She was a quick learner. Just as she was about to drift off, Fiona began to snore. She gritted her teeth. Victoria's description had been apt: the woman sounded like a foghorn. Fiona continued without a break, gaining momentum until Abby felt that the room was actually vibrating.

She tiptoed over and rolled the Scot on her side. The respite only lasted minutes. Fiona gurgled and flipped back over and the bellowing began again. Then Abby remembered seeing a couch in Victoria's room. Time for desperate measures. As quietly as she could, she stripped the top sheet off her bed, grabbed a pillow, and crept to Victoria's door. She sizzled out a relieved breath to find it slightly ajar. The curtains on the bay windows were tied back and the full moon pooled a soft glow over the bed. Victoria lay curled up, her back to the window. Relieved to see that she hadn't imagined the couch, Abby stretched out and tucked the sheet around her.

A kookaburra's laugh, raucous and loud, woke Abby. By the faint light that stole over the windowsill, she guessed it was around five thirty—time to beat a hasty retreat. She glanced over to the bed. Victoria faced towards her now, still asleep under the brightly coloured doona. Her face in repose seemed younger, more vulnerable. Abby's heart gave a lurch; she pushed back an overwhelming urge to go over and stroke the cheek that nestled against the pillow. She knew she should go but she couldn't bring herself to move. She lay there dumbly, with the cushion to her face. And then it was too late.

The dark eyes opened and looked straight into hers. For a moment neither spoke. In those unguarded seconds, Victoria's face lit up in welcome, but the look quickly disappeared. An amused, slightly sardonic expression settled in its place. "So, she does snore after all, does she? I wasn't a whinger as you intimated."

Abby's good humour vanished. "I said I didn't hear her night before last, not that you were a whinger."

Victoria shrugged. "Same thing. Now you better get back to your room before Fiona wakes up. I've got my reputation to think of."

"Huh! You can go in with her tomorrow night. I'm having your bed."

"That's not an option. She can have this room. I'll have a word with her."

Some lingering traces of anger remained as Abby nodded her thanks. She gathered up her bedclothes and without another word, walked off. Victoria's soft laugh followed her out the door.

* * *

Victoria, dressed in her German Sonne Reiter jacket and jodhpurs, made a bit of a fashion stir at the breakfast table. Abby managed a mumbled hello before she ducked back to her meal. Fiona gave the outfit a nod of approval.

"My, you do look smart, Vic. What sort of horse did you have?" asked Ellen.

"A thoroughbred mare retired after a few years on the racing circuit. I was even a member of the Sydney Ladies Riding Club for a while." She grinned. "Hence my rather flamboyant clothes.

They're probably a bit much for out here but I thought I could get some more wear out of them. I've had them hanging in the cupboard for years."

Bill chuckled. "A ladies riding club doesn't exactly sound like you, Vic."

"God, no, not my scene at all. We even had to ride around with a coin between the knees to keep our balance. 'The proper English way of riding,' they called it."

"I'm sorry I'm not giving you a more spirited animal after hearing that, but the horses have already been taken up in the truck. You're going to be riding old Major, a pretty steady fellow. Eat up. We'd better be off soon; the boys are there waiting."

At the yards, Bill passed Victoria a handheld, two-way radio. "Take it so we can keep in contact. The blokes will muster the flats while you and I will see what's at the range dam. The summer's been dry so there's not much grass up in the hills. By the time we get there, the stock should be at the water. We'll bring what cattle are left there down to the yards."

Victoria pulled herself up into the saddle. The chestnut gelding was a big horse, some seventeen hands high and quiet as a church mouse. As he plodded along sedately, she seethed. Steady wasn't the best word to describe Major's pace. *Lethargic is more like it.* She would have loved a sprightlier animal; at any rate, she barely kept up with the cattle. She prodded Major along and cracked him with a switch every so often to keep her mount from falling asleep. By ten o'clock the heat was so stifling and oppressive; Victoria hoped the dam wasn't far away. Perspiration trickled down her back and her buttocks ached. It was hard work keeping the horse moving and he had such an uneven gait.

Finally, over a ridge, the dam came into view. Victoria squinted in the over-bright sunlight as she looked at the cows crowded around the water's edge. Many had calves at foot. Flies swarmed around her face when she pulled Major to a stop to wait for directions.

"Go round to the right. I'll take the left side and we'll push them into a bunch," Bill called out.

Victoria nudged her mount, happy to see Major come to life with the activity. The cattle were quiet; those at rest lumbered to their feet with little protest. Dust puffed up in explosions of red talc as they edged the herd together, then urged it past a corrugated-iron tank to an open wire gate on top of the slope. Three eagle hawks on the bank, rose with a flurry of wings as the cattle trotted by. The smell of nature hung in the air, and the sails of the windmill clanked in the slight breeze.

"Right, let's take them down," said Bill as he wheeled his horse into a trot.

The cattle moved quickly along a well-worn path, and it wasn't long before the other herd on the flat came into view. It was just past one o'clock when the last of the cows dived through the yard gate.

The other three women were already there, waiting in the shade of a group of gum trees near the ramp. Victoria felt like clapping; it was lunchtime—she could get off the damned horse at last. Her bones creaked in protest as she dismounted. The morning had been the longest stint she'd ever had in the saddle and she wasn't exactly a spring chicken anymore. She gave the others a nonchalant wave, ignoring her aching muscles. She refused to give Abby the satisfaction of seeing her in pain.

"Tuck in, girls," called out Bill. "There's still a lot to do."

After lunch, the calves were drafted off the cows and the branding commenced. Dust whirled as the first calf ran up the crush. Bill slammed the calf-cradle shut to pin it in place. The branding iron hissed through the hide and the smell of burning hair reeked in the air. While Victoria and Abby looked on, Fiona made mewing sounds of disapproval. As the steer was castrated and dehorned, she began to look sick. Bill winked and threw a testicle on top of the branding plate to cook. He offered the 'bush oyster' for the Scot to eat and she turned a dull shade of green. For the rest of the afternoon, she sat in the truck.

The last calf was through two hours later; Bill turned off the gas and wiped his hands on his jeans. "I'll clean up here and the boys can take the cows away. We'll wean the bigger calves. Can you ride Major home, Vic? We'll need him in the morning. I'll follow after I finish. The girls can go via the main road to shut the gates."

Victoria looked with longing at the truck, her aches more acute now that she'd cooled down. "No problem, Bill. I'll see you all at the house."

With a superhuman effort, Victoria crawled back into the saddle. Major started off sedately enough and then a slow current seemed to spread through his body. Victoria could sense his quivering excitement build as he realized he was headed home. He broke into a canter and, before she could gather her wits, he launched into a full gallop. As he tore down the winding track, thoughts of coins between the knees never entered her head. All her strength was needed to keep her balance. She pulled frantically on the reins. The horse clamped more aggressively on the bit and tugged her forward.

A gully came into view. With an enormous leap, he cleared it in one bound. For an awful moment, Victoria defied gravity before she smacked back into the saddle. Her tailbone shrieked. She wished desperately that she could turn into a butterfly and just flutter away.

But her mind soon emptied of everything except the need to hang on. She yelped as the horse scraped past a sharp branch overhanging the road. A knee of her jodhpurs ripped apart. Victoria moaned. Her imported pants were ruined, the right leg flapped like a piece of washing in a hurricane. Eyes closed tight, she clung on desperately. She heard the horse's strident breathing and smelt the stench of his sweat as she was forced lower over Major's sloping back. Victoria felt like Ichabod Crane with the Headless Horseman hot on her heels. As her body slipped sideways, she abandoned her grip on the reins and clutched the pommel with both hands. It took all her remaining strength just to stay upright. She was overcome with blind terror and for the first time in a very long time, Victoria prayed. She burbled out her acts of contrition and pleaded for salvation.

Miraculously, with an abrupt shudder and loud blurt, her mount stopped. Shaking badly, she opened her eyes to find they were at the front gate of the house. She dismounted awkwardly and jelly-wobbled into the house. Nobody was home—she'd beaten the truck back. With as much speed as her screaming joints allowed, she went upstairs to change. Unable to find any painkillers, Victoria drank a large scotch from the decanter on the sideboard and went out onto the landing. With enormous relief, she lowered her body into the squatter's chair. The canvas sling sagged. Almost immediately the car drove in.

"Hello, Vic. Back already?" asked Ellen in surprise.

Fiona gaped and Abby looked impressed.

Victoria's laugh rippled on the wind. "Oh, I've been back for ages. Nothing like a bit of a gallop to end the day."

CHAPTER TEN

Abby appeared at the door of the patio. "Can I get you anything, Vic? You must be tired."

Victoria stared at her in surprise. Did she just detect warmth in her voice? Abby had abbreviated her name too. Was she actually offering an olive branch? That ghastly ride had obviously gained Victoria some brownie points. "A cup of tea would be nice."

"Right you are. I'll pop into the kitchen and make you one."

Five minutes later Abby appeared with a cup and a piece of chocolate cake and after depositing them on the small table, she patted Victoria's arm. "Call me if you want anything else."

"This is more like it," murmured Vic.

After she finished her afternoon tea, Victoria decided to go to her room to look over the prospectus she intended to present the following morning. Reluctant to push Abby's sudden goodwill any further, she attempted to rise, but found it impossible with the canvas so low to the ground. Her muscles were lead, her tailbone on fire and her joints had seized up like an old engine without oil. *Why the hell did I choose the ruddy squatter's chair to sit in? There's no way I'm going to ask Abby to pull me out of it. I'll have to wait for one of the others.*

Patience, though, had never been Victoria's strong suit. Within ten minutes she called out for Abby to bring down her briefcase. The younger woman marched out almost at once. "There's no need to yell. You'll wake the others. They're having a rest. I'll get it after I finish my phone call."

A stab of jealousy shot through Victoria. "Chantal again, is it? Tell her to get a life."

Abby bristled. "My personal affairs are no business of yours. You'd do well to remember that. And as for Chantal, she's charming and considerate, things you are definitely not. Take a lesson out of her book."

"Who the hell do you think you're talking to? I'm your boss and you *will* respect me."

"You've got to *earn* my loyalty first. I'm not one of your office toadies."

Victoria wished she could get out of the chair. She was at a distinct disadvantage with Abby towering over her. "Just get me the damn briefcase."

"After I've finished my phone call." Abby wheeled round and stalked back into the house.

Ten minutes later she reappeared and dumped the case on her lap. "Wanker!"

Bill, grinning sympathetically, pulled Victoria out of the chair; every muscle in her body protested. "I understand how you feel. I suffer if I haven't been in the saddle for a length of time. I'll get you some anti-inflammatories. You'll be fine by tomorrow if you take them every four hours, so go and have a rest."

After she swallowed three tablets, Victoria tucked the packet into her pocket and navigated the steps. Pain hampered her progress. She clutched the banister to take the weight off her aching joints and pulled herself up step by step like a swimmer doing the Australian crawl. By the time she reached her room she was sweaty and shaking. Gingerly, she eased onto the bed to wait for the medication to kick in.

Relaxed again, her thoughts drifted back to the night before, to Abby on the couch, her blond curls shaggy and disordered, her cheeks flushed with sleep. Desire clouded Victoria's mind. The artist had looked so adorable she'd had the urge to go over and run her fingers down over her face, then climb onto the couch and cuddle in close. She wondered what it would be like to wake up in the mornings beside her—it had been far, far too long since she'd been that close to someone.

She shook away the thoughts and stretched her legs to test the muscles. The pain had lessened enough for her to stand under a shower to let the water soothe her limbs. Refreshed, Victoria went in to see Fiona. Thankfully, Abby was nowhere to be seen.

Not feeling up to a prolonged conversation, Victoria dispensed with any preamble and came straight to the point. "I want you to change rooms with me, Fiona. You snore badly."

"Nay, do I really? Abby didn't say anything this morning. She looked like she had a decent sleep."

Victoria felt her cheeks heat. "I heard you at the hotel. I'll sleep in here until we leave, so make sure you book a single room for yourself for the rest of the trip."

Fiona frowned at her over her glasses. "It isn't an excuse for you to continue to pick at that bonnie lassie, is it? She deserves some peace away from you."

"You snore like a jet engine," said Victoria, mirroring her frown, "so don't dump that rubbish on me."

"Huh! Why don't I believe you?"

"It's no damn business of yours how I treat her."

"You're going to get more cooperation out of her if you make an effort to be nicer."

Victoria felt the flush deepen and her voice roughened with anger. Her authority was not only diminishing, it was sliding into free-fall. Two days and Abby had her dour assistant wrapped around her little finger. "Just do it, Fiona."

* * *

Though neither woman spoke, it was obvious to Abby when she emerged from the bathroom that something was going on. Victoria looked cranky while Fiona's brows were knit together disapprovingly. "Anything I've missed?" she asked. Without a word, Victoria hobbled out of the room.

Curious, Abby turned. "What was that all about?"

Fiona pulled at the material of her slacks, clearly upset. "I have to change rooms. Apparently, I snore." She gave a beseeching look. "Is it really that bad?"

Abby patted her hand, feeling pity for the woman and annoyance with Victoria for not being more tactful. "A little. It's not an insurmountable problem though. Just look on the bright side—you'll have your own room for the rest of the trip. You don't have to be worried about it," she watched Fiona carefully, sensing her struggle, "so don't let it upset you."

"It's not that. It's Vic. She's normally so pleasant, but she's been flying off the handle for very little reason lately."

"Pleasant? Huh!"

"Aye. She's an excellent boss."

"How long have you worked for her?"

"For twelve years, ever since the company was formed. She's been very good to me over the years. In fact, two years ago I was sick with glandular fever and she paid for my mother's plane fare from Scotland." She pinched her lips with her fingers. "Vic hasn't always had it easy. People envy her because she has everything, but in the beginning she had to work very hard to build up the company. Success comes with a cost—once on top, the workload increases. She never has time for herself anymore."

Her tone was sincere; the woman genuinely admired her boss, Abby realized. "Has she had any lasting romantic attachments?" Once the words were out, she couldn't retract them as much as she wanted to. Why had she asked such an impertinent question? She didn't have a clue. The words just spurted out of somewhere.

"Oh, from time to time she's had her photo in magazines escorting someone to one function or another, but there hasn't been anyone special for years. I can't understand why not. She's so bright and beautiful. I sense she's lonely."

Abby didn't stop to analyse why her heart executed a little two-step at this information. "Maybe it's because no one understands the demands of her work, or if they do, they aren't prepared to put up with it. I can relate to that. My life is madness most of the time, trying to paint as well as earn a living. I'm always too tired to go out to meet someone. I…" She stopped talking abruptly, embarrassed as she realized what she was doing. She was comparing her life to Victoria's. It was ludicrous, for they weren't even on the same planet. Their situations were worlds apart.

Fiona merely nodded in agreement. "That's true, though I believe it's more than that. With such a domineering personality, it's hard for her to mesh with just anyone."

"Huh! You can say that again. She would expect complete submission from a partner. No matter who she was, she'd have to roll over and sing for her supper." A vision of a woman lying on her back with her legs in the air like a puppy while Victoria scratched her stomach popped into Abby's brain. She shook it away.

"Nay. She wouldn't be happy with anyone like that. That's the crux of the matter—she'd be bored after two minutes. It'll have to be a union of minds as well as bodies. Whomever she chooses must be her equal or she'll never be happy."

Abby checked her watch with reluctance as the light dimmed through the window. A pity they had to go, the conversation was absorbing. More questions needed to be asked to satisfy her curiosity. "Come on, it's nearly time we joined the others. I'll help you shift your things into the other room before we go downstairs."

At the dinner table, Abby was more in her element than on the previous evening. Her eyes shone as the discussion shifted from people she didn't know to focus on world affairs, politics and items in the news. Her intellectual comments and balanced assessments about the topics seemed to strike a chord with her hosts. They deferred to her frequently, soliciting her opinion and beaming at her like a teacher might at a particularly clever pupil. Victoria didn't contribute much; she moved her body at regular intervals to sit at odd angles, then slid two tablets in her mouth and washed them down with merlot. Even though the roast lamb was excellent, she seemed to be having trouble staying awake. At the end of the main course, she excused herself for the night.

Ellen raised her eyebrows at her husband as the door closed behind her. He shrugged. "She's feeling the effects of the ride. It looked like her back by the way she was sitting on the chair. That's the second lot of tablets I've seen her take in two hours and washing them down with alcohol should be a real sucker punch. She'll be knocked out 'til morning."

Two hours later, Abby found Victoria sprawled out cold on the bed, her mouth open, drooling on the pillow. "Not such a superwomen after all, are you," she murmured. Her pulse quickened as her eyes wandered down the sensuous planes of Victoria's body, then without thinking, she tucked a stray curl away from her face. She trailed the tip of a finger down her check, marvelling how soft her skin felt. It was like silk, and not pale either, but glowed with life like it'd been blessed with a touch of springtime. Abby examined the full mouth. What would it feel like to kiss it? She imagined it would be like a feathery caress. With a sigh she pulled the covers over Victoria and turned to her own bed, feeling totally frustrated. At the rate she was going she'd never find out what it was like to kiss a woman. But then an unwanted thought came. She really didn't want to kiss just *any* woman.

As she tried to sleep, she looked over at Victoria and Fiona's words rolled around in her head. She would have liked to have found out more about Victoria's past. What drove her to be such an achiever? An overachiever in fact. She had everything yet wasn't prepared to slow down. Was it the result of a financially deprived childhood, or was Victoria simply someone who was so competitive she had to be the best?

Abby wormed into the bedclothes, annoyed. Why did she psychoanalyse everyone? She should follow her mother's "live and let live" philosophy. Abby's job at the Legal Aid hadn't helped: troubled people cast shadows across familiar things, and turned everything into off-kilter versions of normality. Their plights made Abby realize life wasn't black and white, just numerous shades of grey. Everything had a cause and effect. She was a classic example. The death of her father when Abby was sixteen left her mother to struggle to make ends meet. Abby grew up fast. The best things in life might be free (as the saying goes), but lack of money certainly didn't equate to happiness.

She glanced again across at the shadowy form in the other bed. Why was she having such confusing thoughts about Victoria? They'd never get on. But as Abby drifted between consciousness and sleep, another image appeared in the haze: She lay with her legs in the air like a fluffy tiger cub while Victoria scratched her belly.

CHAPTER ELEVEN

Victoria was all business in the morning, a side Abby hadn't yet seen. Assertive rather than superior. She gestured for Abby to sit and took the chair opposite. "Some meetings are better held outside the workplace. This one in particular. The family has owned the land for three generations and need reassurance that our proposed coal mine won't impinge on their remaining grazing enterprise. I came out to personally negotiate the sale to give us much more of a chance to clinch the deal. Developing initiatives to minimize the impact is one straightforward way to make all parties happy. Even though it's government policy to grant mineral rights over grazing, our company prefers amicable solutions instead of running roughshod over landholders."

"So do you expect to finalize the sale?" asked Abby.

"I'm determined to finish it today," said Victoria firmly. "If we do, it would end months of negotiations. I want to go through the details before we see them. You can sit in. I don't expect you to understand much, but listen and you might learn something. One of your duties on the trip is to help Fiona with recording data. I hope you're reasonably au fait with computer filing."

Abby just shook her head at the statement. The woman was insinuating she didn't have an ounce of grey matter between her ears. "I'm sure I can handle it." She expected to pull her weight. She'd be bored out of her brain if she wasn't given something to do. Well, she'd just have to show Victoria she was capable of managing a workload and knew how to be a good employee. To prove her point, she slipped into the role of a diligent subordinate. She asked pertinent questions with a deferential air. Fiona bestowed admiring glances at some of her queries, though Victoria's manner remained closed. It was after eleven when they folded the spreadsheets and powered down the computer to adjourn to Bill's office to begin discussions.

"You bring the prospectus, Fiona, and Abby can bring the rest of the gear."

Discussions took the rest of the day to iron out remaining problems. Finally, Bill stood up and shook Victoria's hand. "Right. I believe it's time to sign those papers you've waved under my nose for months. Break out that bottle of champagne you've been saving, Ellen. After we're finished here, we'll pop the cork."

Abby relaxed as she thought over the day. She hadn't expected to grasp the mechanics of the business so easily. In fact, she had been fascinated with the whole scenario of planning a new mine. She was keen to see one in operation. Once the sale went through, Victoria explained that the next step would be the environmental study for government approval. She was to help Fiona collate some preliminary figures to submit to their planners. Abby looked forward to the challenge.

She could see that her boss was in the mood to celebrate and by the way she sat with her legs elegantly crossed, the effects of yesterday's ride must have vanished. After an hour, Abby was in that euphoric state a few glasses of good alcohol produced. While the others talked, she studied Victoria. Her fingers were long and tapered like a pianist and as she talked she waved them for emphasis. Abby's eyes moved up her shirt where the two open buttons showed the cleft between the swell of her breasts. Victoria certainly had a great body, though it was a crime her personality didn't match her looks. *How could anyone who looked like her be such a bossy-boots?*

"Well, Abby?"

"Pardon?" She snapped to attention. Ellen's eyes were focused on her. "Sorry, I was daydreaming. What did you ask me?"

"How long have you been working for Orianis Minerals?"

Abby glanced at Victoria, aware of her scrutiny. "Not long. I've...I've just recently joined the planning division and am learning the ropes on the trip."

"And do you find it interesting so far?"

She leant forward, not bothering to hide her enthusiasm. "Very much. I found the discussions extremely so."

"Your background isn't in mining?"

"Um...no. I did two years of an IT degree and afterwards worked in a legal department for years." Abby shuffled in the chair. She hoped she sounded employable.

"She's multilingual as well," said Victoria, "which was a requirement for the position."

Ellen gazed at the younger woman with approval. "How clever of you. How many languages can you speak?"

"My father was a cross-cultural business consultant, so I went to school in China and Japan. Paris, too, for a time. I've never had any trouble with languages, even as an adult," said Abby.

"You didn't finish your degree?"

"My father died and the money ran out when my mother became ill. She has to have continuous treatment for severe rheumatoid arthritis, so I support both of us. Her invalid pension's never enough."

Ellen patted her arm. "I'm sorry, dear. It's been hard for you, so forgive me for sounding like I gave you the third degree. Victoria must think very highly of you to bring you on the trip."

Abby couldn't resist a dig. "She values my computer skills."

Fiona, who was not a drinker and had been persuaded to imbibe in two glasses of champagne, was glassy-eyed as she propped an elbow on the table. "I think the lassie is going to be a great help to me. You should be pleased you asked her to come, Vic."

Good old Fiona. Abby stretched with contentment on the lounge like a cat who had just found a hidden saucer of milk.

"I'm confident she will be an asset to the company," said Victoria in a bland monotone.

Abby delivered a satisfied grin. "How nice of you to say that, boss. I wasn't quite sure how I'd go, but with that recommendation I'll be much happier."

"As long as you do what I tell you, everything will be fine."

"I'd like to think I can bring some new initiatives to the position. I doubt you hired me to be a robot."

Victoria rapped a long finger on the arm of her chair. "I realize you don't do things automatically. That's why I chose you. However, I expect absolute obedience of my employees."

"Though some autonomy must be given surely? If you don't delegate tasks and trust them to be carried out, business would grind to a halt," said Abby, her temper tightly reined in. "What do you think, Bill? You've managed plenty of staff."

He looked at her with approval. "You're right, Abby. Trust is an important component of any working relationship. It gives an employee a sense of worth, as well as getting much more out of them in the long run."

"That's not what I meant. You're twisting my words. Naturally I expect my staff to be able to think for themselves," said Victoria, plainly disconcerted.

Abby made a humming sound as the adrenaline buzzed. "I'll be able to make some decisions by myself?"

"Of course." The answer was brusque.

"Good. I'm glad we cleared up that point."

Ellen must have sensed the undercurrent in the air, for she rose quickly. "On that note, we'll move to the dining room. Would you sit next to me Abby? I'd like you to tell me about all the places you've lived. I've never been anywhere much, and now that the sale is going through, I hope we'll be able to do some traveling."

* * *

Victoria adopted a relaxed pose but inwardly stewed. Abby continued to provoke and undermine her authority, which put her increasingly on the defensive. She didn't understand why, but the artist's thinly veiled contempt bothered her more than usual. Maybe it was because their pre-meeting had shown that the younger woman had much greater business acumen than she had given her credit for. Her quick grasp of the facts and figures was remarkable. It was one thing to be confident that her own intellect far outstripped Abby's, but now she was not so sure. Abby was nobody's fool. Victoria felt frustrated. A shift in their power struggle had happened and it didn't favour her.

"Where are you off to next, Vic?" asked Bill.

"I'm taking the opportunity to look over our mine in the Bowen Basin. We'll stay a night then head to Perth."

Ellen tilted her head. "You're doing a long trip this time."

"We're going on overseas after Perth. All in all, we'll be gone nearly six months."

"That long? Don't you usually send one of your associates or lawyers to handle these negotiations overseas?"

Victoria shook her head. "Things are getting tight worldwide with orders. As much as I'd like to sit in my office in Sydney, my high-level clients and potential new markets will expect to deal with the CEO. Trust me, my experience and instincts are going to be necessary to seal the sorts of deals we're looking for."

"Are you happy to be going?"

"Surprisingly, yes. It'll do me good to get away. I've become an office hermit. Every day I'm locked away with reams of never-ending paperwork." Her eyes took on a gleam. "I haven't been back to Western Australia for years. I got my degree there, and then went to London for post-graduate study. I came back to WA to start my first job as a geologist. My old stomping ground will be a walk down memory lane."

"That's where you started your company too, wasn't it?"

"I met Malcolm at Port Hedland and we became friends. We formed a small exploration show with a very tight budget. We hit a seam of iron ore and the rest, as they say, is history. Bit of luck, really, finding the deposit. We were down to our last hundred dollars so we had to work on the drilling rig ourselves. We couldn't afford many staff." She laughed. "I literally had the ass out of my pants."

"I hadn't heard that story. I guess people only see success and not the struggle to achieve it."

Victoria patted her stomach. "Those were the days when I was fitter. I'm five-star accommodations now."

"What about you, Abby. Ever been to Western Australia?" asked Ellen.

Abby peered at Victoria with a bemused expression. If she didn't know better, she would have thought it smacked of approval. But no way would that be right.

Abby blinked before she answered her hostess. "No. I've always wanted to have a look over there. I'm excited about going." She turned back to Victoria. "I'd like to see you with the ass out of your pants." Ellen grinned and Fiona let out a low hiss. Abby sucked in a breath. She screwed the napkin as she stuttered, "I...I didn't mean...that didn't come out right. What I meant to say, I'd like to have met you in those days with your ass out of your pants." She flushed red. "When you were poorer, I mean."

Victoria's mouth twitched into a ghost of a smile. "I can assure you I wasn't very interesting. All sweaty and grimy out in the field."

Abby's fork nearly missed her mouth at that vision, then she pulled herself together and said firmly, "Huh. You underestimate how refreshing it is to see someone working with their hands. There's nothing wrong with good old-fashioned sweat. And life's not so predictable. Tied to a desk doing the *same old, same old* every day is boring."

"You're spot-on, Abby," said Bill. "That's why I love life on the land so much. Every day's an adventure."

"Personally I dislike not being in control, not knowing what's going to happen from one moment to the next," said Victoria, aware she only argued to annoy Abby. Privately, she agreed with Bill. Her life over the last few years had become a source of frustration. She'd been much happier in those days without much money, enjoying the thrill of the chase.

"Pish," said Abby. "Routine is boring. Habit is a mindless state, needing very little brain power."

"Nonsense! Having a business run smoothly requires a great deal of intelligence. If there's no routine, things can dissolve into chaos," said Victoria, her voice sharp.

Abby leant further over the table. "If we want to get into a philosophical argument, mathematicians maintain that chaos can give us insight, power and wisdom."

"Hypothetical theories don't make good business practices," growled Victoria.

Fiona, lost in the argument and determined to quell the spat, hastily intervened. "What each of you is saying has merit."

Victoria whipped round. "Oh? Please elaborate."

Abby too frowned at the secretary. "I'd like to hear what you think as well."

Ellen rose from her chair as she watched Fiona squirm under their scrutiny. "As much as I would like the fascinating discussion to continue, I believe the cook wants to clear the table. Shall we move to the lounge for coffee? Or a glass of liqueur, if you prefer a nightcap?"

Fiona looked at her with gratitude. "I think I'll retire. It's way past my bedtime."

Once they had settled in the lounge, Bill steered the conversation to less contentious subjects. Later, Victoria sat out on the balcony until Abby went to bed, then slipped into the room without saying a word.

* * *

They started off mostly silent on the trip back to the airport. Fiona refrained from backseat driving, or saying anything much for that matter, and Abby was consumed with her own thoughts. The quiet was only broken by the rush of wind against the windscreen and the steady purr of the engine. After half an hour, the lack of conversation grated on Victoria's nerves, especially since she was still on a success high.

"Cat got your tongues?" she asked in a jovial voice.

A snort erupted from her assistant. "I dinna have anything to say. Ye don't listen to me."

"Come on...don't take it so much to heart. We all can get a bit snippy at times. I would have thought you'd be in a good mood with the finalization of the sale. What about you, Abby?"

"I've been thinking over something. I'll run it through with Fiona with the data. I noticed your recording system needed some fine-tuning when we were going through the spreadsheets yesterday. Especially the mapping. I believe I can devise a program which will simplify the process."

Victoria heard the words with surprise. She found herself continuing to gain a grudging respect for Abby. For all her own arguing to the contrary the night before, she valued keeping things fresh and inventive. It was one of the hardest things to achieve in a large organization like Orianis, as each section had to fit in with the overall plan of the company's goals. Anyone going off on an independent tangent meant confusion down the track. Staff tended to follow practices which held little potential to disrupt the status quo. While conformity had its merits, it also discouraged innovation. She nodded her approval. "I'll be interested to see what you can come up with. You'll find seeing the mine will give you more of an idea how we build the infrastructure to fit into the contours of the land. You'll have time on the plane to Perth to enter some of the figures."

Victoria was pleased to see Abby's face brighten. She still remembered prickling disappointment when her first boss arbitrarily dismissed her ideas because she was too young. The rest of the trip passed quickly as they threw thoughts back and forth to challenge the orthodox methods in place. Before they knew it, they reached the turnoff to the airport.

They walked through the terminal to where the company jet waited on the tarmac. Bruce waved a welcome as they approached. The flight attendant was silhouetted at the door of the plane and Victoria let out a heated, "Dammit! It's Stephanie."

CHAPTER TWELVE

Abby caught the tone with surprise and glanced at her boss. Victoria looked angry. Marcia had been replaced by a slender, tawny-haired woman who eyed them with assertiveness. As Abby climbed the stairs, she struggled to contain her irritation. The way the woman watched Victoria was not quite decent. In the close quarters of the entryway, Stephanie yielded little, forcing Victoria to brush against her. Then Stephanie flicked her eyes over Abby when she reached the top and flashed a cocky grin. "Welcome, Ms Benton."

Abby offered a curt nod, miffed. Evidently she was dismissed as no threat for Victoria's affections. She didn't understand why it annoyed her so much. "Where's Marcia?" she asked gruffly.

A satisfied smile appeared on Stephanie's face. "On her days off. I was lucky enough to jag this assignment. I've put a magazine on the seat next to Fiona for you."

"Up yours too," Abby muttered as she crawled into the seat and jerked the seat belt around her waist. Beside Fiona, Abby suddenly saw the funny side of the situation. It would serve

Victoria right to have to fight Stephanie off until they went overseas.

Abby took the opportunity while they were in the air to ring her mother. She had organized daily home-help with the first payment from Orianis, and was reasonably happy now about leaving her for such a length of time. Her mum's friend next-door, Joyce, would be a tower of strength, Abby knew. She had barely finished the call when the plane began to descend. The view out the window was mind-boggling—coal mining dominated the landscape. Huge draglines towered into the air and greyish mounds of overburden blotted the countryside like a foreign invasion. The piles circled open pits, gaping black holes in the earth. Mine after mine went on into the horizon. She had no idea a place like it existed. On landing, she could see the parking area of the airport was filled with multiple rows of four-wheel drives.

Abby turned to Fiona. "Why are there so many vehicles here?"

"They belong to the fly-in-fly-out miners. The newer companies tend to build camp accommodations as opposed to housing their workforces in the town."

"Really? Most people usually live where they work."

"Not in these mining towns," said Fiona. "In the early seventies when the mining booms began, it was a governmental requirement for the big companies to build towns to house their workforces. Now there are mining corporations who will only employ staff from other areas. They fly or bus the crews out. Orianis Minerals is not one of them. Our policy is to support the local towns. It's been a contentious issue for quite a while now in the industry."

Two men, in bright orange jackets with silver stripes slashed horizontally across the chests, waited at the small terminal to greet them. The elder of the two, a whiplash of a man with a long earnest face, shook Victoria's hand with an appreciative look and led them to a Toyota. "I'll take you out to the mine and Paul can drive the plane crew to the motel."

After leaving the town centre behind, they drove fifteen kilometres to the mine turn-off and entered the site through a guarded boom gate. The rest of the day was spent discussing business with the various division managers and touring the open-cut mine. Abby was overwhelmed by the sheer scale of things. The pit was so deep the huge trucks looked like cars at the bottom. The dragline that moved the overburden was as high as a four-story building. Its boom was as long as a football field and the bucket as big as a backyard swimming pool. Fascinated, she could have stood all day watching the bucket swinging back and forth, scooping and dumping its load. It reminded her of a prehistoric monster the way the steel teeth bit into the rubble.

* * *

Dinner certainly smelled appealing after the dirty sojourn to the mine. A long shower had been needed to rid Abby of the coal dust that seemed to infiltrate every pore on her skin. In a private room at the motel, the staff had prepared a feast fit for hungry travellers: pork tenderloin, steamed artichokes, garlic mashed potatoes and slices of fresh melon.

Victoria sat with the general manager and his wife, and in the predictable pecking order, Abby had been relegated to the far end of the table. She sat with three engineers: Bob, boyishly round-faced, with sandy hair and an engaging grin; Adrian, with a lined, tanned face and a killer dry wit; and Frank, Italian swarthy and ruggedly handsome. They proved great company. It was liberating to be the centre of attention from these genuinely fun people, making her feel happier as the weight of the recent past months slipped away. At one stage, Abby laughed loudly at one of the jokes and glanced up to catch Victoria's frown. She continued in defiance. *Blow you. I'm on my own time.*

After the meal, Frank began to flirt. Abby was flattered, especially as the other two seemed enamoured with her boss. They glanced at Victoria periodically with cow eyes. Not that it didn't happen all the time—every man who met Victoria seemed to suck in his stomach and thrust out his chest.

By the time she wove her way back to the room it was after midnight. Frank had persuaded her to stay for a nightcap after the others retired to their rooms, and insisted that he walk her back to her room. From the way he kneaded her hand, Abby was grateful she was sharing her quarters with Victoria. She opened the door and he looked at her with expectation.

"I'm sorry I can't ask you in, Frank. I've got a roommate."

He moaned his disappointment. "Just my luck." With a quick movement, he pulled her into his arms and planted a firm kiss on her lips. "That's to remember me by." He took a card out of his pocket and pressed it into her hand. "Give me a ring. I'd like to see you again one day."

Abby deftly avoided a second kiss, and tapped him on the cheek before she walked in. "Maybe."

After closing the door as quietly as she could, she felt her way in the dark to the bathroom to change. She hoped Victoria was asleep. At last under the covers, she let out a relieved breath. No sound had come from the other side of the room.

Victoria's bed was empty when Abby woke. She felt seedy, her mouth dry and a persistent throb drummed behind her eyes. Even though the thought of breakfast turned her stomach, she knew it would be sensible to have something. The plane trip to Perth would take five hours. She took some juice and toast from the buffet.

Stephanie stared at her. "You look like death warmed up. Heavy night?"

Abby sniffed. The damn woman didn't sound sympathetic at all. "A little too much to drink. I'll be all right shortly."

"You sure were having a good time," said Fiona. "They looked like nice young men, especially Frank."

"Um…yes, they were great fun."

Bruce jumped up with a grin. "I'll get you a small brandy. Hair of the dog, that'll fix you."

She dutifully drank it and gagged as the fiery alcohol hit her stomach. Five minutes later, a flush of calm spread through her body and the nausea receded. She smiled at the pilot. "I feel much better, thanks. I must remember that remedy."

Victoria, who had ignored her so far, raised her eyes. "It won't be happening again for you to have to remember it."

Abby bit the toast with a snap, chewed it thoroughly and swallowed before she said, "Whatever."

Victoria scowled at her for another moment before she turned to Bruce. "We'll get going as soon as we've finished breakfast. The car will be here to pick us up in half an hour."

Abby ignored a bout of dizziness as she packed. She still felt light-headed, though at least her stomach was no longer turning somersaults. After popping two painkillers, she folded her clothes into the suitcase before she lay down to close her eyes. Victoria hadn't said a word since Abby entered the room, which was starting to ping her off. Just because Victoria had had staid company, didn't mean Abby shouldn't have enjoyed herself.

As she drifted off, Victoria spoke. "No use going to sleep. We're going in a minute."

"I'll get up when the car comes. I'm packed and ready. What's your problem anyway?"

"I'm not the one who got drunk."

Abby propped herself up on her elbows and glowered at her. Victoria was starting to sound like her mother. "For frig sake, I was not drunk, just pleasantly primed."

Victoria slammed down her case and towered over the bed. "Rubbish. You were giggling like a teenager at dinner and allowed Frank to slobber all over you at the door."

"Oh, please. All he did was give me a kiss, which, might I add, I didn't see coming."

"What did you expect? You batted your eyelashes at him all night."

"It's none of your goddamn business whom I flirt with. What's it to do with you anyhow? You're so prim and proper, in fact an opinionated prude who's dull as dishwater."

"I'd like ..." The tirade was interrupted by a call outside the door to tell them their ride had arrived. Without another word, Victoria hauled her case off the floor and stalked out.

As soon they boarded the plane, Abby sank into the seat next to Fiona. "Can I have a half an hour nap before we go over the figures?"

The Scot patted her arm. "Go ahead. I've got plenty to do on the laptop for a while. I'm researching my Scottish ancestors who immigrated to Australia."

"Are you really?" Abby leant over to look at the screen. "How long have you been doing that for?"

"A few months. It's really fascinating…I found some cousins in Melbourne and an aunt in the Barossa Valley."

"You'll have to tell me all about it when I'm not so tired. Now I really must get some shut-eye or I'll be good for nothing when we get to Perth."

It seemed she'd only just closed her lids when Abby felt a hand on her arm. "Wake up. Victoria gave me a message for you on her way to the toilet," said Fiona and handed her a note with the words, *do your job.*

Abby stared at it, puzzled. "What does she mean?" she whispered.

Fiona looked down the aisle at her boss, who was in the front seat with Stephanie beside her. She had her arm draped over Victoria's shoulder. "I think she wants ye to get Stephanie away from her."

"Why doesn't she just tell her to buzz off?"

"That hasn't worked in the past. She's very persistent."

"Oh, for Pete's sake." Abby jerked off her seat belt and stormed down the aisle. She reached the front seats to see Stephanie stroking Victoria's knee. A stab of anger shot through Abby. *How dare she touch her like that?* Without a thought, she leant down, and grasped Stephanie's wrist.

"Would you mind not touching my girlfriend?"

Stephanie jerked her wrist from Abby's hand. "Excuse me?"

"Oh, there you are," stammered Victoria. "I thought you had nodded off…"

"That, darling," Abby said gently, "was your fault entirely…" She leaned down and took Victoria's face in her hands and kissed her. The shock of the soft lips against hers made Abby's senses reel. *Oh my, oh my, so this is what it feels like.* Instead of the chaste peck she had intended, the kiss blossomed into something so arousing she let her mouth linger. She slid her tongue lightly along the bottom lip and then over the top one.

All restraint vanished as an exquisite sensation spread through her body. With a breathy moan, she pushed her tongue firmly against the mouth to demand permission to enter. It opened and she slipped it inside. Their tongues began to duel, twirling in a heated dance. Abby was on fire as the slow sweet burning built into a flame. A loud hiss from Stephanie broke the spell and she pulled away. She raised her eyes to look at Stephanie. "Have I made myself clear?" Abby asked evenly.

Stephanie paled, rose quickly and hurried behind the curtain at the top of the cabin. Not daring to look at Victoria, Abby plopped into the seat beside her. "Satisfied?" she whispered. No reply came. When she heard footsteps, she reached over to take Victoria's hand and laced their fingers together. "Just in case she didn't get the message. Now I'm going to get some sleep."

CHAPTER THIRTEEN

As the plane banked over the sea to begin its approach into the Perth airport, it was well into the afternoon. Victoria looked down at the blond head pressed against her shoulder and decided to let her sleep until they were on the ground. She trailed a curl through her fingers and itched to massage the scalp. That would be so...*not sensible*. The kiss had not only unsettled her, it had twisted her in knots. Was Abby simply playing the part she was being paid to do? If so, she was a damned good actress.

Somehow the idea that Abby may have been acting depressed her. Hell, it seemed so real. If it had gone on any longer, Victoria would have reached under the shirt to stroke the nipples that pressed against her chest like two small bullets. She had never experienced anything so erotic.

She pinched her lips together. She could never lose control again. Anxiety swept over her. How on earth was she going to keep her distance? Abby was employed to be her partner for the trip, which meant they had to look like they were in a loving relationship. They definitely had to stop fighting, for it only seemed to magnify their awareness of each other. And she must turn a blind eye if Abby flirted with anyone, for as long as it was discreet, she had no hold over the younger woman. Her face tightened. She remembered the moment that she had seen the engineer take her in his arms. It had taken all of Victoria's willpower not to leap out of the bed to hit him.

And Chantal. Had Abby kissed her too? Hell, the way Abby kissed, the Frenchwoman would never give up. How could she hope to compete with such a stunning creature? Abby raved about Chantal being charming and considerate while she called her dull and boring.

The thud of wheels on the runway thankfully blunted her panic. She couldn't comprehend why it mattered what Abby thought of her, but it did. It did a lot. The plane rolled to a stop, Victoria gently shook her shoulder. The blue eyes slowly opened and gazed into hers. Desire clouded them like a soft haze for a brief moment before the lids fluttered and the pupils focused. Abby pulled away and offered a shy smile. "Sorry, I didn't mean to make you uncomfortable by sleeping on your shoulder. Are we here?"

Victoria looked at her in anguish, her emotions in turmoil. She was totally confused by the feelings. One part of her wanted to kiss Abby senseless and the other screamed caution. *She thinks you're a dull, boring prig, you twit, so get a grip. She's only here for the money. You'll become a joke she'll be able to tell her friends about after she gets home.* She swallowed and said in a rough voice, "We've just touched down. You'd better get back to give Fiona a hand with the gear. She probably wanted you to help her enter the data on the trip so you'll have a lot of catching up to do."

For a fleeting moment, hurt suffused Abby's face before her demeanour changed to disdain. "Of course. I've got a job to do. I don't want you thinking I'm a shirker." And without another word she walked off down the aisle, leaving Victoria with an awful feeling she'd washed something very precious down the drain.

* * *

Abby fought an overwhelming desire to cry as she pulled her carry bag from the overhead compartment. How stupid she'd been to think Victoria had found the kiss as arousing as she had. She squeezed her eyes shut. God, what had she done? She'd tongue-kissed her boss. Waves of self-loathing ebbed and flowed as she berated herself for not having more self-control. One thing was sure; she wouldn't let it happen again. The thought of never kissing Victoria again made her even more dejected. They would see each other every day in the coming months; how could she turn off her emotions like a leaky tap?

"Are you all right?" said Fiona.

The assistant's homely face looked at her with concern; the presence of the sensible woman brought everything back into perspective. Things weren't as bad as she imagined. She'd done her job well with Stephanie; there'd be no more unwanted advances.

And as for the kiss—Victoria had kissed her back, hadn't she? And she'd even pulled Abby in closer when she'd pressed against her, which meant she wasn't too repulsed. So what if it hadn't turned her on? So be it. Abby knew where she stood. Why did she ever think such a gorgeous woman would be remotely attracted to a nondescript thing like her anyway? The best thing to do would be to carry on as if nothing had happened.

She gave Fiona a bright smile. "I'm fine. I completed my task successfully. Sorry about not helping you."

"Don't worry about it, lass. I had a sleep myself so we'll both be fresh tomorrow to start. We're staying a week in Perth because Vic has some meetings."

"We're not working in the morning," said Abby in a firm voice. "We're going shopping and I'd like to treat you to a haircut."

Self-consciously, Fiona's hand dug into her loosely wrapped bun. "A haircut? I know this is old-fashioned, but it serves me well..."

Abby quickly pulled Fiona into her arms in a quick embrace. "You've been so good to me, Fi. Let's have a girls' day out."

"But Vic expects the reports to be done tomorrow."

"Does she need them urgently?"

"Not for a few days."

"Good. She promised me clothes and I'm going to get them. We'll work extra hard in the afternoon to catch up." She ignored the dubious look on the Scot's face.

As the taxi sped into the city, they were silent. With Fiona in the front seat, Abby was content to sit quietly to take in the view. Victoria sat unsmiling, preoccupied. A calypso jangle filled the car. As Abby reached for the phone, she caught Victoria's miffed but restrained disapproval. "Hello, *chérie*. Are you in Perth yet?"

Abby grinned as she recognised the low purring voice. "Hi there, Chan. We're in the cab on our way into the city. I'll give you a ring back in an hour."

"I'll be waiting. It'll be good to have a chat again."

"*Je suis impatient d'y entre*," replied Abby. Switching to French ratcheted her self-esteem up quite a few notches. At least she was desirable to someone. And it didn't hurt Ms I'm-so-fussy Myers to understand that too.

At an apartment block in the inner city, the cab pulled into the kerb and the driver popped the boot. Victoria didn't say a word as two porters hastened out to take their luggage. The decor of the foyer of the apartment building was so lavish Abby gaped. *So this is how the other half lives.* The manager greeted them personally, fawning over Victoria. Abby rolled her eyes. So tedious to watch yet another man fall under Victoria's spell. Abby had an urge to drop a suitcase on his foot, or at least to whisper nastily in his ear that he hadn't a hope in Hades because he was a male, and an unattractive one at that.

The porter led them past the main elevators to one tucked around the corner. The inside had a delicate fragrance of lavender. The fragrance was nothing like the antiquated lift at her home apartment building, which usually smelt of stale food tinged with cheap aftershave. The lift slid all the way to the top and the door opened, not to a corridor, but to a small space with a single door.

"It's the penthouse suite," said Fiona. "The company owns the building and Vic designed the interior. They keep it for visiting dignitaries."

The entrance hall led into the main lounge area. The room was spacious, with mahogany-panelled walls and a colour-toned mosaic floor. Paintings and objets d'arte filled the space, lit by hand-blown Italian glass fixtures. Chairs and two tables sprouted from the floor, and a deep chocolate leather lounge suite nestled in the other corner. Abby murmured her approval at the paintings on the wall. She was pleased to see some of the works were from Australian artists. Her delight was infectious as she bounced round with enthusiasm.

Victoria's ill humour vanished as she watched with amusement. "Have a look at this," she said with pride. She flicked a switch and a huge TV and sound system appeared from behind a panel.

"I love it. I love it. It's fantastic. And look at the deck outside. Scarlett O'Hara would be at home here," said Abby.

The bedroom also got her attention, with its plush carpet and brocaded bedspread. The en-suite was complete with a Jacuzzi, as well as a wall-mounted TV. Music played in the room at the press of a button. Abby smiled. She was going enjoy living the high life.

* * *

Victoria crossed her legs with a whisper of friction as she settled into the chair. "Did you make reservations for dinner, Fiona?"

"Aye, I booked a table at Opus for seven thirty. The others are meeting us there."

"Good. That'll give us time to unpack and get ready."

"Where is the crew staying?" asked Abby.

"At a motel near the airport. They're scheduled for flights all week in WA."

As she watched the other two disappear into their rooms, Victoria sank into the lounge chair. Abby's vivacity was contagious—she felt in a much better mood. It had been a long time since she'd been in the apartment. Designing it had been fun, but she hadn't created anything as challenging since. Maybe after the trip she should rethink where her life was going. Abby was right to say Victoria was boring and predictable. She needed to get out of her comfort zone and spread her wings again. The ringing of her phone interrupted her thoughts and a throaty drawl purred in her ear. "It's Fran, Vic."

Victoria gave a pleased *whoop*. God, she hadn't seen Fran for such a long time. "I'm in Perth. I was going to ring you."

"Malcolm rang to tell us you were coming in today. He told me you needed to get out and have a good time. We're dying to see you. What about joining us tonight? We're off to our old haunt, the Shady Glen, for a birthday party."

"You bet. I'm dining with the staff so I'll be there about nine thirty. I can't wait. How's Wilma?"

"She's good, keeping me in line as always. She says to wear those sexy leather pants of yours—there'll be plenty of ladies to meet. Did you pack 'em?"

Victoria laughed softly. "Actually I did. Hope springeth eternal."

"Well, tonight's the night, babe. No more of your usual picky attitude."

"Yeah, who knows? Maybe I'll get lucky. See you there."

As she rose to go to her room, the blanket of depression that had hovered over her these last months, settled again. She knew deep down what bugged her. The feeling was loneliness. She needed someone to share the next adventure with, someone who understood her. Time to start seriously looking for someone to share her life.

Victoria slid on the hugging leather pants then pulled on the long leather boots. She unbuttoned the form-fitting shirt to the cleavage of her breasts and looked in the mirror. The outfit should do nicely for the bar. She was ready for some action.

When she entered the room, Abby looked up and went pale. "Ready to go?" Vic asked.

Fiona dispensed a long look before she remarked, "Ye don't look like you're dressed for a quiet night."

"I'm going out with friends afterwards."

Fiona nodded with approval. "That's good. It's time you went out and enjoyed yourself."

In the taxi, Abby sat quietly in the corner. Victoria wondered if she was upset but dismissed the idea almost before it was fully formed. She probably was just tired from the trip. But Victoria missed the bubbly enthusiasm Abby had displayed in the suite. She hoped she'd perk up during dinner. The driver pulled up outside the restaurant where Bruce and Stephanie were waiting.

"Where's Marv?" asked Fiona.

"He went out with friends tonight," replied Victoria.

Abby turned with a hard stare. "Stephanie is dining with us?"

"Yes. Didn't I tell you?"

Her eyes turned dark. "I'll have my work cut out tonight with you looking like that. And for heaven's sake, button up your shirt."

Before Victoria could think of a suitable retort, the other two were out the door and the driver waiting to be paid. As they walked across the footpath, Abby took Victoria's hand. Stephanie glanced at their clasped hands and strolled into the restaurant without a word.

Victoria found making conversation harder as time went on. Bruce never said much at the best of times, Fiona was only interested in the food and Abby was unusually sombre. Stephanie's constant chatter seemed to be forced. As well, Abby began to stroke her arm with her fingertips, which made it increasingly difficult to concentrate. By the time the meal was finished, Bruce and Fiona were ready for bed, and Abby was massaging her arm.

"We'd better be off, Steph. We've got an early flight in the morning," said Bruce.

As soon as they disappeared out the door, Abby straightened and dropped her arm. The warm glow in Victoria's belly faded with the loss of the soft body. She cleared her throat, embarrassed by her yearning to reestablish the contact. "It's time to go. I'll call you ladies a cab."

Abby got up and stretched. "You take the taxi, Fiona. It's a lovely night so I think I'll walk home. I adore cities at night."

"Okay. I'll leave the door unlocked."

Victoria hummed her disapproval. "You can't walk around in the dark by yourself."

"Nonsense, I'll stick to the main streets. There're plenty of people out at this time of night. It's not late."

"Take the damn cab."

"No."

"Well, do what you like. But don't come whining to me if you get mugged."

"Really, Ms Know-all, you can be so infuriating."

After Abby walked off down the street, Victoria turned to Fiona with a shake of her head. "I was only trying to look after her."

"You've got to try not to use standover tactics. Be a bit more diplomatic."

"Why do you always take her side? Can't you give me any credit?"

Fiona's bottom lip jutted out. "That's not fair. It's not a question of favouring her over you. The lassie's very sweet, so why shouldn't I be friendly with her?"

Remorse swept through Victoria. She shouldn't take her frustrations out on her assistant. *Frustration—is that what the feeling is? I'll have no qualms about getting someone tonight. That should fix things.* She patted Fiona on the arm. "Sorry I've been so cranky lately. Now here's your cab. I'll see you tomorrow."

* * *

Abby wandered through the streets and headed down to the Swan River walkway. It was a grand night for it, the reflection of the moon danced on the water like a mirror ball. A lover's delight, her mother would say. A warm breeze blew, couples walked arm in arm and city lights shimmered like masses of golden stars. So why was she feeling so lonely? Maybe talking to Chantal would chase away the empty feeling. She took out her phone, but halfway through dialling she clicked it off. It was no use. The image of Victoria in her sexy leather gear was so deeply imprinted in her brain she couldn't possibly talk to another woman. Logic and unbridled emotions duelled in her head. They caused an ache to throb behind her eyes. She wondered if Victoria exuded some high-powered magic pheromone which lingered after she was no longer there. Abby had never felt anything like it in her life, a yearning that wouldn't go away no matter how hard she tried to ignore it. A voice called out and dragged her back from her musings. "Are you all right?"

She opened her eyes to see a group of women looking at her with concern. She leapt up from the seat. "How embarrassing, I must have dozed off. Just as well you woke me."

A tall woman, somewhere in her forties, walked forward, "Are you waiting for someone?"

"No. I'm on my way home from a dinner engagement and decided to walk instead of taking a cab. It's such a glorious night."

"You look like you need a bit of cheering up. We're all nurses from the Royal and off to the pub for a drink. Do you want to join us?"

Because they were strangers, sensibility dictated she should go home but they looked like fun people. Exactly the company she needed. So she said, "I'd love to. I'm Abby."

"And I'm Jessie." After introducing her to the five other nurses, Jessie led the group down the street to a pleasant hotel. Inside brimmed with friendship. Despite the fact her nerves were still on edge, Abby enjoyed herself. The women were good company and had an easy companionship which came with working together in stressful situations. Although a lot of the hospital jargon went over her head, Abby still got most of their jokes. She sipped gingerly her rum and Coke as she studied them. They were all ages, the eldest in her fifties. It was nice to be in a group who were content in each other's company and not there to pick someone up.

Only two didn't have wedding rings. One looked fresh out of college. The other, Patsy, a stocky woman around Abby's age, was entertaining with a great sense of humour. Gradually Abby began to relax, to lose herself into a completely new zone for a few precious hours. Time flew. It was only when they rose to leave, did she think to check her watch and saw that it was past midnight. Damn, she hadn't let Fiona know she'd be late. She hoped the Scot had gone straight to bed and not waited up for her.

"Can I walk you home?" asked Patsy as they said their goodbyes on the footpath.

Abby glanced at her, surprised at the unexpected offer, but then twigged. The nurse had flirted with her half the night. She blushed as she remembered the knowing looks. "If it's not out of your way, I'd love the company," she replied with a smile. Her ego ramped up a few notches. Patsy was a charmer.

As they walked down the streets, they talked comfortably together and found they had a lot in common.

"Have you anyone waiting for you at home, Abby?"

Abby hesitated as the image of Victoria swirled into her mind. She forced it away and replied, "No. And you?"

"I'm still looking. I've dated a few girls, but there's been no one special."

Abby studied her. Her first impression when they had met was that she more handsome than pretty. Now Abby saw beyond that. Handsome, yes, but there was a softness, too, about her that was captivating. Her eyes were a warm brown, framed by the longest lashes. They were honest eyes. Her light brown hair, though cropped short above her ears, looked silky and shiny. She was solidly built without any sign of fat—wholesome was the analogy that came to Abby. Her personality was lively, with an attractive dry wit.

By the time they reached the apartment building, Abby felt a little dejected. Why couldn't she have *la grande passion* for someone like Patsy? The nurse was an uncomplicated good woman who would make a wonderful partner. In all those years of loneliness, she could have met her then. They probably would have been very happy together. But now, that damn Victoria had wormed her way inside her affections and ruined any prospective relationship. *Crap!*

"Would like to go on a date?" asked Patsy at the door.

Abby shook her head. "I'm off overseas for months and then I go back to my life in Sydney. It wouldn't work."

"Where overseas? I'm going to Europe next year for a holiday. My family are shouting me the trip for my thirtieth birthday. My sister is going with me."

"Southeast Asia then some sightseeing in Europe, I think."

Patsy's face lit up. "Wow. Maybe we'll be in the same city at some stage." She dived in her purse, scribbled on a piece of paper and passed it to Abby. "Here's my email address. What's yours?"

Abby rattled it off and kissed Patsy fleetingly on the lips. "I hope we can get together overseas. I really enjoyed your company and thanks for walking me home. That was sweet of you; I had a great time." She gave one last peck on her cheek with a soft, "goodnight" before she stepped into the foyer.

Fiona was nowhere in sight when Abby walked into the suite. She crept over to her door, satisfied she heard snores inside. Finally alone in her room, Abby felt the tension roll out of her body. The night with the nurses had been a breath of fresh air, something she'd remember as one of the highlights of the trip. They were just decent ordinary women without any hidden agendas, willing to include her into their group because they sensed she needed cheering up. But Abby couldn't ignore the nagging guilt that hovered in the back of her mind. What would salt-of-the-earth Patsy have said if she had known Abby had allowed herself to be bought by Victoria?

CHAPTER FOURTEEN

Victoria stepped into The Shady Glen and the blare of noise hit her with a blast. The club hadn't changed much in ten years. The décor was the same, gaudy revolving disco lights still hung from the ceiling and it still looked warm and welcoming. Women of all ages were dancing energetically to a Beyoncé tune, while others chattered together at tables and at the bar. A waving hand in the corner signalled where her friends sat. Fran jumped into her arms and they swung round with delight.

"You look wonderful," said Fran.

Victoria couldn't keep the grin off her face. "So do you. Ten years and you don't look any older."

"Don't look too closely. There're plenty of lines and sags in places they shouldn't be."

A petite body leapt up to clasp her in a hug. "Hi Vic. My, you're getting more gorgeous as you get older."

"Wilma, I'm so glad to see you. Come on, let's have a drink and tell me all your news."

As they talked, Victoria studied her friends fondly as she remembered back to the days when they had first met. Fran had been her best friend at university where they both studied geology. She was the charming, boisterous one, long and lanky like a frisky colt. After Fran met Wilma, a feisty little redheaded accountant who swept her off her feet, the two had fallen deeply in love, and their days of playing the field had come to an abrupt halt. Vic felt a pang of envy. They both still had that wide-eyed look as if they couldn't believe their luck at finding each other. Two children later, domesticity had settled comfortably over them like a favourite well-worn blanket.

"We've got some exciting news. You better get your glad rags ready 'cause we're getting married in New Zealand next year."

"Good for you. Some country had sense to change the law. What date? I'll be away six months."

"It won't be 'til October. I'd like you to be my best man, Vic. Damn. I don't know whether to call you a best man or bridesmaid but you'll be the one in the tux anyhow."

A lump formed in Victoria's throat. "I'd be honoured."

Fran pulled Wilma to her feet. "Now that's settled, I'm going to dance with my girl. You can take your pick 'cause the whole crowd is staring at you."

Victoria bought another drink and snagged a stool at the bar. She scanned the room, searching for the player who won the ladies without trying. That arrogant one who always stood out. For a moment she hesitated at the blonde with the dimples. Did she have blue eyes that sparkled as she got angrier, could her kisses send her soul into orbit? *Get a grip you fool. No one like Abby tonight.*

Then she saw her. She was dancing with two partners, her lithe muscular body swayed to the music. Her short hair was tousled carelessly, her disinterest with her dancing partners apparent. She looked over; Victoria raised her glass and turned back to the bar. Victoria turned away invitations to dance with a shake of the head while she waited. The next tune began. The player approached Victoria to claim her hand with no expectation of refusal. The woman danced well, the light pressure of her body offered a subtle promise it would be closer next time. The bracket ended, and Victoria pivoted and left her alone on the floor. Victoria smiled. Give the woman half an hour tops and she'd be back with a little less arrogance next time.

Fran looked bemused as Victoria sat down. "Gina's hardly your type. Slumming it a bit, aren't you? The room's full of really nice professionals I can introduce you to."

"I'm looking for a love-'em-and-leave-'em type tonight. No strings."

"That's not like you, Vic. What's the matter?"

Compelled to answer truthfully by the concern on her friend's face, she said with some discomfiture, "Fed up with my life, I guess. Christ, all I do is work. I live like a nun, cloistered in my office."

"Nobody's sparked your interest over all these years? You were always so damn fussy."

Victoria's cheeks burned. "There's no one."

Fran offered her a searching look as she caught the blush. "Ah, methinks thou doth protest too much. Doesn't she..."

A hand tapped her on the shoulder. "It's midnight, luv. The babysitter will want to go home," said Wilma.

"Okay, we'd better go. How long will you be in Perth, Vic?"

"We leave Sunday."

"Would you like to come over for dinner Friday night? I'll invite Bev and Emma; they're about the only ones of the old crowd left. Have you anyone with you?"

"Two admins."

"Bring 'em with you. I'm sure they'd appreciate a home-cooked meal."

"Sounds good. I'll bring the drinks. See you then." As they went out the door, Victoria looked at her watch. Five more minutes. On cue, she felt pressure on her shoulder. "Would you care to dance?"

This time, Gina pulled her close and ground her body back and forth to the beat of the music. No subtlety was in the movements. After a few minutes Victoria took control, and guided them to a dark corner where she ran her hands down the woman's back. Gina buried her head in Victoria's neck and nibbled.

"Is there anywhere we can go?" whispered Victoria, though she wasn't yet aroused.

"A room out the back." Gina had panted her reply.

By the time they stumbled into the room, Gina had stripped open her shirt. She sucked wildly at Victoria's neck as she rocked her thigh between Vic's legs. No more foreplay was offered. As Victoria felt the fingers slide under the waist of her pants, her little bit of arousal vanished like a puff of smoke. She went into a cold sweat. *Hell, what am I doing?* She didn't feel any attraction, any passion, only an emptiness that could never be filled by this mindless coupling. She didn't even like the woman. Victoria wanted to shout she had been turned on earlier in the night by someone just stroking her arm that Gina wasn't even remotely in Abby's class. But she was in a ghastly scene she hadn't written properly, as she allowed herself to be mauled for a reason she could no longer remember. She pushed Gina away and buttoned up her shirt. "Sorry. It's not working for me tonight."

"You've got to be kidding me. I'm all worked up. Can you finish me off?"

"I'm sure they'll be plenty out there lining up for that job," Vic flung over her shoulder as she hurried out the door.

"Damn tease." Gina's accusation followed her down the hallway.

Victoria felt washed out and numb as the cab sped through the city. Tonight's fiasco was one of the worst decisions of her life. Shame flooded through her. She suddenly felt an overwhelming desire to cry, though the tears didn't come. *Our family never cries*—that had been drummed into her often enough by her father.

As the taxi approached the apartment building, she could see two women come round the corner, hand in hand. She blinked in surprise as the security light from the entrance glowed over them and she recognised Abby.

"Keep going. I'll get out at the next corner, driver."

As the cabbie drove off, she moved back into the shadows to watch. She stared as Abby bent forward and kissed the woman before she disappeared inside. Victoria felt such a surge of anger she nearly screamed out, "*Who the hell are you kissing now, Abby? You were supposed to be home hours ago.*" But she didn't say a word. She waited in the foyer for ten minutes before she crept up to bed. And as she lay under the covers awake, her own indiscretion faded away as the more urgent problem surfaced. What had Abby been up to and who was the woman she was kissing? Was she going to see her again?

* * *

Abby woke up totally refreshed. She hummed a tune as she poured a bowl of muesli and remembered the fellowship with the nurses. It was good to be alive. She would take Fiona to get her hair cut in a more flattering style and they would buy some clothes. A shopping spree got the juices flowing. A sharp click of the latch told her the Scot was back from her morning walk.

"Want some breakfast?" Abby asked. "There's plenty of cereal, bread, fruit and yogurt. I see there's a fancy coffeemaker here. I'll put it on."

"That sounds good. I'm sorry I was too tired to wait up for you last night. What time did you get home?"

The scrape of a door opening sounded and Victoria appeared wearing a bathrobe and a glare. "Yes. What time *did* you get in, Abby?"

"I..." She stopped suddenly as she peered at Victoria in horror. "What's that on your neck?"

"Vic! How could you?" squeaked Fiona.

Abby narrowed her eyes and spat out the words. "It's a damn hickey, isn't it?"

Victoria didn't speak as she looked down shamefacedly. She groaned and walked quickly to her room. In the mirror, she could see a round, bright red patch above her collarbone; it couldn't be mistaken for anything other than it was. Half an hour later she came back to the kitchen, dressed in her pin-striped grey suit for the morning meeting with the white blouse underneath buttoned up to the top. She tipped some cereal into a dish, not looking at either of them as she began to eat.

She finished, dabbed her mouth with the napkin and said to Fiona, "I'm seeing the accountant of the Hillside Mine today. Could you start on the costing for the shipping this morning? I'll need it by Friday."

As Fiona fidgeted, Abby interrupted. "That's three days away. I'll give her a hand to enter the figures so it won't take all day. We're going shopping for a few hours. I'll have to get those clothes you promised me and Fiona needs some too."

Victoria frowned at the Abby. "Do whatever you want but don't dare tell me what Fiona will do."

Abby flicked her eyes down to her neck and back again. It was over in a blink. When she spoke, her tone was mild with no trace of anger. "I would like her to go with me if you could spare her, please. She really needs new clothes to go overseas with. I'm prepared to work tonight if we're not finished by dinnertime."

Victoria moved her shoulders in a defensive hunch. "All right, she can go, but finish that work today."

Abby waggled her fingers in the air. "Credit card, please."

Victoria bypassed her and handed it to Fiona. "Make sure you get receipts," she said curtly before she marched out the door.

Shopping—how Abby loved it. With no budget worries, she danced on air. After leaving Fiona with the hairdresser under strict instructions for the style, she waltzed down the street to the exclusive boutiques. An hour later she already had three parcels when she went back to pick up the Scot.

Abby had a vague notion what the improvement a good styled haircut would make to the older woman, but was not prepared for the transformation it made. Fiona looked ten years younger.

"Fiona, you look fabulous. Now for some nice suits for work first."

Rather guiltily they snuck back to the apartment after two and made arrangements with the manager to collect the parcels they hadn't been able to carry. Abby lay back in the chair completely satisfied. It had been a fruitful day, though more things were needed which she figured could be bought in Japan. They had enough clothes for the time being. The dressing up parade with the new purchases, which was the best part, unfortunately would have to wait. Work had to be done. By the time Victoria arrived back they had almost finished. "All done?" she called out.

"We will be in half an hour," replied Fiona.

"I'm going for a swim in the pool. Dinner's at seven at that Italian place across the street."

"Right-oh."

After the last entry was recorded, Fiona sighed with relief. "I'm glad ye were there to help me. It's so much easier with two people."

Abby smiled at her. "We make a good team, don't we?"

"Aye, lass, we do. You caught on very well to the business. You should think about this kind of work after we get home."

"As much as I enjoy the challenge, my art comes first. Now put on that lovely green dress and blow your boss away."

Abby slipped on the new blue dress and went to look in the mirror. Simply fab. The design was unpretentious; it fell softly over the contours of her body with the hem just above the ankles. But oh my, she looked a million dollars. No doubt you got what you paid for and the dress had been very expensive. She told herself though, she must be more conscious of the price in future. It wasn't her money. Abby slid on her silver sandals and went into the lounge, anxious to see Fiona dressed up. Underneath that frumpy exterior she'd discovered an attractive woman ready to burst forth.

CHAPTER FIFTEEN

"Chop, chop, you two. I've booked a table for seven thirty," Victoria called out.

At the sound of footsteps she turned, a lump caught in her throat. Abby looked stunning. The blue dress matched her eyes, and the frock really brought out her curves. Victoria couldn't keep her eye off the hint of nipples poking against the fabric. Her own nipples had begun to harden. *Damn it! Down girls!* She was tempted to swat them back into submission. She pulled herself together and said nonchalantly, "New dress?"

Abby twirled. "You like?"

"Um—it looks good."

"Wait until you see Fiona."

At the sound of her name, the Scot appeared. Her dull secretary had been transformed into an attractive, fiftyish siren, buxom rather than large, her stylishly layered hair made her look handsome rather than wholesome.

The expletive burst out before Victoria could think. "Fuuuccckkk, Fiona. You look awesome." She looked at her slyly. "Better watch out. I could go after you myself."

Her assistant simpered and batted her eyelashes. "Ye know I'm straight, Vic."

Victoria winked. "I can always use another toaster."

Fiona disappeared into the bedroom for her purse. Victoria rested her hand on Abby's shoulder and whispered. "Thank you."

A murmur came back. "You're welcome. She was in there all the time. I only brought her out."

* * *

Friday arrived to everyone's relief. They'd been busy all week, with virtually no time to see the city except for a quick double-decker bus ride one evening through Kings Park and the botanical gardens. Fiona preferred a quiet night, but Abby was eager to accompany Victoria to Fran and Wilma's. She needed the break.

She liked the couple immediately. They were chalk and cheese, yet obviously very happy in their relationship. While they sat talking over predrinks, Wilma fed their two small children, Mel and Tim, and bundled them off to bed. There was no mistaking which woman was their biological mother; both had the cutest red curly hair. Abby watched wistfully as their parents kissed them goodnight. Maybe that could be her one day.

She was fascinated to see another side of Victoria as she and Fran ribbed each other, discussing old times as if it were yesterday. Bev and Emma made up the rest of the group. Abby presumed that they too were gay, until Emma mentioned her husband, though Bev with her close trimmed hair, androgynous face and muscular body, shouted she was a lesbian. Victoria introduced Abby as an assistant. They smiled politely and made her feel welcome, though struggled to include her in the conversation. She didn't mind, happy to sit back and listen.

In the dining room, Victoria pointed to the chair beside her and Abby found herself relaxing as they ate.

"Are you still unattached, Vic?" asked Bev.

"Yep. I'm the perennial bachelorette, married to the business. What about you?"

"I'm still on my lonesome."

Victoria looked at her with amusement. "What, nobody snaffled you up yet? A good-looking chick like you."

Bev leaned forward over the table with a glint in her eye, "I'm waiting for you, lover-girl. Just give me the call and I'll be over in a jiffy."

Abby glanced at her in surprise. By the adoration on her face, the woman wasn't joking.

Fran sniggered. "Give it up, Bev. She made it plain years ago she wasn't interested."

"Times have changed, moron. She's still available and I'm thinking of moving to Sydney. I've been offered a job with the firm over there." Bev looked Victoria directly in the eye. "Would you be interested if I did?"

Victoria slid her hand over the table until it touched Abby's. "You never quit, do you? Come on, Bev, we're good friends, so leave it be." She turned to Emma. "What have you been up to?"

Thankfully, once Emma got started on her husband and children, nobody else could get a word in. Then when Vic's hand nudged hers, Abby nearly laughed aloud. For all her self-assuredness, Victoria was just a big ol' wimp. She began to stroke Vic's knuckles with her fingertips as Emma waffled on.

Wilma gave their hands a quick glance and said, "What was your last name again, Abby?"

Abby slipped her fingers off, embarrassed by Wilma's interested regard. No need to continue anyhow; Bev was frowning at Abby like she'd cheated her out of her last dollar. "Um...Benton."

"How long have you been working for Vic?"

"Not long. I was hired to accompany her on the trip."

"She's came with us because she's a wizard at languages," piped in Victoria.

Wilma gave another quizzical look. "I thought I'd heard your name somewhere."

Abby squirmed in her seat which seemed suddenly too hard. "My main job was an interpreter. I was pleased to get the position so I can put those talents to good use."

She was rescued by Emma who rose from the table. "I have to get back to the kids, unfortunately." She looked at Bev. "Are you right to go or do you want to catch a cab?"

Bev looked at Victoria and Abby, and said with more than a little resentment, "There's no point in me staying. Oh, I forgot to tell you, Vic, I ran into Gina yesterday. She's rubbishing you around town about what happened the other night at the club."

Abby turned quickly to Victoria. Spots of red coloured her cheeks. Victoria shrugged. "Don't believe everything you hear, old friend. Her version would have been rot."

After they drove off, Fran threw an arm around Victoria's shoulder. "Don't think you're going yet. Ten years has been too long."

While the others sat down in the lounge to talk, Abby ranged through the room to examine the paintings on the walls. It was something she loved doing. Usually she found some gem and here was no exception. A small Margaret Olley hung in the corner.

"Exquisite, isn't it," murmured Wilma behind her.

Abby cast an eye reverently over the oil flowers on the canvas. "It is indeed. You have wonderful taste. All your pieces are delightful." She turned to look at the redhead. "It's good to see you have a lot of originals and not the usual reproductions." She smiled. "Prints of the masters excluded, of course. Nobody can afford those."

"Vic's got a few. You'll have to get her to show you her collection."

Abby's eyes widened. "Has she indeed? Now that's interesting."

Wilma moved on to the numerous photos on top of the piano. "Here we were in our heyday."

Abby studied them. Victoria featured in many, younger and more carefree, her hair a little longer; her posture seemed somewhat more relaxed, but still held the same slightly defiant bearing. "It's nice to have these to look back on, isn't it? She and Fran must have been really good mates."

"They were. Vic broke Fran's heart when she moved east."

Abby's smile faultered, her next remark caught in her throat. A framed picture stood at the back, a print of her Archibald entry.

Wilma, following her gaze, chuckled. "Did you go and see it? Fran thinks it's priceless." She took it off the top. "Come on. I want to see Vic's face when she finds out we have it."

Abby was barely able to grind the words out. "Don't, please. I really mean it. You can't bring it up now."

"Why not? It'll be a laugh." She deftly avoided Abby's clutching hands and took it over. "Have a look at our latest artwork, Vic."

Fran rolled out a hearty laugh when Victoria went rigid. "Terrific likeness, old girl. The artist's got you down to a T." She poked Victoria in the ribs. "What'd you do to him—cut off his balls?"

"Let it go, Fran. I don't want to discuss it."

"Yes, let's get on to another subject. Victoria hates the painting, so give her a break," begged Abby.

Fran chuckled. "Are you kidding me? I've being dying to have a go at her about it. So come on. What did you do to him when you saw it? Knowing you, you wouldn't let it go."

"Damn nothing. Now are you satisfied? Talk about something else."

Abby shot forward on the seat. "I wouldn't have called it damn nothing," she snapped.

"Oh, wouldn't you?" Vic growled.

"Considering there were no male appendages to cut off, you managed very well to be an arsehole and think of something."

"What I did was deserved. You humiliated me."

Abby pressed her lips together. "I painted what I saw."

"And what exactly was that?"

"A self-important woman who had little regard for me or my talent," Abby replied evenly.

"You're the artist?" Fran's face was a mask of incredulity.

"Abby Benton," Wilma interjected. "I knew I'd heard that name before."

"But, we've moved beyond all that," Abby continued.

"If you say so," murmured Victoria.

Abby turned to Wilma abruptly. "I've got to go to the loo." She looked with apology at Fran and Wilma and fled the room.

* * *

Fran cleared her throat, and started to say something, but then closed her mouth shut again. Wilma stepped into the breach. She took Victoria's glass. "I think you need another drink."

"I guess."

"I'm really so very sorry. I didn't realize she painted the portrait, though I had the feeling I'd heard her name. I ignored her when she asked me not to show you. You're different with Abby, Vic. You like her, don't you?"

"There's something about her that strikes a chord with me. She irritates the crap out of me sometimes but if she's not around, I miss her. I can't help myself." She clicked her tongue with irritation. "And I don't know whether I'm even going to get past first base with her. She's very friendly with an old friend of mine."

"Who?" asked Fran.

"Chantal Du Bois."

"Chantal! God, she's every lesbian's fantasy, rich and drop-dead gorgeous." Fran's face was a study of disbelief and amusement as she slapped Vic's arm. "Damn girl, you've got some serious competition there. So what the hell were you doing with sleazy Gina when you had Abby all to yourself?"

Victoria snarled. "'Cause I had a brain fart, you idiot. Not everyone's as clever as you."

"It'll do you good. You've ignored every poor woman who's tried to win you, so you're getting some of your own back." Fran began to laugh.

The sound of the door opening silenced any more conversation and Abby entered the room. "Sorry about that. I'm sure you've got heaps more to say to each other and I don't want to spoil your evening."

"Do you want something more to drink?"

"A cup of coffee would be great, thanks."

True to her word, Abby sat back in the chair not offering a word. Victoria began to relax again as they talked into the night. It was getting late when Fran asked. "Do you ever see your father?"

Victoria's voice thickened. "I haven't seen him for twenty years."

"Isn't it about time you did?"

"He disowned me, don't you remember?"

"Come on, Vic. You've got to see him, if only to have closure. If you're free of him, you won't need to push yourself so hard. You need a life."

Angry disgust flared over Victoria's face. "Hell can freeze over before I see the mongrel again." Without warning, she began to shake and gasp for air.

Abby moved quickly to her side and took her arm. "Shush. Come on. Take some big breaths. In out, in out. That's it, honey, puff the tension out."

After the attack subsided, Abby moved away. Fran, looking mortified, muttered, "I'm sorry, Vic. It was none of my business."

Victoria gave a tight smile. "No, it's me who should be sorry. I just made a total ass of myself and my only excuse is I've been under a lot of stress lately. I always did let him get to me. I think we'd better be going. We'll keep in touch about your wedding."

On their way home in the taxi, Victoria, no longer able to contain curiosity, asked the question that had been plaguing her all week. "Who was the woman you were with the other night, Abby?"

"You *saw* me with Patsy?"

"Patsy...was that her name. Where on earth did you pick her up?"

Abby pursed her lips. "I didn't pick her up. I met some nurses and they invited me to join them for drinks. Patsy escorted me home, which was extremely nice of her. Anyhow, you seemed to have a good time with Gina, a very good time by all accounts, so what's the problem with me meeting someone?"

Victoria sank back in her seat and mumbled. "I just asked. I was surprised, that's all, considering how friendly you are with Chantal."

Abby remained quiet for a moment before she said, "Yes, Chantal has become a good friend."

Victoria turned to study her; she needed some kind of a yardstick to gauge what exactly Abby thought of the Frenchwoman, but Abby's expression remained closed.

With a sigh, Victoria huddled back into the corner of the cab. It was going to put a damper on their trip if Chantal continued to hover in the background.

CHAPTER SIXTEEN

It was mid-November when they landed in Tokyo. Abby shivered, the sharp chill in the air was a shock after the Perth heat. Their accommodation put her in a better frame of mind. It was enchanting; a traditional style Japanese home, with sliding doors, rice paper screens, an entranceway with a wooden floor and the hallway on the outside. Built in a half square, it allowed the bedrooms and main living area a view of the courtyard. The garden was equally delightful, peaceful and serene, with its pond, rockery and bonsai trees.

She dumped her bags in the bedroom, then, taking note of the simple aesthetics, unpacked and tucked the cases out of sight before she went out. The Japanese had the art of uncluttering down pat; it would be a shame not to conform. The others were in the lounge when she entered; Fiona closed the lid of her laptop and remarked, "It's a pretty place, isn't it?"

"Very," agreed Abby. The décor was quintessential Japanese, with hand-painted Shoji screens, lanterns hanging from the ceiling and tatami mats on the floor. "Everything's so streamlined and uncomplicated. This culture harks back to the principle that the simpler the life, the richer it is."

"How long were you in Japan, lass?"

"Four years. I went to school in Tokyo."

"Exactly how well do you speak Japanese, Abby?" asked Victoria.

"I'm quite fluent. I'm one of the main interpreters at my office in Japanese and Mandarin. I can handle some of the other Southeast Asian languages, though not well. We have lots of Vietnamese coming through the courts too."

"And you haven't been back to Japan since your schooldays?"

"No. I'm interested to see how it's changed."

"Then let's do a double-decker bus tour of the city tomorrow. Fiona and I are keen to see it as well," said Victoria.

Sightseeing the next day was an eye-opener for Abby. The view of Tokyo as an adult was far different than it had been as a schoolgirl. The megacity excited her, with the crush of humanity in its streets and its bright lights and loud signs. The trees on the pavements were dyed in glorious autumn colours, and chrysanthemums created enchanted displays in the parks and gardens. Over the coming months, she was looking forward to interacting with the tech-savvy people and she knew the shopping would be fantastic.

Work began in earnest after that and life became busy. One week blurred into the next as they travelled across the country to visit steel mills and meet with prospective buyers. Victoria insisted they negotiate in person. "Phone conferences frustrate me," she announced after the first meeting. "Face-to-face will win them over every time, especially now that there's more competition for the markets. It'll be a dog-eat-dog situation for all the companies until things improve worldwide."

Abby's relationship with Victoria entered an unexpected phase. Instead of the simmering antagonism that had plagued them earlier, they became comfortable with each other and gradually respect grew. From the moment they stepped onto Japanese soil, Victoria treated Abby like a valued employee, careful to listen to and appreciate her opinions. The three of them settled into a routine, each taking time off for themselves when possible after work. Victoria swam at a nearby hotel, where she'd made an arrangement to use their indoor heated pool. Abby took the opportunity to stroll down to the antique shops to forage for bargains (her favourite site the Tsukiji Outer Market and Bazaars), and Fiona settled down with her laptop to surf the ancestry sites. Abby's trusty Canon camera was a fixture on her arm; she captured many provocative shots, worthy of editing for paintings.

Abby knew Victoria had come to rely on her at the negotiation tables. Her command of Japanese and its nuances made it less likely for the buyers to successfully haggle down the price. Abby could tell if they were bluffing. With their busy work schedules, apart from the obligatory luncheons and functions, Abby, Victoria and Fiona were content to eat at home. Victoria was an expert in Japanese cuisine and Fiona was no slouch either in the cooking department.

Abby discovered she had been so wrong about Victoria. She was not self-absorbed, but thoughtful, kind and very smart. A little overbearing at times, though Abby figured that came with the territory of her high-powered position. As Victoria's official partner, she dutifully went along to all the functions, and it was easy to pretend they were a couple, for the Japanese were not ones for outward displays of affection. She found them to be careful and meticulous in nature: from the trains that ran dead on time, to the sublime works of art. But rural Japan interested her the most. While the metropolitan centres were mostly westernized, the provinces still held many of their traditional customs and the pace was slower, the people friendlier. Beautiful landscapes of wooden houses dotted vast rice fields and fishing villages clustered in hives against the backdrop of the sea.

Abby morosely threw a piece of bread to the birds in the garden. *It's Christmas Eve and if all's so peachy, why am I not content?* She knew why, of course. She was happy with work but more confused than ever by her attraction towards Victoria. She admitted to herself now that she liked Vic far more than she should. The feeling was becoming more acute as the weeks wore on. Every accidental brush or touch sent a shiver of delight through her. It was as if her body had a mind of its own; Abby found she deliberately put herself in positions where they would have to come into fleeting contact. Embarrassment spiralled through her at how she was behaving. She had fast become consumed with wanting to touch Victoria and a concerted effort was needed to quell the impulse. She was only tormenting the shit out of herself. *I can now be officially classified as pathetic.*

At the sound of a step, she turned. Victoria stood in the doorway, dressed in woollen slacks, a warm jacket, gloves and a blue knitted scarf protecting her neck. It was very cold; winter had arrived with a bitter wind and a flurry of snowflakes. "Ready?" Vic asked.

Abby buttoned up her coat as she took in Vic's scarf arrangement. No matter what she wore, she always managed to look elegant. A hard act to follow. "I'll grab my purse and I'll be with you."

"We'll take a walk first after the taxi drops us off and have a look at the decorations. Fiona's waiting outside with the cab."

The inner-city streets were ablaze with lights. Even though Christians only made up one percentage of the Japanese population, lavish, spectacular decorations dotted the city. Here Christmastide was more a time to spread happiness rather than a religious celebration, but all the universal symbols were evident: nativity scenes, Xmas trees, reindeers and Holiosho, the Japanese equivalent of Santa Claus. They strolled and took in the sights, until finally Victoria looked at her watch. "Okay, let's eat."

"Where are we going tonight?" asked Fiona.

Victoria grinned. "Fried chicken is a traditional Christmas Eve food in Japan." She moved to the middle and took their hands in hers. "We're off to Kentucky Fried Chicken."

Abby couldn't remember when she'd had such a fun night. They washed down the meal with Coke, and lingered over coffee and Christmas cake while they exchanged anecdotes of their lives. Fiona was particularly carefree as she kept them amused with her stories of her childhood in Scotland. However serious she was now, she seemed to have been a wag in her youth. Before they rose to leave, Victoria pulled out two small packages from her coat pocket and handed one to each of them. "Christmas Eve here is something like St. Valentine's Day at home. Well...," she gave a little cough, "at the risk of being sentimental, I want you to know you're my favourite people."

Abby caught her breath as she looked at the diamond earrings in the blue velvet box. They were gorgeous. Fiona had tears in her eyes when she pinned on her brooch, which was fashioned in the shape of bagpipes with a sapphire set in the middle. Abby was at a loss for what to say as she stared at her gift. Her life flashed in front of her—the loneliness of being truly alone. Nobody had ever given her something so precious. Emptiness swamped her. She had never awakened in the arms of someone she loved, never touched a lover in true passion. Her eyes wet with tears, she leant over and kissed Victoria on the cheek.

The intensity of Victoria's gaze startled her, the eyes luminous in the muted light and there was something in their depths Abby had never seen before. She opened her mouth to speak but musical rings in her coat beat her to it. Aware of the dark eyes studying her as she pulled the phone out of her pocket, she groaned when she read the number. *No—no—no. Not now, Chantal.* She was tempted to switch it off, but didn't have the heart. She flashed an apologetic smile and said, "Sorry, I've got to take this." She got up and walked to the corner to answer. "Hi, Chan. We're still out on the town so I'll ring you first thing tomorrow. Okay?"

"All right, *chérie*, 'til then. Bye."

Abby knew when she got back to the table the real connection was lost. Victoria, though still pleasant, seemed to shrink back into herself. Abby felt the sudden distance like a cold hand against her skin. They kept up the bright chatter though, as they wandered through the street homeward bound. Abby chewed over the events of the night. Victoria's gifts were as unexpected as they were emotionally overwhelming, not only to her, but also to Fiona. The Scot had been really affected by the present.

Victoria was proving to be a paradox. Abby didn't really know if Vic even liked her as a person. She had come to value her as an employee but like...?

And Chantal was another puzzle. Did she look on Abby as merely her friend or something more? The phone calls had become routine: nearly every night they would chat and discuss their day. Abby looked forward to the conversations, and knew she would miss the comfort of knowing someone cared about her. Even though they had only seen each other twice, Abby felt she was coming to know the Frenchwoman very well. The more they exchanged confidences, the more Abby liked her. She guessed it was probably no different from Internet dating; same thing, only their way was more personal. Chantal intended to meet her in Hong Kong and Abby would know then what the woman's attentions meant.

Christmas Day dawned to an early snowstorm. Victoria announced they'd stay in and have a traditional roast turkey dinner with all the trimmings, even though it was not a holiday in Japan. Tomorrow, work would start again in earnest. They opened their presents from home, and exchanged gifts in front of the artificial tree, decorated with coloured balls and tinsel from a yen store. Much to Abby's relief, her phone call home found her mother was in good spirits. Her sister had arrived from Hobart for a week's stay over the festive season. Her mum gushed over the Christmas present Abby had sent: an attractive hand-painted ivory fan from one of her sojourns through the bazaars.

After the heavy meal, they rented videos and spent the afternoon like couch potatoes. At nine o'clock Fiona got up with a yawn. "I'm going to bed. See you both in the morning."

Abby made a motion to follow, but Victoria waved a hand. "There's no rush." Her voice was gentle. She turned off the main lights, leaving the fireplace to illuminate the room. "Nightcap?" she asked.

"That would be nice," Abby murmured. Victoria retrieved a bottle of port and two glasses from the small galley kitchen.

Abby kicked off her shoes and tucked her feet underneath her. The setting was cosy; Victoria looked quite lovely as she sat cross-legged on the thick rice-straw tatami mat. Lights flickered over her eyelids, like images across a computer monitor.

For a while, they remained in companionable silence with their drinks. "What do you want out of life, Abby?" said Victoria suddenly.

The query caught Abby off-guard. She hesitated for a moment. "That's a loaded question, Victoria. My standard answer would be to say I want to paint and be able to support myself with it, I suppose, and of course give mum an easier life. I could be cute and throw in world peace as well. But I'm probably no different from anyone else. I want to be happy—to love and be loved. And I'd like some children of my own one day. What about you?"

"Oh, I've never really thought too hard about it. I've done what I had to do, although I'd like to slow down, do something for myself for a change."

"Why don't you? You've got everything you'll ever want. Enjoy yourself before you get too old."

Victoria toyed with her glass, twisting it in her hands. "Maybe I will."

Abby watched the fingers twiddle on the shiny surface. Strange that something so innocuous could captivate her. She wondered what it would be like to have them touch *her* like that. "Why are you still alone, Vic?" The words sprung out before Abby could suppress them.

By the look on Victoria's face, Abby knew she had struck a nerve. "You think no one can put up with me?"

"Annabelle would."

A frown creased Victoria's forehead; Abby thought she'd gone too far. But Victoria merely shrugged. "We're good friends. We've never been lovers and never will be."

"I'm sorry. I shouldn't have said that. It's none of my business."

"You needn't apologise, Abby. I must seem the proverbial loser in the romance department to you."

Abby stifled the urge to stroke her cheek; she hadn't thought anything she could say could have the power to draw emotion from the confident woman. "No, of course not. I was out of line. You're entitled to be fussy; you've got much more to offer than most people."

"Like money?"

"Is that what you think? Everyone's after your money?"

"It'd be a great incentive."

"Oh, for heaven's sake, with that attitude it's no wonder you're still single," muttered Abby, then regretted the words immediately, fearing Victoria would retreat into her shell again.

But instead she laughed. "Money doesn't impress you much, does it?"

"Nope. You can't make love to dollar notes."

A gleam appeared in Victoria's eyes. "And you would be the expert...?"

Disconcerted, Abby felt on the back foot. "I'll meet someone one day."

"Like Chantal?"

Abby tried to appear detached as she answered. "Maybe."

"I'd be careful there if I were you. She's an extremely sophisticated woman and you...well...seem inexperienced to put it mildly. Don't get too dewy-eyed over her," said Victoria, a little too sharply.

They locked gazes and Abby's heart plummeted as a thought hit. Maybe that was why Vic disliked Chantal and Abby's friendship. "You want her back, don't you?"

"What! No!"

Abby flashed a sceptical look. "You can't fool me. You're cranky every time she rings me."

"What Chantal and I had together is way in the past. She's a friend now, that's all," Victoria replied impersonally.

Abby recognized the shift in tone and assumed one to match. "That's nice to hear, because she's my friend too. She's coming to see me in Hong Kong, by the way. Now I really am tired, so I'm off to bed. I'll see you in the morning."

In her room, Abby sank heavily onto the bed. Their conversation had left her heavy-hearted and exhausted. She was no further discovering the real Victoria and she desperately wanted to know what made her boss tick. "I'm torturing myself," she whispered as her eyes closed, ready for sleep.

CHAPTER SEVENTEEN

Time flew, and before Victoria knew it, their business was concluded. Seated in the lounge, she watched Abby come out of her room. The younger woman had blossomed in the job since they had left Australia. Abby's command of Japanese had been such an asset and she turned out to be something of a computer whiz; Fiona constantly sang her praises. So far, new sales had exceeded all her expectations, due in no small measure to Abby's efforts. Victoria grimaced—it was getting harder to keep her distance. She never dreamt they would work so well together. But it wasn't Abby's work ethic that intrigued Victoria. She knew she had begun to care for the artist.

Though they had had such a rocky start, there was no doubt their personalities suited each other, even with their tussles of wills (or perhaps *because* of them). For once in her life, Victoria wasn't bored with someone after a few weeks. If anything, she looked forward to seeing Abby every day. And they seemed to be always brushing against each other, which made Victoria increasingly aware of Abby's body. Tantalizingly sweet, yet elusive. At the fireside at Christmas, Vic had had the strangest desire to take Abby in her arms and assure her that all her dreams for the future would come true. When Abby disappeared to bed, her departure had left Vic feeling slightly bewildered and oddly bereft. She feared that their personal—if somewhat blunt—exchange had pushed Abby away, but the next day Abby had greeted her warmly and even touched her lightly on the arm.

"Abby, please tell Fiona to come in. I've got something to say." Victoria went to the fridge to uncork the champagne especially bought for the occasion. The Bollinger label twinkled in the light.

"Come on over here, you two. Let's celebrate for a job well done. I want to thank you for your efforts. If we do as well in China, we'll be laughing."

They savoured the exquisite taste with appreciation and after two glasses, Abby bounced around with enthusiasm to Madonna's *Vogue*. She waved her hands. "Come on. Let's rock."

Victoria didn't argue. She was ready to let her hair down, and even Fiona allowed herself to be coerced onto the floor. For half an hour they gyrated to tunes that belted out from the audio system. Finally the Scot collapsed into a chair. "That's enough for me," she panted. "I'm feeling my age and since it's my turn to cook, ye won't be getting any dinner if I go on. And no more alcohol for me."

Abby giggled, kicked off the house slippers and stretched out on the low chaise lounge. "That was fun. Well I'm ready to have another drink. It's about time we had a blow-out."

Victoria winked. "You bet. I'll crack open another one." She dashed to the bar and then sat on the floor beside the lounge. Bubbles frothed over the rims as she poured the champagne into the flutes. "Bottoms up."

Abby tipped up her glass. "Ah—that's wonderful."

Victoria grinned. "It should be. It's verrry expensive."

"How much?"

"Seven hundred dollars a bottle."

Abby eyes widened. "That's decadent."

"We've earned it. The company's a lot richer with our new contracts."

Abby stretched out and murmured, "Good. Let's drink some of the profits."

"I hoped you'd say that. I put three bottles in to get cold."

"I could live like this," said Abby as she took another long drink. "We've never had any money to have the finer things in life. The champers is great stuff."

"Isn't it just? Nectar of the gods." Victoria squinted at Abby. She looked adorable with her curls tousled and a shimmering layer of perspiration filmed her soft cheeks. "Have you enjoyed Japan?"

"Oh, yes. And I love the business side of things."

Victoria propped one elbow on the seat to face her. "We make a good team, don't we?"

The blue eyes regarded her with appreciation. "You're great to work for."

Suddenly feeling vulnerable, Victoria drained her glass and topped them up again. "You like me now?"

Abby took a strand of Vic's hair and twirled it round her fingers. "I've never really disliked you, honey. You just have the knack of irritating me sometimes."

Victoria's heart skipped at the endearment. "Bring us another bottle in the ice bucket, Fiona."

The Scot frowned her disapproval as she handed it over. "Don't drink too much."

"Don't be an old fuddy-duddy," Victoria said, and, without a thought, she reached over to lightly stroke the exposed patch of skin on Abby's stomach. Abby began humming softly and slid closer. They sat gazing into each other's eyes as they drank on. By the end of the third bottle the stroking had developed into kneading, while Abby massaged Vic's head firmly.

Then Fiona was standing over them with a glare on her face. "Ye lassies will be sick in the morning. Either come to the dinner table or go to bed."

Abby gave a hiccup. "I think I'll go to bed. I…hic…have had quite e…e…snuf."

* * *

Abby's head felt like it was splitting open. She cautiously opened her eyes, then jammed them shut again as the light through the window flashed like an incendiary bomb. She groaned in pain. Her eyes were sore enough as it was, for in her alcoholic stupor she hadn't taken out her contacts. How much champagne had she consumed? Bits and pieces of the night filtered back into her brain like unwanted flotsam. She wished she were one of those people who forgot what happened, but the few times she'd over-imbibed, she'd remembered every last embarrassing moment.

With a great deal of caution, Abby edged out of the bed and made her way to the bathroom. The jets of water made her feel half human again, although her head still pounded. She took out her contacts and put on her glasses; her eyes needed a spell for a while.

Fiona was in the kitchen eating breakfast as Abby went to the medicine cabinet for some painkillers. The secretary eyed her keenly. "Are you all right?"

Abby winced. Why did the woman have to talk so loudly? "If you want the honest truth, I feel terrible. I'm usually not much of a drinker," she whispered. Even her own voice throbbed in her skull.

"Ye shouldn't have drunk so much."

Abby popped two tablets into her mouth and gulped them down irritably. "You're not very sympathetic."

"Nay. I've learnt when the wine goes in, strange things come out."

"Did we make fools of ourselves?" asked Abby as she felt her face flush.

"You and Vic were getting very chummy."

"Everyone looks awesome when you're drinking." The words were groaned out.

The Scot's eyes twinkled. "There's an old saying, lassie. 'Wine gives a man nothing—it only puts in motion what has been locked up in the frost.'"

"Huh!" said Abby unable to think of a suitable reply. She was saved from more conversation with the astute woman by the sound of Victoria coming through the door. She looked as bad as Abby felt.

"Ye don't look so good," said Fiona with a small smile.

Victoria winced. "I'd be better if I could find a place to bury my liver." She padded over to the medicine cabinet and searched inside. "Where are the headache tablets?"

Abby pushed over the packet. "Here." She stood up with caution. "I'm going back to bed, otherwise I won't be fit to go out tonight."

* * *

Victoria stared morosely at the toast and wondered if her stomach could take it. She noted Fiona's frown. "What are you looking at me like that for? It's only a hangover, not the end of the world."

"Ye should be careful how you conduct yourself with Abby."

Victoria ran her hand through her hair as she shot a wary glance. "I don't understand what you're talking about."

"The poor lamb's not used to women like you."

"Women like me? What's that supposed to mean?"

"She's not worldly or sophisticated like your set. If you continue to carry on like you were doing, she'll get a crush on you and have her heart broken."

Victoria tried not to look as stunned as she felt. Fiona had no idea what was going on. Victoria was liable to be the one hurt, not Abby. "We were merely having a few drinks together to celebrate."

"Just be mindful when you're with her, that's all I'm saying. You were touching her inappropriately when she didn't have her wits about her."

"I was not."

"Yes, you were and you know it. Abby's not someone you can toy with."

Victoria struggled to keep her anger in check. "I don't *toy* as you so crudely put it. And she's a mature woman so doesn't need your protection."

"Unlike you, she seems to be a little guileless in matters of the heart."

"Give me a break, Fiona. You sound as though I should have 'Lock up your precious daughters' tattooed on my forehead."

"Don't be flippant, Vic. I won't mention it again but I see things. She's beginning to like you a lot. It wouldn't be fair to take advantage of her."

"We were just having fun. Why do you have to make a drama out of everything?"

"I'm not picking on you and I've come to respect you a lot over the years, Vic, and I know you've been lonely. But Abby's employed to work and doesn't need the extra stress of an emotional entanglement. We have to live closely together for another three and a half months, so just leave her be."

Victoria opened her mouth and closed it shut again, aware it was no use arguing. Fiona had obviously taken up the banner to protect Abby's virtue. She huffed testily and walked outside for some peace. Even though her mind unconsciously registered the beauty of the courtyard, she absorbed the words, "Abby's beginning to like you a lot." Her heart performed a little stutter and a flood of desire shot like an arrow straight between her legs. Then a wave of nausea rolled through her stomach, which forced the erotic thoughts of eating an ice-cream sundae off Abby's bare belly to melt in a puddle of self-pity.

CHAPTER EIGHTEEN

When Victoria appeared dressed in a dolce tuxedo, Abby mewed a muffled moan. The coal-black tailored suit with the crisp white shirt and dusty pink vest delivered a new meaning to elegance. And the silver stilettoed shoes were awesome. The effect of raw sensuality left her slightly breathless and off-centre. She gave a nervous blink, aware she stared. "Great outfit," she murmured.

Victoria's silent appraisal was also appreciative, which made Abby pleased she'd found the blue chiffon dress in one of Tokyo's side street boutiques. As the dark eyes strayed down to the flash of her skin exposed by the low-cut bodice, Fiona made a hushing sound and took Abby's arm in a firm grip. "Let's go."

Vic was left to trail them out the door.

They alighted from the limousine outside the Sheraton Hotel; Victoria offered her arms to escort them up the staircase to the foyer. The Scot's mulish countenance softened only a little at the gesture. Abby wondered why the secretary was so annoyed with her boss. However, she didn't dwell on the matter as she took in the splendour of the reception room. The magnificent hall was resplendent with plush carpets, chandeliers and dining tables adorned with crisp white cloths and fine silverware. The tables were arranged in a semicircle around a polished dance floor in front of a five-piece band. Through the glass door on the side, the room's own private garden area displayed a riot of bougainvillea and lilies.

People mingled in the room while white-gloved waiters moved through offering drinks. Victoria left her associates to greet the guests, dignitaries of the city and company representatives. A half an hour later she signalled to the maître d' to begin seating. Abby sat between the Deputy Chairman of Nippon Steel and the curator of the National Museum of Western Art, while Victoria had chosen to sit with the Lord Mayor and his wife at the far end of the table. The Japan banquet was a sumptuous affair, with culinary delicacies to die for. A bevy of different wines was served with each course, or if the guests preferred, dry sake served cold. Abby's dinner companions were well versed in world affairs, and to her delight, were familiar with her paintings. The bombshell came as she was finishing the last crumb of her chocolate torte.

"Would you be interested in doing a series of three large paintings for our Nippon head office block in Tokyo, Ms Benton?"

Abby looked quickly at Akio Fujimori and wondered if she had heard him correctly. The grey-haired gentleman gazed at her quizzically. She provided a half smile to indicate her interest. "They'd have to be themed, presumably? Japanese or Western style?"

He bowed his head in acknowledgment. "Ah, you are one to come to the point immediately. Good. I have chosen wisely. Could you incorporate both in the panels?"

Abby eyed him thoughtfully, designs already flashing through her brain. "I don't think that would be too difficult, and since there'll be three paintings perhaps the last could be a combination of both—a merging of the traditional arts. It would be a fascinating concept."

"You would think seriously of accepting the commission? We are prepared to pay a hundred thousand dollars for the works."

"I would be extremely interested but unfortunately I am committed to Orianis Minerals for the next three to four months."

Akio bowed his head. "That wouldn't be a problem. The building is in the middle of renovations so there is no need to start immediately. Perhaps in the next few months you could send us some conceptual drawings."

"I will confirm my acceptance by the end of the week after you furnish me with the details of the size, etc." She placed her hand on his in a gesture of friendship. "And thank you, Mr Fujimori, for the opportunity."

"My name is Akio and I would be honoured if you would use it. Come, the band has started to play. Would you care to dance?"

Abby smiled shyly. "Please call me Abby and I would be delighted."

Happy, she tucked away thoughts of the unexpected commission to concentrate on enjoying the night. By midnight her feet began to ache—she hadn't danced so much in years. On a break, she saw Victoria make her way through the crowd towards her. Vic bowed and held out her hand. "Would you do me the honour?"

Abby looked at her in surprise. Was it acceptable for two women to dance formally together in Japan? She didn't have a clue. And she had never danced ballroom style with a woman before, let alone in a foreign country in front of so many people. It was a far cry from the usual scene at parties at home, where the music was invariably loud, fast and anyone still breathing could join in the action, with or without a partner. But Victoria looked composed, entirely in command. So she put her hand in hers and allowed herself to be led onto the dance floor.

Their bodies moved together with little effort. Victoria guided with such grace Abby felt as if she were floating. They danced sedately apart for a while and gradually edged together.

She became lost in the warmth of the body against her, feeling protected in the curve of the arms that hugged her close. They glided across the floor as Victoria steered her towards the door to the garden. Outside it was much darker, only lit by shafts of light that glowed out through the glass partitions and from the streetlamps on the pavements. Neon lights twinkled like stars in the background.

They were alone in the garden. Still joined together, Victoria gently allowed her hands to rest on Abby's waist. She pulled her closer. As Victoria's lips dipped to brush across her neck, Abby felt an ache of desire down to the tips of her toes. She squeezed against her, feeling a pleasant tingle as her breasts nestled into Vic's waistcoat. Without a thought she squirmed against the fabric to create friction on her nipples. Caught up, it was so easy to imagine they really were lovers. Victoria pulled her even tighter and Abby whimpered. She could hear her heartbeat thump faster and shivered as puffs of hot breath softly blew in her ear.

The feeling was so magical Abby trembled. Hands moved down to stroke her back. As the dark head lowered to meet hers, hot ripples flushed through Abby and she puckered her lips for the kiss. Suddenly the moment vanished. Victoria jerked back a step and stared at the doorway. Abby turned to see Fiona, arms crossed, wearing disapproval like a plastic mask. The Scot glared for a full minute before she disappeared back into the room.

Victoria cleared her throat and dropped her arms to break contact. "Fiona looks ready for home. You better go with her and I'll stay to see the rest of the guests off." All warmth had disappeared from her voice, although it remained polite.

To Abby the tone seemed worse than a slap on the face. What on earth had just happened? Victoria had gone from a lover to a virtual stranger in a matter of seconds.

She closed the gap between them again and pressed into the tuxedo. "Please. I'd like to stay with you. Fiona will be fine taking a cab home by herself." She knew she begged but she didn't care. Being in Victoria's arms was the most wonderful thing she had ever experienced.

"No. Go on home. I'm sorry for leading you on."

"Why must I go? I thought the dance was wonderful…that I was beginning to mean something to you."

Victoria stared down at her shoes, her shoulders slumped. "I didn't…I didn't intend to let it go so far."

Abby fought to control tears as her emotions plummeted. She blinked rapidly to hold herself in check. "It meant a lot to me," she whispered.

Victoria took her hands in hers. "You're my employee so it was wrong of me."

"I didn't fight you off, Vic."

Victoria shuffled her feet and jammed her hands in her pockets, a catch evident in her voice when she answered, "I know, but it was still a lapse of judgement on my part."

"Why must everything be so damn black and white to you?" Abby muttered and turned quickly to leave.

* * *

As she watched Abby hurry out the door, Victoria felt hollowness in her chest. What possessed her to say those things—to be so callous? Why had she taken notice of Fiona when all she wanted was to hold Abby in her arms and never let her go? In a way, she knew where Fiona was coming from. She was only trying to keep things on an even keel, and an emotional entanglement would certainly rock the boat. Sensibility dictated they shouldn't become involved, for maintaining a good professional relationship was enough to handle without the confusion of a personal one. Winning the contracts needed all their skills at the negotiating tables; the trip was too important to be stuffed up.

All of it had sounded fine in theory, but the clash of emotions in her breast shattered any logic. She had been cruel to someone she liked, which was unpardonable. *Why couldn't I have been honest about my feelings? I should have told her I was jealous of every man she danced with, even Akio, who's old enough to be her grandfather.*

Victoria went into a cold sweat. Remorse was not the bitterest seed to swallow; she was more alarmed by the consequences of her actions. Abby was meeting Chantal in Hong Kong tomorrow and Vic had virtually pushed her into the Frenchwoman's arms. *Shit!*

CHAPTER NINETEEN

Abby looked down the street outside the Mandarin Oriental hotel. Hong Kong—another Asian city that bustled with activity. As she followed the other two inside, she was barely aware of even a twinge of excitement. She scarcely noticed the people crowding the foyer as she stood to one side waiting for Fiona to check them in. Her hands curled into fists, hating how she felt, hating how, in spite of everything, her skin still prickled with desire when she looked at Victoria. The feeling was so strong; all reason went out the window as her body embraced the sensation.

She'd spent the plane journey from Japan trying to figure out the enigmatic Victoria Myers. Such a complex person— alluring, private and secretive, wedded to her work, frustratingly competent and yet unsure of herself in personal relationships. Victoria, she believed, had been as affected as she when they had danced; how could she still push her feelings aside?

As Fiona moved away from the reception desk, Abby reached for the bag with the business papers and laptop. Immediately Victoria appeared at her side and grasped her wrist. "I've got it."

For a moment, they both stared at Victoria's hand on her skin. Out of the corner of her eye Abby saw Fiona in time to catch the edge of protectiveness reflected in her face. She looked back at Victoria who stood with a hint of defiance. "I'll carry the bag," Vic said.

Perplexed, Abby grounded herself to the floor, at a loss to understand what was going on. And then the penny dropped. Of course. It was Fiona who interrupted them in the garden. She'd been crabby with Vic ever since their champagne-soaked night; she was obviously trying to protect Abby from her boss. God knows why, but she'd succeeded very well. *Damn the meddling fool.* Still, Abby couldn't help feeling a little happier. At least Victoria hadn't rejected her because she hadn't felt anything in the dance. It was some consolation, be it a minor one.

No one spoke as the lift slid up to their floor. Abby found the three-bedroom suite delightful, with a huge lounge area and a balcony overlooking a magnificent view of the harbour. She held her enthusiasm in check though, conscious of the strained atmosphere in the room. Then her phone rang, and when she answered, "Hi, Chan," Victoria strode off to her bedroom and slammed the door.

"Have you checked into your hotel yet, *chérie?*"

"A half an hour ago. What time shall I meet you tonight?"

"I'll come over to your hotel about four thirty. I'd like to catch up with Vic before we go out, if that fits into her plans. It'll be good to see her again." The Frenchwoman's voice lowered to a husky sound which curled into Abby's ear like a warm breath. "It'll be more than good seeing you again, my sweet."

Abby let out a contented sigh. It would be wonderful to see Chantal too, to feel comfortable with someone without drama. Nervously, she glanced at Victoria's bedroom door and wondered how Vic would react to Chantal. "I'll check with her but I'm sure it'll be fine. We're at the Mandarin Oriental. I can't wait to see you."

"Me too. Bye for now."

Victoria emerged from her room as the lunch tray arrived, apparently more relaxed. Her hair was still damp from the shower and she'd changed into casual clothes. Without intending to, Abby's gaze travelled the full length of her body. She noted the cute bare feet with nails painted a burnt apricot, and Vic's low-slung jeans snuggled over the flare of her hips. Her eyes lingered for a moment on the tantalizing swell of the pert breasts beneath the tank top. Abby's body pinged into instant arousal. *Hell's bells. The woman is a sex goddess.* Abby felt the blush rise as their eyes met. Victoria was grinning like a Cheshire cat. *Damn. She's caught me checking her out.*

For a heart-stopping moment she thought Victoria was going to pass a smartassed comment, but Fiona interrupted. "Time for lunch," she said.

Abby cleared her throat as she took a seat at the table. Now was as good a time as any—Vic's good humour mightn't last. "Chantal intends to come over at four thirty to catch up with you. We're going out afterwards," she said.

Before Victoria could answer, Fiona stepped in with a cheery, "That'll be nice. You and she are great friends, aren't you, Vic?"

"Yes, we are," Victoria responded. "But now Abby seems to have that honour."

Nonplussed at the snipe, Abby glared at her. "That's a strange attitude, Victoria. Why can't I be friendly with Chantal too?"

"Ha! You can't seem to make up your mind who you like."

Abby felt a rush of hurt. "That's not true. Yes, I admit I liked you a lot but take note; the operative word in that statement was *liked*. I take people as I find them and I actually thought you were someone worthy of my admiration."

"It's best not to have romantic attachments while working together," murmured Fiona.

Abby swung around to the older woman. "I'm grateful you want to protect me, Fiona, but there's no need. I'm in my thirties, not a teenager, and I am quite able to look after myself. I've been doing so since I was eighteen."

Fiona fidgeted, looking subdued. "I didn't mean to interfere in your life, lassie. I just felt that…"

Abby waved her hands and said a little sharply, "I can't understand what you're going on about. Even if Victoria and

I felt something more than friendship, which we don't," she hastily added, "she's my boss and I am infinitely capable of respecting her and of observing appropriate business protocol. Now I'm going to have a rest before I get ready for my date. I know you both will make her welcome." Without a backward glance, Abby marched to her room.

* * *

Victoria fought to dismiss the unfamiliar disquiet she felt after Abby's words, but the facts couldn't be ignored—she had been judged and found wanting. Never in her life had she felt so exposed. Poor Fiona looked like someone had stolen her last cupcake. Victoria pushed the plate of sandwiches across the table and said, "Finish your lunch."

The older woman averted her eyes. "I'm not hungry."

Even though she felt some degree of sympathy for her distress, Victoria couldn't bring herself to absolve Fiona of her guilt. Abby was right: Fiona had set herself up to judge affairs that were not her concern. And Vic had to share the blame as well for listening to her.

"Go lie down," Victoria said softly. "I'll wake you at four. We had better be on our best behaviour when Chantal gets here."

After Fiona disappeared into the bedroom, Victoria wandered onto the balcony and gazed absentmindedly over the harbour. The tension in her chest eased, but her thoughts continued to swirl in a jumble of self-righteous anger and self-recrimination. As she calmed, for the first time in many years, Victoria studied herself in a critical way. How had ambition taken over her life to the extent that she no longer valued love and friendship? When had she become so arrogant? Why did she let the agony of her father's abandonment deter her from finding someone to share her life?

She went into a cold sweat; she was at the crux of the matter. Why was she pushing Abby away? Listening to Fiona had only been an excuse. In a moment of clarity, she faced the truth.

I'm crackers about her.

Now that she'd thought those words she wanted to scream them out onto the wind. Float them out over the harbour. It was crazy, wonderful, scary, and so liberating to finally embrace her feelings. If someone had asked her two months ago if she knew what real attraction was, Victoria would have laughed. She'd had her fair share of dates. Women constantly asked her out, beautiful desirable creatures, but the zip, the zing, the thrill had never quite been present. Dating had become unexciting and predictable. Victoria grimaced. She'd never considered love-making reduced to only sensation without emotion, satisfying. To share one's body should be the ultimate joy and surrender. No, she hadn't had any concept of what true connection meant until Abby. She'd never met anyone that touched her secret inside places like Abby did with so little effort.

Truth be out, the artist had interested her from the very beginning. When she had caught Abby checking her out before, she'd had an overwhelming urge to take her to the bedroom until she screamed out Victoria's name in passion. But she had no idea how experienced Abby was. She had never mentioned ex-girlfriends, even in passing, so it wouldn't do to rush into anything. No matter how much Abby had awakened her desire, making her affection known would call for kid gloves.

Victoria's exercise in self-analysis vanished in an instant as erotic thoughts blanketed her. As she visualized Abby writhing naked on satin sheets, Victoria clawed at the balcony handrail. But maybe it was all academic. She had had her chance with Abby and blew it. Chantal would be the likely winner.

With a despondent sigh, Victoria massaged her temples as a ripping headache began to rise. She went inside to find some painkillers.

CHAPTER TWENTY

Victoria took the cocktail platter and drinks from room service, and knocked on Fiona's door. "Nearly four thirty. Time to get up." She listened at Abby's door, heard the shower running and moved away.

Fiona appeared, not looking her in the eye. She set up the glasses and crockery without saying a word and Victoria, feeling a surge of pity, placed her hand on her shoulder. "Buck up. Abby will forgive you. Let's show her we can be good hostesses."

As the Scot offered a wan smile, the doorbell rang. Victoria opened the door and a flash of jealously enveloped her at the sight of the Frenchwoman. The low-cut dress fitted her like a glove; to Victoria it looked like it radiated an *I'm-available-if-you-want-me* message. She had forgotten just how truly stunning Chantal was. She thrust aside her feelings and swept Chantal up into a hug. "My, my, old girl, don't you look good enough to eat. It's lovely to see you again."

"Ditto, *mon ami*. Travel certainly agrees with you," Chantal remarked.

"Too much restaurant food, I'm afraid. I've put on a bit of weight. Come, take a seat and tell me what's been happening with you. What'll you have to drink? We've got a fair selection."

"A dry white wine will be nice. Abby has been keeping me up with the news of your trip. Where is she, by the way?"

"Still getting dressed. She'll be out in a minute."

On cue, the younger woman emerged from her room. A flash of heat shot straight through Victoria's body and she barely managed to muffle the gasp that exploded deep inside her throat. Abby looked breathtaking in a dress which was the mother of all little black dresses. The top left little to the imagination and the bottom just covered her bum cheeks. An inch off either way and she'd be guilty of indecent exposure. She glanced sideways at Chantal. The Frenchwoman looked even more stunned, with her mouth open and eyes saucers.

"Chantal. It's great to see you again. I've been looking forward to it for weeks." Abby clasped Chantal in her arms. A muscle twitched in Victoria's jaw as the embrace was returned with equal enthusiasm.

Chantal held her at arm's length and chucked her under the chin. "You look wonderful. I can see I'm going to have to keep an eye on you tonight. I fear I neglected to bring my pistol to ward off all the suitors."

Abby brushed at the fabric and pinched at the hem of her new frock. "You like? I found it in a shop in Tokyo and couldn't resist it." She smiled. "I've always wanted a little black dress. Now I believe our guest needs a drink and something to eat."

Fiona rose immediately. "Yes, yes, of course. You get the drinks, Vic, and I'll get the platter."

Abby sank down and patted the spot next to her on the sofa. "Come and sit down beside me, Chantal. I've given you a running commentary of our adventures on the phone, now the others might like to tell you some of the funny incidents."

Fiona gave a grimace when she described the bush oysters. "I dinna think it funny at the time."

"That's what makes humour," said Abby. "It's only after chaos settles down that we can see the funny side."

Victoria chuckled. "I never told you about the horse ride, did I?"

After she finished her recital, Abby burst into laughter. "Do you mean to tell me you couldn't get out of the squatter's chair?"

"I swear on the Bible I couldn't. My backside was too sore after being Ichabod Crane for kilometres."

The laughter was doused when Chantal cleared her throat. "I'm sorry to break it up but our reservation is for seven thirty. We shall have to go."

Victoria's smile didn't reach her eyes. "Of course. It was lovely to see you again, old friend. Maybe we can get together before you go. How long will you be here?"

"Four days. I fly to Rome the day you head off to China. I came specifically to see Abby so we shall see each other again."

"Oh...right...I'm sure we will. Have a good time, tonight," Victoria said casually, though she felt anything but dispassionate as Chantal took Abby's arm and led her to the door. As the sound of their footsteps faded, she headed for the fridge to pour herself a scotch. A very large one!

* * *

Dinner proved a truly stellar experience for Abby at the Lung King Heen restaurant in the Four Seasons Hotel. They feasted on steamed lobster and scallop dumplings, the signatures dishes of the chef, and Chantal proved an ideal dining companion. Throughout the meal the conversation was lively, though they didn't touch on any subject too personal as they ate.

"Would you like to look at the dessert menu?" asked Chantal as the last dish of the main course was whisked away.

"I don't think I could fit it in. A cup of coffee would be nice though."

"Yes, I agree. I've had enough as well." Chantal signalled to the waiter who hovered close by, and placed the order. She turned her eyes back to Abby.

Aware she was being scrutinized, Abby gave a timid smile. "What?"

"I was just thinking how good it is to see you. You have really come out of your shell—you're blooming." Chantal fiddled with her spoon with a slightly nervous gesture. "I've really enjoyed our phone conversations; in fact I've become a little addicted to them."

Abby impulsively leaned over to take her hand. "Me too, Chan. We've become really good friends, haven't we?"

"Are we just *friends*? I thought we were…had become a little more. We talk on the phone most nights, and…well…I'm finding that we suit each other very well." She clasped Abby's fingers tight before she could pull her hand away. "I'm not asking for anything you're not comfortable with, but I would really like us to get to know each other while I am here. Can't we enjoy each other's company and see where it leads us? I'd like you to at least give us a chance."

Abby heard the words with some misgivings, but could think of no reason not to agree. She did like the Frenchwoman very much and Victoria didn't seem interested in her. She'd made it quite clear after the dance in Japan that Abby was only *a lapse of judgment* to her. So she said, "Of course. It will be great to share time with each other."

"*Mais oui*. So come. Let's take a double-decker bus ride and see the city sights."

By the time they arrived back at Abby's hotel suite, it was after midnight. Abby opened the door. "What time tomorrow?"

"I'll pick you up at nine thirty." Chantal moved closer and gently took her into her arms.

The kiss was slow and sweet, and when Abby thought Chantal might take things further and was poised to pull away, the Frenchwoman moved out of the embrace. With a soft "goodnight," Abby slipped over the threshold.

After the click of heels faded down the hallway, Abby remained pressed against the closed door. *Damn it! What on earth am I going to do? She expects more than friendship.*

"Did you enjoy that?" The question whispered in the gloom.

Abby swung round. *Shit! Victoria. Can things get any worse?* "You were looking at us?"

"How could I avoid it? You weren't exactly discreet. You were standing in the open doorway under the hallway light. Blind Freddy would have seen you." In an instant they were face-to-face. "You didn't answer my question."

"What business is it of yours?"

"Tell me if it was as good as this." Immediately Victoria's lips were on hers, insistent and demanding. Abby grasped her shoulders to push her away, but as she felt Vic's tongue slide into her mouth, she pulled her closer. She sucked it in deeper. Heat shimmered across her skin. Victoria slid her hand through her hair and gently eased her head up until Abby's neck was exposed. She dipped her mouth to feather kisses on the sensitive skin and then moved up to claim Abby's mouth again. The kiss deepened and Abby whimpered as a sweet burning flared in the moist warmth between her legs. A heavy fullness settled in her breasts and stomach, and when a finger brushed against her nipple, she moved her hands down and massaged Victoria's backside.

She suddenly realized what she was doing; with an effort she jerked away. Her body protested immediately from the loss of contact. It took all her willpower to take another step backward. Breathless, she gasped, "No—no—no, honey. We've got to stop. If you start again I won't be able to."

"I'm sorry. I'm sorry, but I couldn't help myself. I was so jealous when I saw you kiss Chantal." Victoria grasped Abby's hand and sprayed kisses over the knuckles and palm. "Come to bed with me. Please…please, sweetie. I really need you to hold me tonight. If you don't want to do anything more, we won't."

Nearly sick with longing, Abby forced herself to say, "I…I can't. It's not as though I don't want to. God, you've no idea how hard it is for me to walk away from you. All my heart wants is to bury myself in your arms and never surface for a week. But I'm talking with my brain now. When I give my heart and body to someone I must be sure. I won't be taking the step lightly—it's against my nature to be casual with anyone's feelings, especially mine. I…I don't want to be hurt." She stroked the dark hair with her free hand and twirled the strands in her fingers. "You won't like me for saying this, but I have to be fair to Chantal as well. She has flown all the way over here to see me and I can't be sharing your bed while she's taking me out. We've become… well…she expects…"

Victoria went still. "You'd choose Chantal over me?"

Abby's hands shook with frustration. "That's not what I meant. I'm saying she deserves to be treated with respect. She's been only kind and considerate to me and a genuine friend. I won't treat her badly."

"And I don't deserve to be treated with respect?" Victoria rose and backed away, her posture wary and defensive.

"You…you don't understand."

"You're a lot like me, Abby, so I understand what you're saying. I've never been into casual sex and I don't want to be hurt. But I am hurting. In a way, you're also like my father. He didn't think much of me either. I doubt if I'm able to compete with Chantal. She'll put you on a pedestal so she can adore and look after you, but be warned: you'll be so far up in the clouds, any ambition you've ever had will wither and die."

Abby stared at her, alarmed. Before her was a new and totally vulnerable Victoria. She struggled to ease the pain she had caused, but could only whisper, "I'm…I'm sorry."

"*Sorry* doesn't cut it anymore. Just remember, Abby. You can't have your cake and eat it too." She turned abruptly and was gone.

CHAPTER TWENTY-ONE

The next morning dawned bleak and overcast to match Abby's mood. Smog was a fuzzy grey blanket over the harbour; it was nearly impossible to see the junks and ferries. As it was to be their sightseeing day, she dressed in jeans, a T-shirt and slipped on her comfortable sneakers. In the breakfast area, Fiona was seated at the table and looked up with a smile. "What are you two up to today?"

"Chantal's got a trip planned to the Sai Kung fishing village for lunch. What are your plans?"

The Scot shrugged. "Vic's meeting someone for lunch so I'm having a day to myself."

Abby nudged her arm; time to offer an olive branch. "Wanna come with us? It's supposed to be the best food."

"If Chantal doesn't mind me coming along, I'd love to." A bright smile appeared. "I thought you were still angry with me."

Abby flushed with guilt. She had no right to judge anyone. *Let he who is without sin…*"We all make mistakes, Fiona. I should control my temper more and be nicer to my friends. Come on;

let's put it all behind us. Where do you want to have breakfast, here or the dining room?" She glanced round the room. "Where's Victoria?"

"She'll be back in a minute. She's ordered room service for us." The older woman clasped her hand. "You're a wonderful person and I'm very sorry I interfered."

Abby gave a weak smile. If only the woman knew.

She had slept only fitfully, tossing and turning as she relived her encounter with Victoria. God, how could she have been so callous and unfeeling? Victoria had begged her for comfort and Abby had treated her badly. The self-righteous platitudes she had spouted were all a load of crap. In the dark of night, filled with remorse, she finally faced the truth: she didn't know how to handle her feelings for Victoria.

Her insecurities had gotten her into the worst pickle of her life. She'd encouraged Chantal to come to Hong Kong so what was she going to do? The Frenchwoman would probably expect her to stay the night at some point, so how was she going to get out of that one? And Victoria? *I'm going to have to do some major kowtowing there to get back into her good graces.*

As Abby was planning her strategy, the door clicked open and Victoria entered. She didn't acknowledge Abby but addressed Fiona. "Breakfast will be here in a minute. Will you be all right by yourself? I'm sorry I have to leave you here."

"Abby's invited me to join her and Chantal."

Victoria shot a look at Abby and said in a low voice. "That's big of you to share Chantal with Fiona. She's only here for a few days and I am aware you think she deserves your full attention."

Abby's heart plummeted. The friction of last night was still alive. Fiona looked uncomfortable. She reached over to pat the older woman's hand and murmured a light laugh of reassurance. "Heaven's no. Fiona's company will be the highlight of the day. There's only so much two people can talk about. Chan was saying last night she'd like to learn more about Scotland and who better to tell her than a native?"

A beaming smile was her reward. "Aye, lass, I'd like to tell you all..."

Thankfully, the doorbell signalled welcome respite for Abby as the food tray was brought in. They ate in silence. Victoria disappeared into her room as soon as she had eaten and tension rolled out of Abby's shoulders. Time to get out into fresh air to collect her thoughts. "Go and get dressed, Fiona. The car will be here in half an hour. Let's get the show on the road."

* * *

Victoria couldn't believe how her life had disintegrated into jealous bouts and self-pity. She had no control anymore. One minute she went out of her way to antagonize Abby, the next she found herself begging. But the final act was the worst. She'd broken down and heaped the sins of her father on Abby's head. Instead of playing it cool in the morning as she had meant to, she'd sniped immediately. Not that Abby shouldn't share some of the blame. She was full of contradictions. How could she have shared her embraces with Chantal and yet still respond like a tiger to Vic's kisses only moments later?

Victoria took a second to relive the kiss. *Wow.* But Abby's passion wasn't the only thing about her that was exciting. The woman had spunk and a temper to match. What a mate she'd make.

Victoria frowned. *Mate—when did I start thinking along those lines?*

Depression set in again. *I gave her the ultimatum last night; it's Chantal or me, and the damn Frenchwoman's got the inside running.*

Mercifully, the beeps on her alarm brought her out of the doldrums and back to other matters. She had only an hour to dress and get to her appointment with their Asian accountant.

Li Jiao's office was on the third floor of a multistoried office block in downtown Kowloon. Victoria had only met her a few times, their business conducted mainly through Skype video conferencing. The accountant was a striking woman and a particular favourite of the gossip columnists. Her lover was a famous Chinese Kung Fu actress who starred in mass-produced B-grade action movies. It was unsurprising then, that after they concluded their business and went to lunch, the paparazzi, spying Jiao with another woman, began clicking their cameras. Victoria cursed. She hoped their photos wouldn't be splashed across the front page of the daily paper for Abby to see. The pictures would just add a few more nails in the already well-sealed coffin.

* * *

Chantal arrived in a chauffeur-driven Mercedes to pick them up. She was gracious about Fiona accompanying them on the trip, and it turned out to be an entertaining day. The fishing village was a pretty spot, with shrimp and crab dishes to die for. By the time they arrived back at the hotel, the Scot left them to continue to share their evening alone.

Abby and Chantal took a walk through the eye-opening Temple Street Night Market: a rowdy place, where hawkers flogged cheap wares, fortune-tellers clustered in tents, Chinese opera troupes busked, and outdoor stalls sold strange food. A bargain hunter's paradise.

Chantal was attentive, insisted on paying for everything, and was overprotective as they strolled along. Abby couldn't help thinking of Victoria's prediction that the Frenchwoman would put her on a pedestal. As much as she tried to take the lead, Chantal's possessive hand still steered her along. The next two days were the same. They took a sampan ride, visited art galleries and dined at exclusive restaurants, and each time, Chantal took charge. At night, Abby went back to her own hotel where they went no further than kissing. Victoria didn't appear again, much to her relief.

On their next-to-last last night together, Abby knew she couldn't keep Chantal at arm's length any longer. As much as she liked her as a dear friend, any romantic spark just wasn't there. All she could think of was Victoria and what she was up to. To make matters worse, on the cover of the English newspaper *The Standard*, was a full-page photo of Victoria with a sensational Asian woman. The headline screamed—*Mysterious Beauty Cuckolds Chuntao*. Abby ripped the page to shreds.

But she had an even bigger problem. Chantal had made it quite plain she assumed they had a future together. Every gesture, every touch, every look reeked of love and commitment. When she walked Abby to the door, she took her by the hand and stroked her knuckles. "I would like you to spend tomorrow night with me. Tomorrow's our last day together. Why don't I pick you up in the morning?" Chantal paused, and seemed to gather herself before she spoke. "I think it's time to take the next step."

Hell!

Abby gulped, at a loss about what to do. She just nodded. "See you tomorrow."

Coward!

She hardly slept a wink as she spun ideas around and rejected them immediately. In the end, she decided she would be honest about her feelings. How would she explain why she'd been leading her on? Chantal was considered an exceptionally eligible gay woman, and would be highly insulted to be knocked back by someone like Abby. And she didn't deserve to be hurt like that.

A stream of sunlight woke her. Abby felt she'd gone through a clothes dryer, her eyes burned and she had a dull headache. Still dressed in her skimpy night panties and top, she wandered into the kitchen to ease the pain with coffee. Victoria was already there and her eyes lingered on Abby's bare midriff and exposed thighs. A thought flashed through Abby's mind as she took in Victoria's appreciative look. Maybe she should ask her advice about what she should do about Chantal. Then the image of the Asian woman in the paper popped up. *No. Victoria doesn't give a damn now. She'll probably tell me I got myself into this mess so I'll have to get myself out of it. I'm not going to give her the satisfaction of gloating.*

* * *

Victoria hadn't slept well. It was crunch time. Chantal would expect Abby to sleep with her tonight. She'd heard Abby come in every night much to her relief, but if Chantal was serious, there was no way she would leave Hong Kong without cementing the relationship. Even if Abby wasn't quite ready, she didn't have a hope once Chantal got her in her room. She was the mistress of seduction. No woman could resist her, certainly not anyone inexperienced. She'd have Abby's clothes off in the blink of an eye. She wondered why Abby hadn't yet succumbed to her charms. Well, one thing was for sure: Victoria was finished with Abby if she stayed the night. She wouldn't share. Full stop!

When Abby wandered in, hair tousled and clothes barely covering anything, Victoria nearly choked on her egg. *Hell, Chantal must be nearly off her head by now from waiting. She'll go all out tonight.*

"How are you finding Hong Kong, Abby?" she asked, determined to make an effort to be pleasant.

"It's interesting. Despite the East-West clichés you read in brochures, it isn't a bad description. Hong Kong Island is such a modern city, but in parts of Kowloon I felt I was literally in the middle of China."

"I know what you mean, there's no doubt it's a city of contrasts. What's on your agenda today?"

"We're going on a helicopter ride this morning and taking the trolley up the peak for lunch. And you?"

"Off to the races. There's a big meet on."

Abby popped a piece of bread into the toaster and gave Victoria a quick sideways look. "With Jiao?"

Sooo, Abby had seen the paper. "With Fiona. She likes a flutter occasionally. Contrary to the tabloid trash, Jiao and I aren't sharing a secret love nest, nor am I planning to confront her lover, Chuntao, with the intimate details of our sordid affair. Jiao is the chief accountant of our Eastern branch and I went to see her on business."

Abby giggled. "No love nest, huh?"

"If you've ever seen Chuntao, there wouldn't be any confrontation either. She's built like a brick and she's a Kung Fu expert. Just the thought of tangling with her puts me into a cold sweat." Victoria cast a calculating look. "What about the four of us going out for dinner? It's our last night and it'd be nice to share it together. We have to be at the airport by nine so we can get to bed at a reasonable hour."

Abby looked contrite and lightly touched Victoria's arm. "I'm sorry. Chantal wants to cook me a meal herself tonight at her hotel. Maybe you can help me with…"

"Oh, well, it was just a thought. Have a nice time," Victoria interrupted and hurried from the room. She closed the bedroom door behind her feeling miserable. *Abby's going to Chantal's room.*

CHAPTER TWENTY-TWO

Abby checked her watch—her shopping trip had taken a little longer than she had planned. Chantal had the door open almost immediately at the first chime of the bell. "Come on in. Did you see anything you liked?"

Abby placed the bag on the table in the hallway and pecked her hostess on the cheek. "Two great knickknacks at a street market. I was lucky you sent me shopping while you prepared dinner. It was my bonus for the day." She sniffed appreciatively at the aromas wafting out from the kitchen. "Something smells good."

"Genuine French cuisine. Come, we'll have a glass of champagne first. Curl up here beside me on the lounge."

Abby glanced at the glowing candlelight. *Uh-oh! It's started already.* "Just one, okay. I don't want to be tipsy before I eat. I really want to be able to savour every mouthful since you've gone to so much trouble."

With a little reluctance, she allowed herself to be pulled over until her back nestled against Chantal's chest. The scent of perfume shimmered, and Abby nearly moved away as the soft breasts pressed against her. The Frenchwoman wasn't wearing a bra; her nipples were firm pebbles through the silk of her shirt. A leg slid up around Abby's side and the fabric fell away to reveal a creamy thigh.

A whisper tickled her ear, "Comfy?"

Abby took a swig from her flute. "Yes, thanks."

When the lips feathered kisses along her shoulders and a hand slid under her shirt to tickle her stomach, it was enough for Abby. "Come on, Chan. Let's eat. I'm starving."

Chantal registered her surprise with a low hiss. By the time she rose, Abby was seated at the table. Chantal moved to the kitchen and stroked Abby's shoulder as she passed. In between each thoroughly chewed mouthful, Abby continued a stream of conversation. By the time they cleared the table it was already after ten.

"Come dance with me," Chantal said in a tone that indicated she expected no argument. With the flick of a switch, the strains of Celine Dion's "The Power of Love" floated through the air.

For a moment, Abby hesitated before she moved into her arms. Chantal splayed a hand against her back and pulled Abby forward to curve their bodies together. They swayed in a quiet rhythm as Chantal hummed to the tune in her ear. To Abby, it seemed she was being assailed with sensations. The feeling was so delicious she let it go on. She could pull out at any time and her friend deserved a little affection. She had come all the way to Hong Kong to see her; they both could enjoy a little comfort so long as it didn't go too far. Chantal's lips afforded the sweetest caresses and her touches were exquisite.

As they moved to the music, Chantal began on Abby's palms, first with hot breaths and then warm kisses. All the tender parts of her arms were lavished, the dips and hollows nipped and suckled, accompanied by whispered tender words of love. Chantal moved over Abby's face, her neck, her ears, sometimes with mere fleeting touches, drawing sensations from the sensitive flesh like a violinist playing a concerto.

Whispering, touching, kissing—on and on and on—so hypnotic that Abby was unaware she was slipping out of control.

Then she was lying on the couch with Chantal on top, Chantal's hand on her breast. When she felt the fingers squeeze her nipple, Abby came to her senses. "No...no, Chan, please stop."

The hand froze for a second, then began to fondle again as Chantal murmured in her ear. "Oh, darling, let me pleasure you. I'll be gentle, I promise you."

Abby wriggled out from under Chantal, ignoring her muffled protests. She dropped to the floor with her back to couch. "I mean it. Please, I don't want this."

Chantal's voice was filled with indignation. "Look at me, Abby. Don't you dare turn away."

Mortified, Abby slowly swivelled to gaze into the grey, angry eyes. "Um...I think we need to talk."

"That would be the understatement of the year. You knew how I felt about you. Why did you come tonight?"

"Because...well...because I didn't know how to say *no*. You'd made such an incredible effort to see me and I...I felt obliged to go out with you."

"Obliged? That's a harsh word. So, am I not attractive to you?"

Abby tilted her head as she forced herself to keep eye contact. She had hurt the woman badly. "It's not that. You're a beautiful woman and anyone would be proud to be your lover."

Chantal looked defeated. "But not you, obviously."

Abby blanched and ploughed on, Chantal deserved the truth. "I do love you but not in the way you want. I...I...like Victoria. I can't help myself."

"From our phone calls I realized your attitude towards Vic was changing, but I didn't think it had gone so far. Does she know how you feel?"

"She's aware that I like her. But it's...it's complicated."

"Huh! I don't find that hard to believe. She's difficult to have a relationship with. She was never able to let herself go completely when we were together. How do think she feels about you?"

Abby swallowed back a twinge of jealousy as she pictured the two of them together. "Not letting go isn't the problem with us.

When we're together it's like…like spontaneous combustion. If she's not there, it's as if a light's gone out in my world and I think she feels the same. When we kissed the other night, it was difficult not to go further. Well, it was me who pulled away because I didn't want to be unfair to you. She even begged me to go to bed with her." Seeing the look of misery on Chantal's face, Abby was filled with guilt again. "Damn…I'm sorry. You don't want to hear all this."

"*Oui*, it is hard for me to hear. Why can't you love me, Abby? We are very well suited as friends."

"I think because you need someone to care for, to cherish. I want to be my lover's equal and run the show occasionally. Your love would smother me in the end. Victoria and I disagree sometimes, but it's different. It's like we have to have a little one-upmanship in our relationship."

"So, have you been intimate with each other yet?"

Abby felt tears prickle. "No, and we probably never will be. She told me if I came over to your hotel tonight, she was finished with me."

"And did you believe her?"

"Yes. She was serious, not cranky, when she said it. She said she couldn't take abandonment again."

"So why did you come?"

Abby shook her head, suddenly tired. "Two reasons. The first, because I promised you I would. I wasn't intending to sleep with you, just explain how I felt. I should have done that the moment I arrived. I shouldn't have danced with you. I let things go too far. I'm so naïve it sickens me. I can't understand why you and Victoria bother with someone as pathetic as me, to be quite honest."

"Never underestimate the power of goodness or freshness. And the second reason?"

Abby sat up straighter, the mantle of weariness dropped away. "Because nobody has the right to stop me from doing what I feel is right, and I *will not* be manipulated, especially by Victoria. That's not love, its ownership."

"Ah, but you allowed yourself to be bought. Is that not owning? You could have managed somehow, but you chose to take her money."

Abby felt the blood drain from her face and said in a hollow voice, "Yes, I did, and I'm going to have to live with the consequences. I lost my integrity, and as well, Victoria's, yours and my mother's respect by doing so. Mum warned me not to take the job. She said I wasn't calling the tune and I'm beginning to understand what she meant. It isn't a thing easily forgotten. The sad fact is, I should have agreed to go for the amount offered by the company without taking her extra contribution. The wage was more than enough to help set us up financially. But it was never about the money. I was too consumed with sparring with Victoria to think of doing it that way. She has that effect on me."

Chantal stood up and looked down at her. "I think perhaps you were very foolish. Now we'd better get some sleep. We both have to catch a plane in the morning and it is well after midnight. I will get you a pillow and blanket for the couch."

Abby nodded. "I'll set the alarm on my phone and get away at daylight. I won't wake you up."

Chantal returned with the bedclothes, Abby clasped her hand and a tear fell. "Are we still friends?"

Chantal regarded her gravely. "Perhaps we should leave it. In a way it's my own fault that you do not consider me as a suitor. I thought your naiveté was actually an inability to look after yourself, which was stupid and condescending of me. It will take me quite a while to get over tonight, I fear. Maybe one day we shall meet and can be friends again. Good night, Abby."

As Chantal's light footstep faded, Abby began to cry.

At five thirty in the morning, the first blush of dawn crept through the nearly silent street in front of the hotel. Abby stepped out of the lift, took her shoes off and quietly pushed open the door of the apartment. She tiptoed across the tiled hallway floor to the lounge. Fiona always rose at six but Victoria liked a little more sleep; plenty of time to change her clothes before they came out. With luck they wouldn't realize she had spent the night at Chantal's hotel. She looked round; so far so good, the room was empty. A noise made her turn to the dining area and she shuddered. Victoria stood at the breakfast bar, fully dressed, a cup in her hand and her face stern.

Abby waved nonchalantly as she continued to walk to her room. She didn't make the door before the question cut through the air.

"Just getting in?"

Abby, determined not to be put on the back foot, smiled sweetly as if creeping in with her shoes in her hand was as common as chips. "Yes. I'll see you in a bit."

"Come and have a cup of coffee. You look like you need one."

Abby couldn't help glancing down at her crumpled clothes. *Damn! Sleeping in them hadn't helped.* "I'm fine. I have to get on with my packing."

"Now please, Abby, I have something to say." The words were said with authority, in a pitch Victoria ordinarily reserved for difficult clients.

Abby darted her eyes to the door of her room. She felt like she was ten again being scolded by her mother. She dipped her head in resignation. *I may as well face the music now. Victoria will never let it go.* "Yes, ma'am," she said with more bravado than she felt.

Victoria drummed her finger on the marble top. "So, how was Chantal? You stayed the night, did you?"

Abby cast a quick glance at her face. Vic looked angry, but there was something else...something that seemed a lot like disappointment or perhaps something even deeper. Abby decided the best defence was attack. "If you have something to say to me, Vic, use a civil tone. If you want to know my business, ask me properly."

"If you stayed the night, you would have slept with her."

"Why?"

"Because she's so damn beautiful she can get anyone she wants and she's fabulous in bed."

A stab of jealousy shot through Abby again. "You're judging me on *your* experience? You're not the yardstick by which everyone measures themselves."

"Huh! Have a good look at yourself, Abby. Women like her eat inexperienced poor things like you for breakfast. You wouldn't have lasted two minutes in her room before she had you panting out her name."

Abby swallowed, remembering Chantal's caresses and how difficult it had been to ask her to stop. "Not necessarily."

Victoria ran her fingers through her hair, clearly upset. "I can't understand you. You kissed me like I mean something to you and then you spend the night with her."

"Because I stayed at her hotel doesn't mean we made love," Abby muttered.

"What's love got to do with it? It's about sex. You're so innocent you haven't a clue what that means in the real world. You live in a schoolgirl fantasyland where everyone lives happily ever after."

Abby struggled to remain composed. "Don't judge me, Vic. I'm not a child. There is nothing wrong with having hopes and dreams."

"And you think all your dreams will come true now that you've shared Chantal's bed?"

"I didn't sleep with her. I like her but I don't look at her romantically."

Victoria leaned forward until they were nearly touching. "I expected at least honesty from you, Abby. I don't believe you could have said *no* to Chantal. As far as I'm concerned, you betrayed me by going over there last night."

Those last words were too much for Abby. She placed her hands on Victoria's shoulders and pushed her away. "I don't give a damn."

They stared at each other for a long moment. "I'll see you at the airport," said Victoria in a quavering voice. She turned abruptly, picked up her briefcase, and strode out of the apartment.

Abby sank down onto the chair, horrified. She put her head in her hands and cried in agony. "Love's got everything to do with it, you foolish woman."

CHAPTER TWENTY-THREE

The tension between Abby and Victoria continued unabated into China. They landed at the Beijing airport at noon. Fiona, uncharacteristically quiet, must have picked up on the emotional vibes.

Big feathers of snow were falling. Their cab barely crawled through the traffic, which didn't help matters. Eventually the taxi nosed into a parking space in front of their modern hotel, The Opposite House. It was a green glass cube of a building, trendy and up-market with American oak bathtubs, mood lighting and airy rooms. Fiona had ensured that the rooms they shared were outfitted with twin beds. This was to be their base, as the majority of the country's three thousand steel mills were situated in the east and most head offices were in Beijing.

In the first week, the long days were filled with bargaining for iron ore contracts at office tables and boardrooms, but each night was an ordeal for Abby. Although her anger dimmed, Victoria remained distant. Abby found the emotional strain increasingly difficult to handle and began to realize how much her night with Chantal had damaged their friendship. Victoria had warned her, but she'd been too stubborn to listen.

To make matters worse, the hotel suite had an open-air plan; the bathroom was behind a partition which didn't allow much privacy. And while the loo was separate, it wasn't exactly soundproof either. Abby couldn't believe she could be living in such close proximity with someone yet could feel so lonely. In public, Victoria was friendly, though businesslike; in private, she was aloof and remote. After two weeks, sick of being ostracised, Abby decided to try to mend fences.

It was early evening when Victoria came back from her swim. Abby poured glasses of wine and handed her one. "Try this. It's a local vintage."

For a second it looked like Victoria was going to refuse, but she gave a halfhearted nod and took it. "Thanks." Then she opened the paper at the crossword.

"I'm reading Amy Tan's *The Joy Luck Club*, to get a feel for the place," said Abby brightly.

"I've read it," said Fiona, "though you will find Jung Chang's *Wild Swans* more informative as it spans three generations."

"I'll have to wait until we're out of the country—the book's banned in China."

"A bit late I'd say. The novel's been translated into thirty-seven languages." Fiona picked up a stack of mail, "But then there's a lot of confusing things here. Have you seen these ruddy Chinese stamps? I can't decide if they're upside down or right-side up!"

Abby suppressed a laugh and looked at Victoria. She was chewing the end of her pen, frowning at the paper. *Right, one last try!* "Wanna come with Fiona and me to the see the Forbidden City, Vic?"

Victoria didn't look up as she answered, "No thanks. I've got work to do."

"Come on," cajoled Fiona. "We haven't seen much since coming to China."

Victoria placed her pen on the coffee table and folded the paper. "I'm fine. Go and enjoy yourselves. Now have a look at the menu and tell me what you want for dinner. I'll ring room service after I have a shower."

Abby rolled her eyes at Fiona after she disappeared out the door. "I'm at the stage I'm just about ready to kill her."

"You've never mentioned what happened between the two of you. By the way she's behaving it must have been serious."

"It was a total misunderstanding," said Abby with a dismissive, vague wave of her hand. "She took offence at something I… ah…said, and now she's got her knickers in a knot."

"She'll come round then. She's not one to harbour a grudge for long," said Fiona. "Now, what time shall we be off tomorrow?"

"From the size of the brochure, I'd say all day, so let's leave by eight."

The Forbidden City did take the full day to see. The February weather was still cold, though the worst of the winter had passed. Abby was pleased it wasn't the full-on tourist season; she could imagine how uncomfortable it would be contending with perpetual crowds. When they climbed the steps to the Hall of Supreme Harmony, she gave Fiona a poke. "Look at the name. We should have dragged Victoria along."

"Aye, we should have. And to this one too," said Fiona, pointing to the map. "It's called the Palace of Earthly Tranquillity."

For the next month the pattern was much the same, and although Victoria softened a little, she remained remote. Fiona and Abby did trips to the Great Wall, Terracotta Warriors and other touristy sites on the weekends, and Abby began to go to Fiona's room at night to talk before she retired. Even though she tried to ignore the hurt, Victoria's attitude eventually got the better of Abby. She became fed up with China—everything about the place began to irritate her. She couldn't see any beauty, only the teeming masses and pollution. She wished they didn't have to stay so long in the country, but large contracts were nearly impossible to obtain. This meant smaller ones had to be won and negotiations seemed to drag on and on. Finally, Abby had to face the truth: any hope of reconciliation with Victoria had disappeared.

* * *

The wall of indifference Victoria had built grew harder to maintain as each day passed. Neither her feeling of betrayal nor her desire for Abby had diminished. The agony of living in such close proximity was excruciating. Privacy was in short supply; Abby's outline in the shower and her skimpy nightclothes were enough to send her off her head. Her only defence was to whip up images of Chantal and Abby to stoke her anger. But as the younger woman receded into her own world, one that excluded her, Vic realized what she had done. She had, by her bloody small-mindedness, effectively wrecked any hope of salvaging any relationship. All she had left was her pride. And she refused to crawl back to Abby, only to risk more rejection.

Then, after six weeks in China, Abby approached her one morning at the breakfast table. "Do you think I could stay home with Fiona while you visit the Anshan Mill? She could do with help. You'll only be there for two days and the manager speaks English well enough."

The request was the last straw for Victoria. Her detached attitude was forgotten as a burst of anger flared. *How dare she think she can choose not to go.* "No way," she responded sternly. "You're coming with me so don't you dare damn well wriggle out of this one. I need you there."

Abby's mouth sagged, her face bunched into a scowl. "No, you don't. We've already negotiated the terms. The inspection is only for show."

"It's your job, so do it properly."

"What do you care if I'm with you? You don't acknowledge that I'm even in the room most of the time."

"And whose fault is that? You just sit at your desk and sulk."

"Sulk? What rot. I've had just about enough of your cold shoulder."

"Don't you dare turn it around as though it's my fault."

"And you said nothing to provoke me? Please."

"How typical, heaping all the blame on me," Victoria snorted.

"You've got a selective memory," Abby shot back. "I wouldn't have reacted like I did if you hadn't been so nasty and patronising. You were too quick to judge me."

"I'm always the big bad wolf in your eyes. What do you expect me to do, beat my breast chanting 'mea culpa?'"

Abby opened her mouth to reply, but after a moment's hesitation, she began to laugh. Great rolling gusts erupted from deep inside her belly. "Oh, get over yourself, Victoria. I'm staying to help Fiona with the shipping costing because there's a lot to do and that's that. I'll see you when you get back."

As she watched Victoria leave the room, Abby executed a fist pump. Their relationship was alive and kicking. With a spring in her step, she went to find the Scot to start the day's work. But her euphoria was short-lived.

In the early hours of the morning after Victoria had left for Anshan, Abby was woken by screams from the adjoining bedroom. She hurried in to find Fiona writhing in agony on the bed, her face grey and in a lather of sweat.

Afraid and feeling totally helpless, Abby went into a panic. "What's wrong? What can I do?"

As the Scot struggled to rise up on her elbow, she gulped out between sobs, "I've got a shocking pain in my side and back," and flopped down again. Another wave of pain lanced through and she shrieked.

Frantic, Abby phoned reception. She prayed the desk was manned all night. When the receptionist answered, she nearly wept with relief. "This is Abby Benton from room 261. My friend has become very sick. Would you call a doctor, please? It's urgent; she's in a great deal of pain."

"We'll have to ask one to come in, ma'am. If she is really ill, perhaps it would be better to call an ambulance."

"Yes…yes. Do that…please hurry."

She dashed to her own room, dragged on jeans and a jumper and ran back to Fiona. Sweat beaded the older woman's face, now more a dull white than grey. By the time the medics arrived fifteen minutes later, Fiona had started to vomit. Abby felt completely inadequate as she dumbly watched them examine Fiona and load her onto a stretcher. She was grateful that they allowed her to ride in the ambulance. As they sped through the streets to the Chaoyang Hospital Emergency, Abby dialled Victoria's number.

"I'm unable to take your call. Please leave a message at the tone." Abby's heart sank—she was on her own.

At the hospital, after the trolley disappeared down the corridor, Abby plodded over to the nurses station to fill out forms. She brushed away tears as she reached for the pen, which seemed too chunky to hold as she fumbled to write the words. Finally she managed to complete the document, and pushed it across to the woman who was busy with someone else. Abby turned to a line of plastic chairs in the corridor—all she could do was wait. A further attempt to contact Victoria failed, so, defeated, she sent a text message to ring as soon as possible. Abby sucked in a ragged breath to steady herself. At the sight of a drink vending machine down the corridor, her spirits lifted a little. Just what she needed, she was parched. She fumbled in her pocket for just the right change to feed the machine and was relieved to see the can of Coke roll out.

An hour later, a man in scrubs appeared and addressed her in halting English. When she answered in fluent Mandarin, he smiled. "Ah, you speak our language. That makes things so much easier. I'm Dr Chan. Your friend had a large stone in her right kidney which caused the severe pain. Unfortunately, due to the state she was in, we had to remove it by open surgery and insert a small catheter to drain away the fluid."

Abby peered at him anxiously. "Will she be all right?"

"She'll have to be treated in hospital for six days. Barring any complications, she should make a full recovery, though she'll have to rest for a following two weeks. I presume she's covered?"

"Ms. McPherson is an employee of Orianis Minerals; she'll be a private patient. I'll confirm the details of the insurance tomorrow."

"Good. Shortly she will be in the Intensive Care Unit. We'll inform you when you can see her."

Abby trembled at the thought of what would have happened to Fiona if she had gone to Anshan. In ICU, Abby sat beside the bed and stroked her friend's hand. Fiona was still drowsing from the anaesthetic; her face was pale, her grey hair fanned out over the pillow in a knotty tangle and a dribble of saliva trickled down her chin. The Scot looked so alone and lost, Abby gulped back tears. Ten minutes later a nurse entered, changed the bag of IV fluid and went out with only a nod. An acute feeling of isolation swept through Abby—she wanted to get out of the place, she wanted to go home and take Fiona with her. In the lonely room, her emotions stripped bare, Abby thought about what the two women had come to mean to her.

Fiona was a gem; hardworking, stoic, and an enormous support. She had become a very good friend. And Victoria—well—she was now more than a friend. So much more. In a moment of clarity, Abby realized exactly the extent of her attraction to the woman. *I've fallen in love with her.* The epiphany brought a fresh round of anguish. She was under no illusion how different their circumstances were. Even if Victoria returned her affections, would she care that Abby had allowed herself to be bought? She hunched her shoulders, willing herself into a more peaceful state. But the room was stark and sterile; smelling of antiseptic, anaesthetic and the acrid odour of urine. Much worse, however,—broken only by the monotonous beeping of Fiona's monitor—was the unnatural silence.

* * *

Victoria woke late and jumped out bed at the Anshan hotel, annoyed her alarm hadn't rung. Her meeting was in ten minutes, which meant no breakfast. In the car, she checked her phone. *Still in the silent plane mode. Damn!* She scrolled through the missed call list to find three from Abby in the early hours of the morning and a text saying Fiona was taken to surgery. Victoria's face pinched tight when there was no answer. Half an hour later after four more tries, Abby answered with a weary, "Hi, Vic?"

"Where have you been? I've been ringing for ages."

"Calm down. I had to turn my phone off in the recovery room. Fiona was..."

"She's all right, isn't she?"

"Just listen for a sec and don't interrupt. It's been a terrible night and I'm completely zonked out. Fiona had a kidney stone. The operation went well, but it involved more than simple keyhole surgery. She's in ICU. The doctor said she's doing okay. I...I..." The sound of crying echoed at the end of the phone.

Victoria felt a lump in her throat. She longed to comfort Abby. "Go home for a while and lie down," she said. "I'll catch the first plane back."

Abby sniffled. "I will have a bit of a rest. It's upsetting seeing Fiona lying on the bed with tubes everywhere. She hasn't woken up from the anaesthesia and looks awful." Abby's voice lowered to a whisper. "And Vic, honey, hurry back. I...I miss you."

The next available flight wasn't until midday. The plane ride seemed to move at a snail's pace, which allowed Victoria too much time to dwell on everything that had happened. Abby was right; her behaviour had been deplorable. She'd cocooned herself in a bubble of invulnerability to disguise her pain about Abby's rejection. No wonder Abby had sought Fiona's company over hers. Vic felt sick. Life without Abby, she realized, would be too lonely to endure.

By the time the aircraft landed, Victoria was completely frazzled. At the baggage collection carousel, her heart gave a little skip; Abby was waiting for her. Pleasure flushed through her—she hadn't expected her to come to the airport. She extended her arms and Abby fell into them. "I'm so glad you're back. Everything feels better now that you're here," she murmured.

Victoria's arms tightened as she breathed in her familiar scent. "How's Fiona?"

"I've come straight from the hospital. All's fine. The doctor's pleased with her progress and she's awake and talking. Sore, of course, but they're giving her something every four hours for the pain. She'll get transferred tomorrow into a private room. We can go to the hotel first if you like, but she wants to see you."

"Of course. I'm anxious to see her too."

As the cab sped toward the hospital, Victoria put her arm round Abby's shoulder and felt peaceful for the first time since arriving in China. "I'm sorry for interfering in your life and for being so mean, sweetie," she whispered. "I promise not to annoy you with any more advances. I don't want to lose your friendship."

* * *

Abby snuggled into the warm body, though she heard the words with misgivings. Victoria seemed convinced Abby hadn't welcomed her passionate embrace in Hong Kong. Was the woman completely clueless? She must have some inkling of the depths of Abby's feelings by her response. And Victoria had called *her* naïve. It was on the tip of her tongue to declare how she felt there and then, but what if Victoria didn't feel the same way? The declaration would wreck everything and make friendship impossible. She knew Vic liked and desired her, but love? She'd given no indication that her affection was seriously romantic. Love was the ultimate emotion, the final surrender. Abby buried her face into the soft neck and murmured, "Oh, honey. You're important to me too."

Content to cuddle, the two women maintained a comfortable silence until they reached the hospital.

Fiona's face lit up at the sight of Victoria. She looked a little better, her skin a rosier colour and eyes brighter. "Hello, Vic, 'tis good to see you, lass," she whispered hoarsely.

Victoria reached over to tenderly brush the strands of hair back from Fiona's face. "Well aren't you the one, frightening us all like that, old girl. How do you feel?"

"Like a truck's run over me. I feel really bad giving you both so much worry. I canna tell you how much it hurt."

"Well you're in the right place and it's all fixed." Victoria settled down in the seat beside the bed and stroked Fiona's hand. "Just lie still and don't talk. I'm with you now. Close your eyes and go to sleep."

As Abby watched Victoria lean over Fiona so protectively, she only then realized the full extent of their friendship.

CHAPTER TWENTY-FOUR

Abby remained in Beijing to look after Fiona while Victoria went alone to Shanghai. They talked each night on the phone, but it was obvious by her wistful tone that Vic was lonely. Fiona's surgeon had ordered bed rest for a fortnight, which meant most of the business tasks and the caretaking fell on Abby's shoulders. She'd never worked so hard in her life. Her secretarial and nursing duties left her no time to complete the preliminary designs for the art works in Japan; it had become urgent to submit them. She berated herself for not having spent more time on the proposals while she'd had the chance. Fiercely protective of her art, she'd held back mentioning the commission—she never shared her work until a project was completed.

As they planned a five-day break in Seoul, she figured that would be the ideal opportunity for the work. She surfed the net for a secluded spot in South Korea where she could spend the break, and found a pension at Jangho, a small fishing village four hours by train from Seoul. The simple accommodation looked ideal in the brochure—part of the guesthouse with its own private bathroom and kitchen facilities. Taking the plunge, she booked it. The only remaining obstacle left was finding a way to tell Victoria without it developing into a drama.

Fiona was scribbling on a pad at the dining room table, when Abby decided to enlist her help. "Can we talk for a sec?" Abby asked, taking a seat. "I've got something to run by you." Once she had Fiona's attention, she launched into her prepared speech. "You understand how important my art is to me, right? It's only a week until we fly to Seoul and we're going to take a five-day break. Well…as I haven't had a chance the whole trip to pick up a pencil, would you mind if I go off by myself so I can do some sketching? I've found a little fishing village to stay where there should be plenty of subject matter. And I've taken heaps of photos which I would like to get on paper."

"I can see where you coming from, lass, but I was looking forward to the three of us having a good time together. We've been through so much."

Abby winced as she caught Fiona's disappointment. "I think that would be great too, but it is the longest I've ever gone without doing something art-wise. You've heard the expression…use it or lose it."

Fiona stopped fiddling with her pen and eyed Abby intently. "Do you think you'll be safe on your own?"

"I can't see why not. South Korea is a civilized country and I can manage the language. Not as well as Mandarin or Japanese, granted, but enough to make myself understood. I really need this."

"Will you be alone there?"

Abby sat up straighter and frowned. Now Fiona thought she was going there to shack up with someone. "Who would I have with me?" she asked sharply.

"Chantal."

"Oh for heaven's sake, Fiona, you're worse than Vic. If I were meeting Chantal, I would tell you. Why would I lie about it? For your information, I am no longer seeing her. We called it off in Hong Kong."

The older woman's face softened and she patted Abby's hand. "I'm so sorry, lass. You must be very disappointed. I didn't think she was the type to play with your affections, but it's for the best to end it before you really got involved."

"I ended it, not her," said Abby with satisfaction, annoyed at the presumption.

Fiona blinked. "You did? But she's a prize catch."

"So? She was getting too serious and I didn't feel the same way. I'm not going to hook up with someone just because they're rich and good-looking. That's not the basis for a lasting relationship."

The eyes behind the spectacles blinked again. "Ye never cease to amaze me."

Abby let out a sigh. "I guess I'm a romantic, just hangin' out for true love. I want the happy ever after. And even if everyone tells me differently, I'm not going to be satisfied with less."

"Good for you. One day someone will come along who takes your eye."

Abby clasped the edge of the chair firmly. *If only you knew.* "Okay. Now that that's out of the way, can we get back to my art break? Will you support me with Vic? She may be a bit cheesed off about it."

"I will if that's want you really want to do." Fiona shook her head. "I don't understand why, but when it comes to you, she's not her old self. You're both so volatile with each other."

"We can annoy the crap out of each other sometimes." Abby gave an apologetic look. "We must be hard to live with."

"I'm fine. I'm very fond of you both so it doesn't matter. I can switch off. Though I'm puzzled how Vic has changed. I've never seen her like this in all the years I've known her. She's always been so placid. If someone annoys her, she rarely loses her temper, just becomes aloof as though they're not worth the time of day. She's cut many a competitor down that way."

"Has she ever been really keen on a woman?"

"Not that I'm aware of. Not for years anyhow."

"Maybe she's feeling stressed with the pressure of the trip."

Fiona heaved her shoulders. "Perhaps. I hope once she's home, she'll be back to normal."

Abby sized her up; now that they were being frank, perhaps she'd tell Abby more about Victoria. "What about Vic's father?

She mentioned him in Perth. She seemed upset so I didn't like to ask any more."

"I've never met him, but from all accounts he was hard on the family and deserted them. Vic was in her teens. But if you want to hear any more, she'll have to tell you. She doesn't talk about it."

Abby nodded, aware not to pry further though she was consumed with curiosity. "Of course. I wouldn't expect you to betray her confidence."

They chattered on for a while, Abby confident Fiona would support her trip to Jangho. She thought about Victoria. Fiona's words had given her ego a giant boost. *Victoria had never been really interested in a woman as far as Fiona knew.*

* * *

Victoria arrived back in Beijing two days before they were due to leave for South Korea, the last country on their business agenda. Abby's pulse hitched when she entered the apartment. Victoria looked tired, with new stress lines around her eyes, not unexpected with the load she'd carried. Abby, with an urge to smooth Vic's wrinkles away, pulled her into a hug. "Hello, Vic. I'm so glad to see you."

The embrace was returned with gusto, and they remained pressed together until the sound of Fiona's door opening broke them apart. "Hi Vic," called out Fiona as she made her way to the fridge. "I'll be with you in a minute. I'm supposed to drink plenty of water. Can I get you something?"

"Bring two cans of that Hite beer for Abby and me, and then come into the lounge. I've got something to tell you both." She fluffed up the cushion on one of the seats. "Sit here."

Fiona handed over the beers and lightly rubbed her scar through the material. "There no need to fuss. I'm nearly better, thanks to Abby's nursing skills."

"You'll be glad to know we've exceeded contract expectations in both Japan and China. Malcolm's sent an email of congratulations. The last order was the icing on the cake, sooo, he's giving you both a bonus. Ten thousand dollars each when we get back to Australia."

Abby stared at Victoria, astounded. "That's a lot of money."

Vic draped her arm over the back fabric and gave Abby a compassionate, tender look. "You deserve it. It hasn't been much fun lately. I'm taking you out to the Capital M restaurant tonight to celebrate."

"That sounds wonderful. We've been eating in-house since you've been away. We're getting sick of their menu, aren't we, Fiona?"

"Aye, we are. I'd give half that lovey bonus for a plate of sausages and mash."

"Don't worry, all that's going to change. I'll make sure we have an exciting time in Seoul before we start again. I've organized some great tours," announced Victoria with a smile.

Abby felt her throat swell as if she'd swallowed a chili whole. She peeped at Fiona through lowered lids. The Scot had turned two shades lighter and gave a small shake of the head. Anxious, Abby made a show of looking at her watch. "We'd better get dressed if we're going out. You go first, Vic."

"Okay. We can have a few more drinks when we get there. I could do with a hot shower and wash my hair. The pollution was worse than ever."

Once she disappeared into their bedroom, Abby said in an urgent whisper, "What?"

"Now's not the time to tell her, lass. Wait until she's got some nice food in her belly. And she won't argue in a public place."

Abby shot her a dubious look. "I hope you're right. I have a feeling she's not going to be too happy about it." She rolled the beer can in her hands. "Do you think you could tell her?"

"Me?" Fiona squeaked.

"Please. She's gone to all the trouble to plan tours so it's a cert she's going to be miffed. It'll be better if you plead my case."

"Okay, lass, I'll tell her, but I still think it's a shame you're not coming with us. We're…we're going to miss you."

Abby hugged Fiona quickly. She regretted that she hadn't already finished the Tokyo designs. Victoria looked so happy to be back. And it gave Abby a hollow ache to think she wouldn't be sharing Seoul with her friends. She hadn't realized how much she'd missed Victoria until she'd walked through the door.

* * *

Abby found the view delightful. Their balcony table overlooked the towers and statues of Tiananmen Square, ablaze with light. Victoria brought them up to speed with her Shanghai news as they ate the entrée of smoked Norwegian salmon. Halfway through the main course of suckling pig, Fiona sat up straighter. Abby braced herself. *Here it comes.*

"Abby would like a few days off by herself before we start work again."

Victoria stopped in the midst of taking a mouthful and lifted her head to stare at Fiona. "What do you mean? Isn't she coming with us to Seoul?"

"Um…she's going to a village on the coast so she can paint."

"For how long?" Victoria turned her attention to Abby. "Well?"

"I was planning to stay for five days. I really want to do some sketches of local scenes and people and I haven't had a chance to do any art since we left Sydney. The idea is to do small drawings with watercolour. I can reproduce them in oils on canvases. You don't mind if I spend some time by myself, do you, Vic? I'll be back by the time we start work again."

Victoria's face went blank as she took her knife and began dissecting the pork. "Where will you be going?"

"I booked part of a cottage at a fishing village called Jangho on the Korean coast. It's a four-hour trip by train from Seoul." Abby dug in her bag for the printout of the booking. She handed it over in silence and waited for Victoria to read it.

The dark eyes flashed. "So you've got everything organized."

"I think she needs the time away by herself. She's worked hard and been very good to me while I was sick," piped in Fiona.

Victoria suddenly looked defeated. Hurt was evident in her voice. "If you want time off, Abby, by all means take it. You've earned it. Put a hire car on our tab."

"I'm quite happy to take the train."

"Get a damn car."

A quick retort died on Abby's lips. She tried to ease the tension between them. "Thank you, I will. I appreciate the thought."

No more was said on the matter as they began to eat again, though the conversation was more subdued. It was a relief when they finished their meal and left for the hotel.

CHAPTER TWENTY-FIVE

The holiday in Seoul had lost most of its appeal by the time Victoria went down to breakfast on the third day. Her anger had long since dissipated and been replaced by a needy ache. Sightseeing just wasn't much fun without Abby; her bubbly enthusiasm made even the most ordinary places and situations interesting. She knew Fiona felt the same by the way she had moped and displayed so little excitement. Victoria grimaced as she spooned some kimchee over her bowl of rice. *We're like two bloody wet rags.*

To make things worse, Fiona, a worrywart, couldn't hide her anxiety for Abby's welfare, although the younger woman had rung every night in good spirits. Her constant, "I hope Abby's all right," rubbed off on Victoria in the end, and now Victoria suffered similar pangs of disquiet. It wouldn't have been so bad except for the nagging feeling that Abby's art was simply an excuse to get away from them, or more to the point, from her. Suddenly, it occurred to her that Abby wasn't alone but with Chantal. All morning she stewed. In the middle of the tour of the Gyeongbokgung Palace, Fiona murmured an apology to the tour guide and pulled Victoria out into the courtyard.

"What exactly is wrong with you, Vic? You're being downright rude to everybody," said Fiona, her hands planted firmly on her hips.

Victoria bit back a defensive response. "I've worked out why Abby left us. She's gone there to be with Chantal."

"Even if she did, what business is it of yours?"

Victoria grasped for a plausible reason. "I don't want her taken advantage of," she said in her best schoolmarm voice.

"For goodness sake, you're always interfering in her life. Just leave her be. She's old enough to make her own decisions. I went down that road and look what happened. For the life of me, I don't comprehend what your problem is. Chantal is an extremely nice woman and most eligible."

"Huh! You were worried about me but Chantal's different. Is that what you're saying?"

Fiona looked testy. "You're being very childish and it doesn't become you. It was only a flirtation for you, but Chantal's serious about the lass. Anyway, it's water under the bridge—they're not seeing each other anymore. Abby called it off before leaving Hong Kong."

Victoria's grey world burst into technicolour and a wide smile spread across her face. "You're right. It's got nothing to do with me. Come on, old girl. We haven't seen the throne room yet; it's supposed to be spectacular. This afternoon we're off to see the Seoul Museum of Chicken Art if you're up to it. It should be interesting."

Fiona climbed back up the steps with a shake of her head.

* * *

Jangho turned out to be a picturesque spot, with a beach that fronted jagged rocks in jade-coloured water. Tree-covered hills created a backdrop for the tiny village. Abby found it was a haven for folks who loved the outdoor life, and dozens of snorkelers navigated around the rocks throughout the day.

The hamlet had no chain marts, and at local markets only fresh food was available. Seafood was popular in the no-frills cafés that lined the main street; octopus was a specialty. Most tourists disappeared back to larger city centres by nightfall.

Sightseeing took only an hour on arrival and afterwards Abby settled down to work on the drawings. Even though it was such a pretty place, her retreat grew claustrophobic by the end of the second day. Abby found the place no fun without someone to share the experience. Being a people person, she couldn't fathom how anyone got a kick out of travelling alone.

By noon on the third day, the drawings were done and dusted, and emailed off to Akio, which left her wondering what on earth she was going to do. She had no desire to join the swimmers and lacked the enthusiasm to wander around alone. *Another two days and I'll be round the twist. I bet the other two are having a ball.* Just thinking of Victoria and Fiona caused an ache deep inside her chest. She looked at her watch. If she left now, she'd be in Seoul before nightfall. After quickly packing and tidying up, Abby delivered the key to the family next door and hit the road.

By six she'd dropped the hire car off and was outside their suite at the Ritz Carlton. Victoria, towelling her wet hair, opened the door. Abby, unprepared for the assault on her senses, flushed as a flood of heat swept over her body—Vic looked ravishing in a silk robe, belted loosely. It took a few seconds to lift her eyes to meet the dark ones wide with surprise. "Hi Vic," she stuttered.

Victoria pulled her into a bear hug. "You're back!"

Abby registered the pressure of Vic's nipples against her chest and a thigh pressed against her leg. The scent of lavender soap tickled her nose as she tried to keep her breathing steady. Involuntarily, she slid her body up and down Vic's before she moved out of the embrace. Victoria stepped back, a pink colour on her cheeks. "Sorry. I'm just pleased to see you."

"Me too."

"Is there something wrong? We weren't expecting you for two more days."

Without a thought, Abby stroked down the side of the soft face with her fingertips. "Naw. I just got lonely. It wasn't much fun by myself."

Wistfulness settled over Victoria's face as she leaned into the . touch. "You missed us, huh?"

Abby poked her tongue over her bottom lip and gazed at Vic's full, kissable lips. She yearned to press her mouth against them, to run her tongue over them and taste Victoria. She'd been dreaming about doing it for the last two days. Like a magnet, her eyes were drawn downwards to her body and she ached to slip her hands under the robe and cup Victoria's breasts. Their embrace had slipped the robe open further and offered a tantalizing glimpse of a brown nipple. Victoria sucked in a breath as the dark chocolate areola began to pucker and her nipple firmed. Abby stared, mesmerized—her own breasts responded immediately, becoming full and heavy as they strained against her shirt. Filled with longing, Abby dragged her gaze up to the eyes hooded in the soft light.

To her consternation, Fiona's bedroom door opened. "Abby! You're here. What happened?" she asked.

Abby sidled around Victoria to move into Fiona's outstretched arms. "I missed you both too much to stay away."

"We missed you too, lass. We're a bit like party poopers without you to keep us entertained."

As they hugged, Abby caught Victoria's eyes over the Scot's shoulder. They seemed to reflect the disappointment that she knew shone from her own. She hoped so.

* * *

Victoria cursed her traitorous libido as she watched the two women settle into the large leather chairs. She knew Abby had noticed her nipple's response. God, as soon as it had the attention of those sultry blue eyes, it had just popped out. She waited for her pulse to stop racing. Despite the air-conditioning, Victoria felt hot and uncomfortable and realized she was wet between the legs with nothing on beneath the robe. She scooted into her room and called out as she passed, "I'm going to get dressed. The restaurant's not formal tonight."

After another shower as cold as she could stand, she felt composed enough to join the others for drinks.

Fiona turned towards her room. "I'd better get ready as well."

When the door closed behind her, an awkward silence fell between them. Abby rose after a minute and gave Victoria's shoulder a fleeting touch. "Would you like a drink? I could do with one."

"Yes please," whispered Vic, her throat suddenly dry.

Except for a slight layer of perspiration above her top lip, Abby looked remarkably calm as she handed the glass over. "So what's on the agenda tomorrow?"

As she answered, Victoria gazed at her with longing. Abby fascinated her more every day. She exuded a startling mixture of vulnerability and sexual power which made Vic's hormones respond like fire. She'd have to tell Abby shortly how she felt or she'd bust. But she needed to wait for the perfect moment. No stuffing it up this time.

CHAPTER TWENTY-SIX

Abby put on the tailored, white coat over the vest and surveyed herself in the mirror. *Not too bad at all.* Tonight was their last formal function now that their business had been concluded in South Korea. After the five-day break, they'd been busy shoring up deals and the last contract had been signed yesterday evening, much to everyone's relief. Things had gone along without any hiccups, but during that time Victoria and her relationship had fallen into a lockdown mode. Victoria had reverted back to her *just friends* attitude and Abby had been reluctant to express her emotions. Abby was beginning to despair that it would ever change.

When Victoria came out of the room, Abby eyed the mid-length red dress with approval. "Wow, that's a smoking hot dress," she exclaimed.

"Damn Abby, I let you wear the pants tonight! What was I thinking?" said Victoria with a look of appreciation too.

"I just might take control of you, so watch it, lover girl." Then realizing what she had said, she stammered, "I wasn't meaning to…"

"No worries sweetie, I just might let you." Victoria threaded her arm through Abby's. "Come, my fine beau, take me to the party."

Fiona, who had begged off accompanying them—she was "done in" by the sightseeing—indicated her approval with a nod. "My, you look a fine couple."

Victoria winked. "We might just be mistaken for royalty, huh?"

On the third floor, Abby followed Vic into the Kumkang Room to Minjoom Kim's table. Minjoom, an official of the giant Korea Midland Power Corporation, their major customer, was hosting the dinner. The other guests were already seated when Abby settled into the seat next to Vic. It took all her concentration not to look down; Victoria sat with her legs crossed and the hem of the dress rode up to expose an expanse of thigh. A high-heeled satin shoe elegantly dangled from her foot. Vic held Abby's hand and seemed bent tonight on making it plain they were a couple. Normally she was more conservative in public but Abby wasn't going to argue; she relished the intimacy, even if it was only for show.

Throughout dinner, a theatre troupe entertained with traditional dances on the small stage. Legs concealed by billowing hanboks and accompanied by drums and flutes. The artisans performed a variety of fan and dramatic sword dances, much to the audience's delight. After the applause died down, Abby had turned to converse with the elderly Korean lady on her left when she felt Victoria's hand tighten. The pressure firmed until the fingers pressed hard into her bones. She turned quickly to see what was wrong. Vic was staring across the room at a group of men seated in the far corner.

Abruptly, Vic rose and excused herself for an ostensible trip to the loo. Concerned, Abby caught her host's eye. "Do you know who that group of men are over there, Mr Kim?" she asked.

"We are sharing the venue with members of two conventions; a medical team of West German epidemiologists and a firm of import/export lawyers from the UK. I believe they are the lawyers."

"Victoria's upset about something. If you will excuse me, I'll see what's wrong," Abby said quietly, and without a fuss, hurried to the restroom.

Inside, Victoria was hunched over a hand-basin, the white porcelain basin gripped tightly in her hands. Her normal healthy colour had drained away, leaving her sheet-white; she blinked rapidly as if straining to focus. Concerned, Abby immediately draped her arm over her shoulder. "What's wrong, honey? Just relax now." She pulled her close and stroked her hair as she whispered soothing words in her ear.

A woman entered the room, looked at them curiously and ducked into a cubicle. Victoria's body went still and Abby met her eyes in the long mirror. She had a haunted look, her face stretched tight with pain. When two more women came in, Abby took Victoria by the arm and led her down the corridor. She spied a door to a balcony.

Once in the fresh air, Victoria walked to the railing and stared over the city skyline. "I'm all right. I just need a minute to compose myself."

With long slow strokes, Abby rubbed her back. "What's wrong?"

"It's…it's him."

"Who, dear?"

Victoria turned to look at her, her face bleak. "My father."

"What did he do to you, Vic?"

Victoria chewed her lip as she stared out over the buildings again. "It's a sad story. I haven't seen him for years."

"Tell me about it. It always helps to share problems."

Victoria twisted around, agony evident in her face. "He never made it a secret that he disliked me. I was never good enough for him, he desperately wanted a son. Whatever I did was never right; I never met his standards. He kept telling me I'd end up a good-for-nothing with no prospects. I won't go into the sordid detail but I'll only say I had a very strict upbringing. There were few occasions to laugh, and crying wasn't allowed." She stopped to take Abby's hand. "What makes a good parent, Abby?"

Abby gave her hand a squeeze, but said nothing.

Victoria took a deep breath before she continued. "You probably wouldn't have had to think about it much. Your parents were obviously very loving. My father certainly wasn't. It was all about his place in society. I listened to him brag about money while he degraded my mother in private. No physical violence, just putting her down all the time. I guess in a way, that's why I've subconsciously shied away from relationships. I'd hate to treat my own family like that. I do have his genes."

"Don't be so silly, Vic. Everyone makes their own decisions about how they live their lives. If anything, your upbringing should make you more aware of how *not* to treat your family."

"I've told myself that but…"

Abby shook her head sternly. "No buts. You're going to make a wonderful partner and parent. Now go on, why did he leave your mother and you?"

"Things got progressively worse. My announcement that I was gay brought it all to a head. That was the culmination of his disappointment in me, not to marry and give him grandkids— the last straw. He lost control and hit me…hit me hard. I ran to my room and waited until I thought he'd calmed down enough." A sob escaped from Victoria, causing Abby's throat to choke up. "An hour later I came out and found my mother collapsed on the floor. I took her to the hospital in a taxi—he'd broken her cheekbone. We never saw him after that day. She received a token out of the divorce settlement; he was a solicitor and knew how to fiddle his accounts. When crunch time came, he had hidden most of his assets. He moved to England, leaving us without financial support."

Abby looked at her in disbelief. "Did he send any child support payments to your mother?"

Victoria shook her head. "Mum saw to my education by waitressing. They were hard times for both of us but I won't go into that. She eventually remarried when I was in my early twenties."

Abby battled to contain her temper. It was inconceivable to have that sort of upbringing. Her own family had only ever nurtured her. "And he's here tonight?"

"Yes."

"What are you going to do about it?"

Victoria dragged a heel across the floor. "What can I do?"

Abby took her face in her hands and rubbed her thumbs lightly over her lips. "Have you ever had a good look at yourself, Victoria Myers? You're gorgeous, as well as incredibly bright and successful. So don't give me that crap. If you want to get on with your life you have to face him on *your* terms. So let's go in together and damn well say hello. Just remember, I'll be with you and I don't take rot from anyone."

For a moment Victoria stared at her and her face lit into a smile. She reached for Abby's hand to clasp it in a firm grip. "Let's go, tough girl. That's why you're wearing the pants tonight. What are we waiting for?"

* * *

As she made her way past the tables, Victoria held her head high, determined not to show signs of weakness. She grasped Abby's hand a little tighter, reassured by its warmth. Only a few metres away, someone at his table nudged her father and said, "Those two women seem to know you."

He watched them approach, frowned, and his hands bunched into fists.

"Hello, Dad," Victoria said. She studied him as he rose. The years hadn't been kind. His face was etched with deep lines, his nose was sharper now; he was thinner, and his hairline had receded halfway along the scalp. He looked frailer, no longer the big, frightening man of her youth.

"Hello, Victoria."

"Abby, this is my father, Andrew Eggers. Dad, meet Abby Benton."

Abby mumbled a *hello* which was returned with a curt nod.

One of the men hastily pulled two more chairs to the table. Opposite, a florid man with a trimmed ginger beard eyed Eggers with a quizzical look. "You have a daughter, Andrew?"

Victoria ignored the chair and turned to him, expertly concealing her emotions. She'd had years of practice with boardroom politics. "Yes, Andrew has a daughter. Mind you, he left my mother and me high and dry over twenty years ago but I still have some of his genes, more's the pity. I made sure to discard his name though." She swept her eyes round the table. "Is he your boss?"

At the end of the table, a tall, thin man in his sixties said in a clipped British accent, "I'm the senior partner of the firm. Andrew works for me."

Victoria raised her eyebrows at her father. "Not the top dog? Amusing—you always had such high expectations of me and you didn't get there yourself."

The veins in his temple bulged and his face tinged red. "I've done well enough. And what do you do, Vic, that you can be so arrogant? You're still an upstart who doesn't know her place, I see."

Abby spoke up. "Your daughter is a very successful woman, Mr Eggers."

He swept his eyes over her body. "Let me guess. You're another dyke. Are you two pervs together?"

Abby's eyes widened in shock and a look of angry disgust settled on her face. "Excuse me? What century are you from? Our relationship is definitely not open for discussion. And for your information, Victoria could buy each one of you fifty times over with her petty cash. Haven't any of you heard of Victoria Myers of Orianis Minerals?"

A cough echoed from the senior partner, who quickly got to his feet. "Actually I have. Please accept my heartfelt apologies for my employee's behaviour, Ms Myers. I am embarrassed to say you are one of our clients. We handle your European investments."

Victoria frowned, her displeasure clear. "Your firm is Barnaby and Hartford, I presume. And you would be?"

"Michael Hartford."

"Well, Mr Hartford, perhaps I shall have to reconsider our association," she said gravely.

Hartford seemed to shrink a couple of inches. "I hope that won't be necessary. We are prepared to make any changes to our staff you deem necessary."

"I'm sure we can come to an understanding. We will be at the hotel for another day. Would you visit me at eleven tomorrow morning to negotiate my terms? My father owes my mother a great deal of child support," Victoria said flatly.

"Who the hell do you think you are, Vic?" Her father's shout brought startled looks from patrons nearby.

"I'm someone who's no longer afraid of you," Victoria said, completely calm now. "And really, Dad, looking at you here, I wonder why I ever was. You're just a loathsome bully. The only reason you got away with it then was because you were bigger than me. But you're not now."

As she turned to go, her father erupted. His chair upended as he swept it aside and raised his hand. Before Victoria could move, Abby was in front of her. "You touch her, Mr Eggers, and I'll slap an assault charge on you before you can blink. And if you say one more word, I'll accuse you of the intent to do physical harm."

"Andrew!" Hartford snapped. "Go home." To Abby he nodded his approval. "Thank you. Now. Get. Him. Outside," he ordered the other men at the table. He turned to Victoria. "Please accept my sincere apologies. You have my assurances he won't bother you again. We shall take our leave and I will see you tomorrow."

As they hurried off, Victoria reached for Abby's hand.

"Come on, honey, it's time we left. You go on up to the room while I say our goodbyes to our host," said Abby, giving her palm a squeeze.

Victoria felt completely washed out, the adrenaline that had energized her, gone. She simply nodded and slipped out the door.

* * *

Victoria was in the lounge nursing a scotch when Abby came in. "I'd like to thank you for what you did," Vic whispered.

The vulnerable tone forced Abby take a deep breath to stop the threatening tears. She settled down beside Victoria and put her arms around her shoulders. "Your father's a proper swine, isn't he?"

"Yes," Vic whispered in anguish. "I'm sorry you had to see that."

"Don't be worried about me," said Abby, giving her back a comforting rub. "I'm used to confrontation in my legal aid job. We get some nasty stuff to contend with. God, he was only an amateur compared to some of the shitty people I've seen." She pulled back to study Victoria's face and gently kissed her forehead. "I was really proud of you tonight, Vic. Once you settle down you'll realize you're free of him. He's nowhere in your league, so forget everything he's done to you. Don't even think about him anymore. Don't give him that satisfaction. Now I'm going to get a drink? I could do with one after all that the drama."

Victoria gave a hint of a smile. "Yes Ms Legal Aid. You were awesome." She returned with the glass, her voice serious again. "You're a hell of a nice woman, Abby, and I'm proud to be your friend."

Abby curled her fingers around the glass as she heard the words with a few misgivings. She didn't want to be the woman's friend; she wanted to be her lover. She hoped Victoria wasn't going to put her up on a pedestal like Chantal. God forbid.

They sat quietly for a while with their drinks, comfortable in each other's company. "Time we hit the sack. You go in first to change," said Abby.

Victoria was already in bed when Abby finished her shower. Too keyed-up to sleep, Abby heard muffled sobs. Eventually the weeping got the better of her, so she padded over to Victoria's bed and slipped under the covers. She curled her body gently against Victoria's back and the crying quieted a little. Abby threaded her hand under Victoria's arm to stroke her stomach. "Let it all out, honey. I'm here with you."

After a while Victoria moved out of the embrace and turned around. She snuggled into Abby, with her head nestling under her chin. Abby held her close, rested her cheek on the silky hair and sniffed her scent. A moment or so later Vic's breathing slowed and Abby knew she had fallen asleep. The heat of the body against hers made Abby's senses reel, the longing to touch and be touched almost overpowering in its intensity. It took all her willpower to curb the urge to stroke the silky skin. She was only there to give comfort and support. Sheer exhaustion sent her off to sleep.

Abby woke at dawn to a breath on her neck and a soft body pressed against her. Groggy, she opened her eyes to find dark ones staring into hers. Abby made no move to shift; she relished the contact now that her body wasn't demanding instant satisfaction. "Good morning," she said, feeling suddenly shy.

Victoria stretched and Abby could feel her desire rise again like the sun. Abby propped herself on an elbow, though kept their hips pressed together. She extended a finger and lazily stroked Vic's stomach. "You feel better, honey?"

"Um…much better, thanks to you."

"What are you going to say to Hartford this morning?"

Victoria raised her hand to brush a wayward curl away from Abby's eye. "I'm going to tell him that he'd better start docking money out of my father's wages every week until all the back payments are made to Mum. If he doesn't, they'll lose our account."

"No more?"

"I don't want anything from the bastard we aren't entitled to. His humiliation will be the extra compensation."

"Good for you," Abby said. "You're free of him now, honey. You can live your life how you want without any regrets."

"I know. It's like a whole house has been lifted off my shoulders. When I saw him last night it was strange. It wasn't so much hate I felt as pity. He was only a shell of the man I'd feared all those years. A man who'd turned his back on his family and for what? He didn't look happy."

"I'm so glad I was able to help," murmured Abby. She pressed closer.

"You were wonderful," Victoria said in a distracted whisper.

Abby wet her lips and moved her head closer. Victoria's mouth looked luscious, full and moist, ready to be consumed.

Her pink tongue was peeking out, like the centre of an exotic flower. Their mouths were only inches away. Suddenly cups clattered in the kitchen. The sensual haze enveloping Abby vanished like a spent breath of wind. She went still and groaned. "Damn, Fiona's back from her walk."

"Yes," said Victoria in a strangled voice. "I suppose we have to get up?"

They looked at each other and grimaced as Fiona's voice floated in. "Come on you two. Up you get. It's already seven o'clock."

As Victoria disappeared out the door, Abby flopped back on the sheets and groaned, *"Shit!"*

CHAPTER TWENTY-SEVEN

The last day in Seoul, after Victoria met with Harford, they spent the afternoon packing and filing the bookwork. That evening when Victoria went for her usual swim, Abby was tempted to join her, figuring it was time they had a serious talk about their feelings. But in the end she decided to tackle it that night in the privacy of their bedroom. It would be cosier. And she really needed to work out what photos to delete before they left Korea; her picture folder was chockers.

After she settled down in front of her computer, she clicked on her Gmail account before she started. Two messages were from friends, one from her mother and another from an address she didn't recognize, pcorrigan@bigpond.com. She opened it.

Hi Abby,

It's Patsy from Perth. We're in Paris for five days and then we're on to Spain. Where are you? I'd love to catch up with you again.

Cheers—

Patsy.

Abby rested her fingertips on the keys as she reread the message. Patsy the charming nurse. *Well! Well! What a nice surprise.* She replied with the suggestion they meet somewhere in the city and that they exchange phone numbers. She left it to Patsy to get back to her when and where. She decided to postpone her talk with Victoria until after the rendezvous with Patsy. Vic might be more amenable to Abby's heart-to-heart if she thought a rival lurked on the horizon.

They flew out of South Korea the next morning and landed at de Gaulle at five in the afternoon. After a lazy day off to recover from jetlag, the following morning Abby and Fiona went to the Louvre, while Victoria visited the accountant who handled her French investments. The day after, Victoria planned to take them to view a chalet she was considering in Bordeaux.

Victoria was relaxing on the balcony when Fiona and Abby returned from the museum. "How was the Louvre?" she called out.

"Unbelievably crowded," answered Fiona and collapsed in a chair.

Abby tossed the bundle of glossy literature on the table and walked to the railing to gaze over the city. "Good view of the Eiffel Tower, isn't it?" Then she turned and joined them on the deck chairs. "The Louvre was spectacular."

"Did you get to see much?"

"A lot of the famous pieces, but it'd take more trips to see the lot. It's so big." Abby kicked off her shoes and wriggled her toes. "Fiona got tired after a while, so we stayed around the old Dutch Masters in the afternoon. I'm particularly interested in them." She laughed. "Besides, their paintings of drunk and stoned people were far more interesting than all that religious art."

Victoria smiled. "I know what you mean. How do you feel, Fiona?"

"Oh, I've got my strength back. I'm nearly one hundred percent now."

Abby eyed the Scot fondly. Now that the business part of the trip was over, Fiona's worry lines were no longer evident. She was leaving them in a week's time for Scotland, her excitement barely contained at the thought of seeing her family.

"Where are we going tonight for dinner, Vic?" Fiona asked.

"Le Flamboire. The chefs specialize in long-braised meats."

"You two should go out on the town afterwards. It'd be a shame to be in Paris and not take Abby out to see the nightlife. I'll turn in after we eat. I couldn't walk another step," said Fiona.

Victoria raised her eyebrows at Abby. "You wanna go for a stroll down the Champs Elysées?"

"Sounds romantic, but sorry, I'm meeting a friend at six thirty so I won't be going with you to dinner."

"You're meeting a friend?" said Vic, her voice incredulous. "When did this happen? You never mentioned you knew anyone in Paris."

Abby tried for unruffled. "I just got the email a few days ago, and, since she's on a schedule, we've arranged to meet tonight. We were hoping we'd be in the same city at some stage. Bit of good luck really…"

"She?"

"Um…yes."

Victoria tilted her head, her eyes bright. "An old friend?"

Abby began to wilt under the scrutiny. Her plan to try a little jealously with Victoria seemed a tad off now. "No, a new friend I met…I mean I haven't known her very…"

"What's her name?" asked Victoria.

"Her name's Patsy Corrigan." Abby put the emphasis on *Corrigan*.

"Patsy from Perth?"

"Yes, that's her."

"You go out with Abby, Vic. I'm quite happy to stay at home and get room service. I've plenty to do now I've discovered another family line in Melbourne," said Fiona. "It's a cousin…"

"You're quite welcome to come, Vic, but you'll probably be bored," Abby intervened hastily, not only to discourage Victoria from coming, but also to nip Fiona's ramblings about her family tree in the bud. The novelty of the ancestry recitals had long worn off.

"I'd love to come if that's all right with you…and of course Patsy."

The last thing she wanted was for the two of them to meet, but Abby's eyes met Victoria's and her resolve crumbled. "That's great. I suppose we should be getting ready. Just casual. Patsy's backpacking so she won't be wearing anything dressy."

In her room, Abby collapsed on her bed, worried. Certainly, Patsy expected her to come alone. *Crap!*

* * *

"You look smart tonight, Vic. New jeans?" said Abby as she perused the *casual* attire. *Designer* was more like it. Abby had on her sightseeing gear: casual khakis, sandals, a loose chambray shirt. She knew from experience that the backpackers' usual dresscode called for one outfit on and one in the bag, especially if there was a single pack to hump between the two of you.

Victoria threw a winning smile. "I've had these old clothes for years."

When their cab pulled up at the Dans les Landes restaurant, Patsy greeted them on the sidewalk. Abby had texted her to let her know Victoria would be coming as well, which didn't seem to perturb the nurse. Patsy's response said she'd bring her sister to make up an even number. The neighbourhood, filled with cafés sporting colourful awnings and cute outdoor tables and chairs, was the real France to Abby. It was May, and despite Paris's famously fickle weather, the air was fine and warm. Blooming boxes of flowers hung from nearly every building. Abby was entranced. Such a magical place. The crowd was a feisty mix of tourists, bohemian locals, bikers and students.

Patsy gave her a hug, which Abby returned with enthusiasm. It was really good to see her again. They dined at the tapas bar, and ordered carafes of house wine to make it easier for the sisters who were conscious of their budget. Clarissa Corrigan looked a few years younger than her sister, with brown hair tied in a ponytail and a fresh open face dotted with freckles. She seemed in awe of Victoria who, to Abby's immense relief, was going out of her way to be extra pleasant. Patsy seemed reserved with Vic at first, though soon warmed up as they began talking. The nurse's sharp wit was equal to Victoria's, which made scintillating conversation.

Abby studied them both as they conversed. The two women were night and day: Victoria dark, imperious and commanding; Patsy fair, solid and dependable. But Abby couldn't help getting the vibe that, underneath their geniality, there was a power struggle going on. Clarissa seemed oblivious to it and soon fell under Victoria's spell. It was beginning to be a bad case of hero worship as the night wore on.

"Have you seen much of Paris, Patsy?" asked Abby.

"Some. All the touristy spots and we've done the markets as well." She smiled shyly. "I haven't walked by the Seine at night though. I hear on the Left Bank there's a fantastic park at the Quai Saint-Bernard where they dance late into the night. Will you come with me?"

Abby shot a quick glance at Victoria. Her face remained closed. "What about you, Clarissa?" Abby asked.

"We're staying at a hostel around the corner. I'll see her home before we go," said Patsy.

Victoria stretched in her chair, seemingly unconcerned. "You two don't have to head off yet. We still have a couple of dishes to go. We can have another drink and then what about I shout you all dessert." She winked at Clarissa. "There's ice cream."

Clarissa's face lit up. "Awesome."

Abby couldn't pinpoint when she noticed Victoria's demeanour towards her begin to change, for it was ever-so-subtle. First it was just a fleeting touch on Abby's shoulder, then a whisper in her ear to pass the salt, an accidental brush with her arm, a secret smile directed solely at her. By the time dessert was on the table, Abby was quite aware of what she was doing. Victoria was staking her claim on her. Patsy knew it too. She looked deflated, though Clarissa didn't seem to have a clue and kept up her bright chatter.

After the dishes were cleared away, they stood up. Patsy focused her gaze on Abby, her soft eyes holding the promise of the beginnings of a relationship if Abby wanted it. "What about it, Abby? Would you like to come with me down to the park?"

Abby turned to Victoria. She looked totally exposed, with a vulnerability that had never been there before. In that moment, Abby knew that she was no longer falling, but totally in love with this frustrating, wonderful woman. She pulled Patsy into a hug. "I'm sorry. I'm going home with Victoria. You and Clarissa have a great holiday." She gave Clarissa a kiss on the cheek. "You look after your sister, now."

She reached over to take Victoria's hand. "Come on, let's go home."

They didn't say a word in the taxi on the way home, just sat hands entwined, thighs pressed together. Inside the hotel suite, Abby swung to face Victoria. "Your room or mine?"

Victoria's face broke into a grin, her eyes sparkling. "Yours. It's the furthest away from Fiona's room. I'll be back after a quick wash. Put some clothes on after your shower; I want to take them off."

CHAPTER TWENTY-EIGHT

Victoria was at the window when Abby came out of the bathroom. "Get into bed, sweetie," Vic called out.

Instead, Abby stepped behind her, wrapped her arms around her middle and rested her chin on her shoulder. She kissed Vic's neck, nibbled and licked the base of her hairline until goose bumps flushed across her skin. Then she ran her hands down her back and slipped her fingers under the elastic and pulled the silk pants down over Vic's bottom. As she massaged the cheeks and arched against them, Vic's heart raced. Each pump of Abby's hips sent her into orbit. As the movement reached fever point, Abby swung her around and pulled her head down until their mouths melted together.

Their tongues began to entwine while Abby moved her body up and down with a steady rhythm. "Please, on the bed," Vic said breathlessly. "I want to do it properly."

"Hurry, luv. I need you so badly I'm hurting."

Vic ripped open her robe and hurried over to the bed. Abby lay on the top sheet, her face glowing with anticipation.

Vic crawled onto the bed and slid off Abby's top. She glided her hand under the lace panties and eased them down over her ankles.

"Oh, my god, you're lovely," she whispered, and feathered kisses over Abby's face before she claimed her lips.

Abby ran her hands down Vic's sides. "Your skin is like silk. Lie on top of me so I can feel all of you, honey."

Victoria moved her body carefully on top, supporting herself with her elbows while she slid their bodies together with a steady rhythm. When Abby moaned, she silenced her with a long kiss. As she sucked in Abby's tongue, Vic threaded her fingers through her hair. She tightened her grip and moved downwards to kiss her throat. By the time she reached her breasts, Abby was fighting for dominance.

"Oh, no you don't. Lie still. I'm in charge tonight," Vic reminded her.

She turned Abby onto her stomach and lavished kisses on her feet, slowly moving up her legs to nibble at her inner thighs. Ignoring the heated protest when she left that area, she straddled Abby's back and tilted her head forward to nip the skin under the hair. When Abby displayed impatience, Victoria turned her over and nestled her half under her body. With her securely cradled in her arms, she bent again to give her a long, hard kiss. Finally, with a slow, sensual movement, she trailed kisses down her neck and nuzzled her face between her breasts.

After a moment, she pulled back to gaze in awe at them. They were creamy and soft, the pink areola puckered and the long nipples stiff with passion. She cupped them, feeling the weight in her hands, and squeezed them together, then took them in her mouth. By the time she'd finished sucking and licking, Abby was beseeching her to go lower. "Please, luv, I feel on fire between my legs. I need you there."

With a rocking motion, Vic gently pushed open her legs with her thigh and slid her fingers up and down the slick sides. Abby was arching into her now, trying to get the fingers where she most needed them. Carefully Vic searched and touched the small bundle of nerves with slow, deliberate strokes, then harder and faster. Abby began to stiffen. With a swift movement, Vic slipped two fingers inside and pumped as she firmly massaged the clit with her thumb. Abby exploded with a low "ahhhhh" as her orgasm peaked. She then lay gasping in waves of pleasure. It took a moment to catch her breath before she murmured, "I...I didn't dream it would be so wonderful."

"Oh, sweetie," Vic whispered as she pulled her close. "Haven't you ever had an orgasm?"

Abby ran her fingers lightly down Vic's arm, a tear trickled down her cheek. "I've only been with boyfriends. Sure I've had orgasms, but they were nothing like that one."

Vic stroked her hair. "I wish I'd known I was the first. I would..."

"Don't be so silly. That was the best experience of my life."

"Is that so? Well I haven't finished with you yet." She slid down, pushed open Abby's legs and buried her head between them. Minutes later, Abby climaxed again under the Vic's insistent tongue, this time longer and harder. She feel back and panted, "No more—I'm too sensitive. It's your turn."

Victoria propped herself on an elbow and trailed her finger down over a nipple. "It was your night. You must be tired, so I can wait."

"You've got to be kidding me. I've wanted you for ages. I hope I can do what you like, so tell me if I'm not doing it properly. I...I really want to be good for you."

Victoria planted a soft kiss on her lips. "Oh, sweetie, I'm just enjoying being here with you. I know you're inexperienced so don't worry, anything you do will be fine. I'm not far off."

"Okay. I want to kiss you first." Abby began with soft feathery kisses on Vic's palms, then up and down her arms, her earlobes and neck, paying particular attention to all the sensitive hollows. By the time she took a nipple in her mouth, Vic was moaning frantically, "Please...please. I'm nearly there."

"Not yet, darling. This is the first time I've touched a woman like this. Let me love you."

As Abby leisurely suckled and stretched out her nipples, Victoria reached fever point. If Abby didn't touch her soon, she'd burst. It was the sweetest agony she'd ever experienced. "Now, sweetie, please…"

Abby ignored her pleas as she trailed a tongue around her navel then dipped it in and out. Then she nibbed over her stomach until Vic took her hand and pushed it downwards. Abby gave a little laugh and slipped in two fingers until she felt the clitoris. When she began to firmly stroke, Victoria's orgasm rose immediately. She convulsed into waves of blinding pleasure. Then as Abby continued to rub, another climax followed. A cry wrenched out, as the second hit with more force. Vic flopped back like a rag doll and felt Abby climb on top of her. She opened her eyes to see Abby grinning. "You liked?"

Victoria could only nod dumbly.

In the morning, Victoria's body still ached with desire despite the immensely fulfilling lovemaking of the previous evening. She looked at Abby nestled against her, so naked and desirable that it was hard to resist the temptation to fan the flames of arousal again. For the first time in her life, she felt consumed by the need to possess and be possessed. Reluctantly, she slipped out of bed and into her robe. Fiona wouldn't be back from her walk for at least another three quarters of an hour. She padded out to the kitchen to make breakfast.

Victoria was beating eggs when Abby, clad in only bra and panties, entered. She raised the fork in the air. "You hungry?"

Abby pressed her body against Vic's back and grasped her waist. A husky laugh tickled her ear. "I'm famished, but not for food."

She turned Vic toward her, and the fork clattered into the sink. With a swift movement, Abby opened the robe and took a nipple in her mouth. Vic drew in a breath, heat radiating in a flush of desire as fingers tickled the top of her pelvis. She spread her legs quickly to allow entry and shivered as they slid downwards.

"Is this good? You're so wet," murmured Abby.

Victoria nodded.

"And this?"

She moaned her assent.

"What about this?"

"Ohhhh. Yes...yes."

As her fingers stroked, Abby hummed to accompany her groans. When Vic felt her body change, ready to climax, the door opened. Fiona entered and bent to take off her walking shoes at the door. Alarmed, Victoria gaped at her over the top of the blonde head buried between her breasts. Stifling a moan, she hit down sharply with both hands on Abby's shoulders to gain her attention.

A muffled whisper came. "You want harder, do you, honey?" With a sharp thrust Abby drove a knuckle into the quivering little pearl. Vic flew over the edge and her orgasm slammed into her. Her body arched backwards. An involuntary cry of pleasure rose from deep inside and she frantically clamped her lips together; it wasn't enough to stop a grunt escaping.

At the sound, the Scot turned to look. Her face contorted into horror at the sight of the two of them pressed together and her boss in the throes of orgasm.

"Good lord in heaven, lassies. What have they put in the water?" she screeched and fled to her bedroom.

* * *

Once they were dressed, Abby muttered, "You go out first. Why the hell did she have to come back early?"

Victoria stopped pacing round the room and frowned. "Why me? You go."

Abby placed her hands on her hips and stared her down. "Don't be a squib. You're the one going out with Fiona this morning. You told me you were taking her with you to negotiate the sale of the chalet. What time are you meeting the owner?"

"In three quarters of an hour."

"Good. You'll have to go soon."

"Now who's the coward?"

Abby grinned. "Too right! I am. I'll come out and say hello but I'll leave you do the explaining. You're the boss."

"Oh, very well," she muttered and when Abby chuckled, she couldn't stop the laugh. "I hope she's over the shock. I wonder what she's going to say."

"I bet she won't say anything—not for a while anyway. She'll have to have time to digest it." Abby hesitated and took her face in her hands. "That...that was the best night of my life. I...I love you, Victoria Myers, with all my heart."

Victoria became flustered. She wanted to say she loved Abby too, but the words stuck in her throat. Instead, she gave her a quick kiss and walked out.

Fiona stood at the front door and curtly nodded. Victoria avoided her eyes. "I've rung for the taxi. It should be here in a minute," she said in a strained voice.

Abby gave a wave as they went out the door and they walked in silence to the lift. While they waited for it to reach their floor, Fiona asked, "Do you think he'll sell?"

"Of course. I'll offer him a price he can't refuse. If Abby can be bought, anyone can."

A hiss behind her echoed in the corridor. Victoria turned to see Abby standing in the doorway of their apartment. After a moment, she wheeled back inside. The door slammed behind her.

Vic felt the blood drain from her face. *Oh, hell. What have I just done?* She started toward the apartment, desperate to explain her comment to Abby. It wasn't about the money at all. She wanted to tell Abby she admired her and loved her with all her heart. But the lift door opened and Fiona stepped inside. Victoria had no choice but to follow.

* * *

Abby leaned against the door, trying to stay calm. Was that how Victoria saw her: something she had bought...a possession? In her heart she knew Victoria had a right to think that. Abby had allowed herself to be bought, lock stock and barrel, and it would always hang over her head. Regardless of her reason, she had prostituted herself by accepting the money. Her mother was right: she wasn't the one calling the tune and never had been. She was the piper and would never be on equal footing with Victoria, so how would their love ever survive? There was only one way now to regain her self-respect.

She hastily packed and booked the flight. She scribbled out a note to Fiona and one for Victoria, then rang for a taxi to take her to the airport.

CHAPTER TWENTY-NINE

Victoria shuffled through the stack of papers on her desk. It was two and half months since Paris and she still found it hard to concentrate, continually troubled by the same questions. Where the hell was Abby? How could she have disappeared off the face of the earth? Vic had tried to find her; she'd scoured the city, visited every art gallery, every Legal Aid office and haunted the street where she lived. She drove past her mother's house often enough for her car to know its own way.

Her anguish turned into anger. Was that what she had become? A common stalker? Stuff Abby! If that was the way she wanted it, so be it. Taking the piece of paper out of her pocket, she read it one last time.

I'm going away, Vic, for I realize what I have to do. I said I love you and I meant it from the bottom of my heart. You are my life but I shall never be happy knowing you still look upon me as your possession. It was my own fault for accepting the money and I don't blame you in the slightest. But honey, if I don't have my self-respect, I have nothing.
Abby

Victoria scrunched the note into a ball and tossed it into the wastepaper basket. Time to get on with her life. Fiona looked up in surprise when she walked to her desk. "Are you off early?"

A stubborn look settled over Victoria's face. She had at least three hours of work ahead of her but she didn't give a damn. She wouldn't put up with the pain in her heart any longer. She was going out to have a good time. Her friend, Irene, had emailed an invitation to a party, so she was going. Plenty of willing women would be there, ready for a fling with no hang-ups and no whining about self-respect. "I'm going out tonight and I won't be in until ten tomorrow."

Concern flitted across the Scot's face. "Are you all right, Vic? You look angry about something."

"And so I should be. I'm sick of working my guts out in the goddamn office. No one appreciates the hours I put in. I'm off to let my hair down for once in my life."

Fiona reached over and patted her on the arm. "She'll come back soon, dear."

"I won't be here when she does," Victoria roared and marched to the lift.

By the time she reached Irene's apartment, Victoria's anger had settled into a sullen hatred for Abby's scruples. Any other damn woman would welcome the fact she had plenty of money. What was the point of working nonstop to get it, if she couldn't spend it how she wanted to? The door opened and she was engulfed in a hug.

"Vic, it's great to see you again. You've become quite the hermit. Come on—the crew is all here. We're dying to hear about your overseas venture," said Irene as she pulled her into the room.

Victoria smiled, her mood improved by the presence of friends. A drink was thrust into her hand and she took a long sip. She began to relax as she related the events of her time away. It was exhilarating to relive the trip. During the recital though, a moment of fear rolled through her. What if she never saw Abby again? She quelled the thought and went back to being sociable.

By midnight Victoria was pleasantly primed, ready to throw caution to the wind. Why not enjoy someone? Diane, a pretty accountant from out of town, had paid her particular attention for the last hour. As they nestled on the lounge together, the woman shifted to press her full breasts against Vic's arm and slid a hand down to knead her thigh. Victoria's initial arousal quickly faded.

It felt wrong. Quick, easy, meaningless pleasure couldn't possibly heal her bleeding heart. She closed her eyes, willing to enjoy Diane's persistent touch but she couldn't block out the vision of Abby. The image of Abby's naked body sent shivers down Victoria's spine and inspired an acute wave of desire. Rising quickly off the sofa, she muttered a word of apology to Diane and headed home.

Victoria resigned herself to another night of unrequited longing. After a cold shower, she lay down on her bed and dropped her head on the pillow. A tear dripped down her cheek. It was no use. She knew whose body—and love—she wanted; nobody else would do. Would she ever feel that again?

* * *

Abby watched anxiously as the three panels were winched up onto the wall to be secured in place. The last wasn't quite dry, but she'd been away long enough. She climbed the ladder, bolting them in place herself—at this height there would be no danger of the paint being touched. Once the panels had been attached, she stepped back to study the artworks with a great sense of pride. They really did look good.

Akio took her arm. "You must be proud, Abby. They are wonderful. You certainly have exceeded all our expectations. Your art is indeed a masterpiece for the foyer and a fitting reminder of the friendship we enjoy with your country."

"Thank you, Akio." Abby smiled. "They did come out well, didn't they? I think I'm going to collapse for a week now that they're finished. I've hardly taken a day off since I started."

"We understand how hard you've worked. The company would like to give you a complimentary holiday at the Zao

Onsen Ski Resort to show our appreciation. It's north of Tokyo in the Tohoku region. I think you would enjoy the snow sports and there are therapeutic hot springs. They're quite relaxing. The vacation would be a most pleasurable finale for your time in Japan."

Abby gulped. He had been so hospitable; he had paid for her accommodation near his home, and he and his wife had invited her over for many meals. The Japanese gentleman had become a very good friend. "Oh, Akio, I would love to but I really must get home. I've been gone too long already."

He bowed. "I understand. The grand opening of our building won't be for another month, so perhaps you could come back and take the holiday then. My secretary has transferred your fee to your bank account. See her about booking a flight to Sydney when you've made up your mind which day you prefer."

Back in her room, Abby went online, thrilled by the fact her bank balance had swelled by one hundred thousand dollars. After she transferred the sum over to her savings account, she clicked off the laptop and phoned her bank in Sydney.

Abby felt a sense of relief. *All done. Time now to go home.*

* * *

To Victoria's annoyance, the board meeting seemed endless. She leafed through the sheets of paper absently, struggling to maintain focus. The crappy day was getting worse; she'd barely slept a wink after the party and all she wanted to do was crawl into bed.

The manager of their finance division continued to waffle about the costs associated with the upgrade of their loading facilities on the wharf, a familiar rant. She glared at him. The pompous jerk was out of touch. He wouldn't embrace the fact that more modern technology would save the company millions in the long term.

She rolled her pen in her fingers and wished Fiona would hurry with afternoon tea. When her assistant finally arrived, she hurried to Victoria with a letter. Victoria frowned; Fiona knew better than to interrupt her with correspondence at a board meeting. Sporting a Mona Lisa smile, Fiona carefully placed the envelope in front of her on the table and continued to hover. The finance manager stopped talking, eyes fixed like lasers on the letter, as were the rest of the board's. Victoria picked it up and read the words "Victoria Myers—personal" on the front. She flipped it over. On the back, typed in black, were the words "From Abby Benton."

She closed her eyes to steady her nerves. With a heave she rose from her chair.

"Excuse me for a minute," she called out as she turned to hurry from the room. She ignored Fiona's hiss of disappointment as she passed by.

Victoria rushed to her desk and slit open the envelope. A single piece of paper was inside, with a pink slip stapled to the corner with the words "With compliments from Abby Benton." It was a bank cheque, made out to her for the amount of one hundred thousand dollars. Victoria stared at it for a long moment before comprehension sunk in. Abby was paying back her contribution. But what did that mean? Did she want nothing more to do with her, or did she want her again because they were on equal footing? *Crap!* She was more bamboozled than ever. Why hadn't the woman put a note in with the check?

When a knock on the door sounded, Victoria snapped, "Come in."

Fiona sidled into the room. "What did she say?"

Victoria made a chuffing sound as she threw the check over. "She's paid my money back."

The Scot began to laugh though hastily turned it into a cough at the frown on her boss's face. "Good for her. Did she include a letter?"

"No, only the cheque. Damn it, she didn't even say where she is." Victoria rose and began to pace around the room. "Do you think she's giving me the brush-off?"

"You will have to wait and see. Why don't you ring her?"

Victoria shook her head. "Surely you haven't forgotten she changed her mobile number?"

"I meant her home number. She may be back in town. Or you could ring her mother."

"God no! Her mother doesn't like me. What do you think I should do if she's doesn't answer her home phone?"

"There's nothing you can do. You'll just have to wait until she contacts you. Now you'd better get back to the meeting. The board members are occupied with afternoon tea. And please come and check the preparations for the staff party once you've finished. I've asked you twice already. It's only five days away and it is at your house."

Fiona disappeared out the door. Victoria smoothed down her skirt, patted her hair into place and went back to the boardroom. She put on her poker face as she noticed Malcolm studying her. Victoria doubted she could keep her emotions in check for any length of time or absorb a word of business. Her heart raced as she realized that, whatever the check meant, Abby hadn't forgotten her.

CHAPTER THIRTY

On her third morning in Sydney, Abby reached for the phone. She'd organized her affairs and seen her mother, so it was time to take the plunge. Five days earlier Victoria had left a message on the answering machine, but nothing since. Hesitantly, she dialled Victoria's office.

"Ms Myers's office. How may I help you?"

Her heart lurched at the familiar Scottish brogue. "Hi, Fiona, it's Abby."

"Abby, lass, where are you? Why haven't you rung before now? We've been so worried."

She swallowed back a small feeling of shame. "I'm back home. I've been in Japan since I left Paris."

"Japan!" Fiona exclaimed. "What were you doing there?"

"I'll fill you in when I see you. How was your holiday with your folks?"

"Wonderful. I left the day after you, so I had more time with them than I thought I would."

"Oh. You didn't stay in Paris?"

"No. I went to Scotland and Vic flew home."

Remorse swept through Abby. She'd wrecked Victoria's holiday. "Umm...how is Vic?"

There was a brief silence. "Haven't you contacted her yet?" Fiona asked.

"No, not yet. I'm...I'm testing the waters with you first. I guess she's cranky as hell with me."

"Wouldn't you be if she did that to you, lass? But don't worry, she's started to go out socially again and enjoy herself."

Jealousy swirled through Abby. "Has she now? Can you put me through to her, please?"

"Sorry. She's asked not to be disturbed. Our staff party is at her house tonight. Last-minute preparations, you understand."

"Oh...right. I'll catch her another day. Would you like to come over for dinner one night?"

"Why don't you come to the party?"

"I...I wouldn't like to gatecrash. I don't work for the company anymore."

"It'll be fine. Malcolm is anxious to see you about the fine job you did overseas."

"Okay. If he wants me there, I guess I'll go," Abby whispered. She suddenly felt like crying. She'd stayed away too long. Victoria had moved on and Fiona didn't seem anxious to see her. Not that she blamed them. Abby should have swallowed her pride and kept in touch. She'd put them through unnecessary worry while she thought only of herself.

"We'll see you there at six thirty, lass. Wear something a bit dressy. That blue dress you wore on our last night in Japan would be nice. Do you know the address?"

"Yes. I'll see you there. Bye for now."

* * *

Victoria raised her eyes from the computer screen when Fiona approached. "What is it? I have to be home by three to check on the caterers, so I hope it's not important."

"I'm just making sure you're leaving the office at a reasonable hour. Malcolm will be a little late, so he wants to make sure you're there to greet everyone."

"I intended to be, so don't worry. There's nothing here that can't wait until tomorrow." She stared hard at the Scot. Fiona looked like the cat that had just swallowed the canary. Definitely smug. "Do you know something I don't?"

"No, no. Just making sure everything's teed up for tonight. I'll be off in another hour." She reached the door then turned. "And Vic, what about wearing that lovely tuxedo you wore in Japan? It really suited you."

Victoria shook her head in disbelief. She must have completely lost her dress sense if Fiona was advising her about what to wear.

* * *

Abby took out the blue chiffon dress and slipped it over her shoulders. The outfit did look elegant, though it was odd that Fiona suggested she wear it. The woman hadn't displayed any flair with clothes when they went shopping overseas, though she was happy to take Abby's suggestions. After she brushed her hair and applied her makeup with extra care, she clipped the sapphire pendant around her neck and put on her heels. She was ready. Not wanting to be one of the first to arrive, Abby waited until seven to call the cab.

The cab pulled up outside Victoria's home in downtown Sydney and Abby took a few deep breaths. The doorman led her to the lift. "Ms Myers occupies the top level, madam." He ushered her in and pressed the floor number.

The door slid open at the entrance to a spacious foyer. As unobtrusively as possible, Abby slipped into a room occupied by a number of people chatting in groups. She hung back, embarrassed, and blew out a breath as she spied Fiona heading towards her. When she swept Abby into her arms and hugged her tightly, Abby's doubts evaporated in an instant. "Oh lass, I am so glad you came."

"Me too." She wiped away a tear; it was so good to see her. "I've missed you very much."

She held Abby at arm's length to eye her closely. "You've lost some weight. Haven't you been eating properly?"

"I've been painting nonstop. When I get in the zone I forget meals sometimes."

"Is that where you've been doing—painting?"

"Akio offered me a great commission. Three large panels for their new office block in Tokyo. The commission paid well enough for me to repay Vic." Abby took Fiona's hand and pressed it firmly. "You do understand, don't you? I had to give her the money back so I could regain my integrity and pride. I…I shouldn't have taken it in the first place."

"Aye, lass. You did the right thing, although Vic doesn't see it that way. You hurt her badly."

Abby sniffed. "And now she's moved on. It serves me right; I should have told you both where I was. I'm afraid I'm just too stubborn for my own good. I hated she knew I could be bought. Will she want to see me, do you think?"

Fiona smiled. "She's checking on the chefs in the kitchen and will be out shortly. In the meantime, Malcolm is on the terrace waiting to talk with you."

Abby followed her onto the balcony. Victoria certainly had a prime spot; the view was amazing, the city lights breathtaking. The chairman's face lit up. "Abby, how good to see you again at long last. The job you did overseas was excellent and the mapping program you devised has saved us a lot of manpower hours. You're considered quite the superwoman in the company. Did you enjoy your time?"

"Oh, yes, sir. It was a great adventure and I learnt so much."

He looked pleased. "Would you consider working for us? There's a position there if you want it."

"I found the work exciting, but I've made the decision to start painting in earnest. I'm planning an exhibition that will take at least a year to prepare. Thanks to you, I can afford to do it."

"I understand. But remember there's a place here for you if you ever change your mind." Malcolm glanced over her shoulder and back at her. "Have you seen Vic yet?"

Abby fiddled with her dress material. "Not yet."

"You will in a minute. She's coming our way."

* * *

Victoria finished organizing the platters, topped up her glass of wine and went back to mingle. She deftly sidestepped the Manager of Finance and made her way to the balcony. He wouldn't follow her out there—she knew the night air affected his asthma. Malcolm stood by the railing and smiled at her approach. Victoria's words of greeting froze in her mouth when the woman he was with turned around. When their eyes met, Vic's widened in shock.

"Hi, Vic."

"Abby. You're back," she stammered. Aware that a hush had fallen over the conversation, Victoria flushed but quickly pulled herself together. With one hand in her pocket, she sauntered over to Abby but made no effort to touch her. "It's good to see you. Are you being looked after?"

Hurt flickered in the blue eyes. "Yes, thanks. How have you been, Vic?"

"Good. How about you?"

"I'm fine too."

Victoria draped her arm over the railing. "Have you been home long?"

"A few days."

"Where've you been?"

"Japan," said Abby, accepting a glass of wine from the waiter.

"Japan, huh?"

"Yep." Abby sipped.

Malcolm patted Abby's arm. "I've just been congratulating her on how well she worked overseas."

Victoria ignored him. "What were you doing in Japan?"

Abby's face tightened. "This and that."

"No phones where you were?" snapped Vic.

"I went to work, not to chat on the phone," Abby growled.

"You worked all night too, did you?"

"Well, I didn't exactly stay home and not have any fun. Like some boring people I know."

Relief flittered across Malcolm's face when Fiona appeared and grasped Abby's arm. "Come with me to the library. You'll love it."

With a glare at Vic, Abby followed her inside.

Malcolm frowned at her. "What the hell is wrong with…"

"Oh, bugger off, Malcolm," she snarled and wheeled round to stride after them.

Abby was pulling a book off the shelf when Victoria entered the room. "Would you mind if I spoke to Abby alone, Fiona?" asked Victoria.

Fiona pursed her lips. "If the lass is okay with that."

Abby nodded. "I'm fine."

After the Scot left the room, Victoria said in a low voice, "I'm sorry. I was upset." She crept closer. "Will you forgive me?"

Abby ran fingers up her arm. "I should have told where I was. It was mean of me."

Victoria leaned forward to tuck a curl behind her ear. "I missed you. Can I give you a hug?"

"You still want me after what I did?"

Vic bent her head and nibbled her ear. "Yes, sweetie, I've been so lonely. Come here."

"Oh, honey, I've missed you so much."

As she moved into Vic's arms, Abby let out a long sigh. "I'm home."

Victoria nuzzled her neck and Abby arched backwards to give her access to the tender flesh. With reluctance Victoria pulled back. "I'll have to get back to the party." She looked at Abby anxiously. "You'll stay won't you?"

"Wild horses couldn't drag me away."

It was well after midnight when the last guests, an inebriated group from the finance department, staggered out. After the door shut, Victoria turned to Abby. "Finally! Come here. I thought I'd never get them to go."

"Do you think maybe we should go a little slow for a while? We haven't really dated."

"What! We lived together for six months," came the indignant reply.

Abby toyed with the lapel of Vic's jacket. "Okay, okay. I just thought I'd ask. I don't want to pressure you into anything."

"For heaven's sake woman, give me a kiss."

When their lips met, it was as if they had never been parted. They began slowly, savouring every sensation as their tongues began to duel. Victoria shimmered her mouth down Abby's neck, nibbling the tender skin as she went. Abby rolled the chiffon down to her waist and unclipped her bra. When her breasts fell out, Victoria said breathlessly, "So beautiful."

Vic massaged and rolled the nipples between her fingertips until they were taut and long. Abby grasped her head and pulled it down to her chest. "Suck them hard, honey, please." Abby shivered as each nipple was consumed by the wet mouth. "Get you coat off," she moaned. "I want to feel you too."

"Quick! The bedroom!" Vic undid her clothes as they stumbled down the hallway. Abby followed her through the door, ripped off her dress and flopped onto the king-sized bed. Vic shook off her tuxedo trousers, and prowled to the bed, clad only in a pair of hipster hotpants. She growled as she crawled on her hands and knees over Abby, who eyed the hipsters with appreciation. Vic bent her head and claimed her mouth. Their tongues entwined heatedly until eventually Abby pulled away to begin licking Vic's neck with long firm strokes. As the fires flamed hotter they began fighting for dominance, and as they thrust and twisted, pounded and stroked. Their movements developed into a rhythmic dance, building inexorably to a grand finale. With a last thrust of their thighs, they crashed over the edge. They groaned out their pleasure as the waves rippled through.

Abby lay stunned on the bed as she listened to Victoria's laboured breathing beside her. So much for control. Abby rolled over and nibbled her shoulder. "Get those sexy pants off and you may take mine off with your teeth if you like. We haven't even started yet."

* * *

Abby woke pressed between long firm thighs. She eased away, ignoring the acute sense of loss as she slid over to the edge of the bed. Heat simmered in every part of her body as she remembered the lovemaking and the many times they reached for each other in the night. Her toes curled into the soft shag carpet. She found it difficult to stand up, she was so sore. She ignored the tenderness while she searched the room for her clothes. The chiffon dress was a blue twisted mess on the floor. One shoe was in the corner and she had to crawl under the bed for the other. Gently she eased her black lace panties off Victoria's toe and looked round for her bra. It wantonly hung by a strap on the bedside lamp, the cups fronted her like all-knowing black eyes.

She dressed quickly, deciding to forego the bra which she stuffed into her purse. While she folded Vic's clothes onto the chair, she paused for a minute to look at the hotpants. Her libido skyrocketed again. *Get a grip, girl! You have to get home.* Abby reluctantly placed the pants over the tuxedo, before she padded over to the desk to find pen and paper. If she had to wake Vic it would be on again and she'd miss her meeting. After she scribbled out a note, she placed it on the side table and gazed at Victoria one last time. The woman was raw sensuality personified, with her hair tousled, her thick lashes dark shadows on her face. Her soft curves caressed the sheets.

A maid was clearing up the aftermath of the party when she came downstairs. Abby graced her with a nonchalant wave as she hurried down the foyer to the lift. Soon she was speeding along the street in a taxi, wishing she was back with her lover.

CHAPTER THIRTY-ONE

Victoria splayed her hand over the sheets to feel for the warm body beside her. Only lingering warmth and an indentation revealed that Abby had been there. She frowned and turned over to look. She listened for the sound of water spraying in the shower, but heard nothing. Abby must have left, her clothes were gone and Vic's were arranged neatly on the chair. She felt a twinge of petulance. Typically, Abby had disappeared like a will-o'-the-wisp. But any annoyance vanished as she remembered the night. Victoria smelt the sheets to drink in her lover's perfume and the languishing smell of sex. Abby was such an incredible lover, so receptive and passionate. She gave as generously as much as she received. Victoria's mouth set in a firm line. Now she'd had a taste of real love, she wasn't going back to her old life. She would just have to persuade Abby to live with her. It wasn't going to be easy. She had a thing about money.

With reluctance, Victoria heaved herself out of bed, wishing she could stay there in the warmth. After she showered, she noticed the note on the side table.

Good morning, honey.
I have to dash. I've got an appointment at nine with the accountant.
Would you like to come to Mum's for dinner tonight at six? She's
having a few friends over and I'd love you to meet everyone. Text me
if you're coming.
Love,
Abby xxxxx
PS I miss you already.

Victoria felt a zing of pure joy—she was going to see Abby
again tonight. Panic then bubbled. The mother hated her. She
suppressed her disquiet and sent a text to confirm the dinner
date before she went downstairs. Fiona was chatting with the
maid over coffee and the place was clean. Her assistant had that
smug face on again.

"Hi, Vic. You're up late."

Victoria flashed a bright smile and ignored the look. "Late
night. What's for breakfast, Sandy?"

The maid pointed to the stove. "Scrambled eggs are in the
saucepan. I'll put on a piece of toast. I was going to offer some
to your guest but she seemed to be in a hurry."

Victoria felt her face heat as she heard Fiona's titter. "That'll
be great. I'll make my coffee."

"Abby stayed, did she?"

Vic uttered a resigned groan. She may as well tell her,
because the Scot wouldn't let it go. "We made up. I'm going
over to meet her mother tonight."

Fiona's mouth formed into an O. "My, my. Things are
progressing."

"I'm a bit nervous actually. She doesn't like me."

"You'd better be charming. Take her some flowers and
chocolates. That'll help."

* * *

After she smoothed down her slacks, Victoria squeezed the box of chocolates under her arm, clutched the bunch of roses in one hand and pressed the bell with the other. Abby opened the door and gave Victoria an enthusiastic kiss. "You look terrific," she whispered.

Victoria gazed at her starry-eyed. "So do you. That's a pretty dress."

Abby laughed. "Hong Kong. Come in and meet the folks."

"One more kiss before we go in."

"No, I don't want to look rumpled."

"Just as well I've got my hands full or you wouldn't get away that quickly," Victoria muttered.

Abby patted her ass. "Huh! Get thee inside, stud."

Five older people and three women Abby's age were sitting in the room. Her mother was nowhere in sight. The other guests looked at her with interest. "This is Victoria Myers everyone." As Abby introduced her, Victoria began to wonder what she had told them about her. By the way they greeted her, she doubted anyone knew they were a couple. Judy Benton appeared from the kitchen with a plate of nibbles. She transferred the eats to her daughter to pass around, wiped her hands on her apron and nodded brusquely. "It was good of you to come, Ms Myers."

Victoria handed her the flowers and chocolates with a nervous cough. "A gift to show my appreciation for asking me tonight, Mrs Benton. And call me Vic, please."

Judy looked at her without warmth. "Thank you, Vic. There was no need to bring gifts. Now, have you met everyone?"

Vic nodded, suddenly tongue-tied. Damn, it was obvious Abby hadn't told her mother either.

"Vic was Abby's boss on her overseas trip." Judy called out to no one in particular.

At that snippet of information, everyone seemed to relax, which confirmed Victoria's suspicions. The night passed more pleasantly than she anticipated. The three younger women, Abby's friends, were great fun to be around. Once dinner was over, they rose to go and Abby pulled her onto the couch. "Vic will stay for another cup of coffee, Mum."

"You make it, dear. I'll show our guests out."

Victoria followed Abby into the kitchen. "You haven't told her yet, have you?"

"Not yet."

"Why not?"

Abby busied herself with the cups, not meeting her eye. "I'm trying to get the courage. I thought it better if we told her together."

Victoria stared at her incredulously. "You're going to make me damn well do it, aren't you?"

"Umm…we'll see."

"Sweetie, look at me. Aren't you?"

Abby pulled her sleeve with a nervous gesture. "Would you?"

"What do you want me to say? That we love each other."

Abby eyes widened. "Did you just say you loved me?"

Before Victoria could reply, Judy bustled into the room. "Coffee made yet?"

"Go into the lounge, Mum. I'll bring it in."

"Good, I'm ready to sit down." An awkward silence fell as Judy eyed Victoria, who had followed her from the kitchen and taken the seat opposite. "Abby said she enjoyed her time overseas. Thank you for looking after her."

"She was an excellent employee. It was a pleasure having her on the trip. It's a pity she doesn't want to join our company."

Judy brightened and warmth seeped into her voice. "That's nice to hear. She's always been a good girl."

At that moment Abby entered with the cups, handed one to Victoria and one to her mother.

"Put it beside me on the table, dear. My arthritis is playing up."

Victoria said with compassion, "How do you manage your pain, Mrs Benton?"

"Medication mostly."

"I've done some research and there are other ways to help."

Judy stared at her in surprise. "Some of the aids are expensive and it's difficult on my own. Abby does the best she can, but she can't stop working to look after me when I get a severe attack. The disability is something I've learnt to live with."

"It's good you won't have to worry in the future, isn't it? I've plenty of money to get you the best treatments and employ home help."

Judy blinked. "Excuse me? Why on earth would you do that?"

Victoria turned to peer at Abby and frowned. "Do you mean to tell me you haven't you told your mother yet?"

"Told me what?" said her mother sharply.

Victoria rolled her coffee cup in her hands. "I'm sorry, I thought you knew. I wouldn't have presumed to say what I did if I had realized you didn't. Would you like to tell her our good news or shall I, sweetie?"

"You do it, you're doing just fine," Abby whispered.

"Abby and I are in love and intend to live together."

For a second Judy Benton was silent, then she puffed up like a pigeon. "What did you say?"

Victoria swallowed, alarmed. "Um…Abby and I formed an attachment while overseas. We…we want to live together."

Judy plucked a piece of fluff off her sleeve, flicked it in the air and turned to her daughter. "Is that right, Abby? After what this woman did, you want to *live* with her?"

Victoria quailed. The mother made *live* sound worse than *murder*. They both looked at Abby who began to squirm under the scrutiny. For a moment she seemed poised to flee the room, but then she straightened and crossed her arms over her chest. It was a solid gesture, assertive rather than defiant. She looked her mother squarely in the eye. "That's right, Mum. She is the best thing that's ever happened to me and I love her dearly. I expect you to welcome her into your home and our family."

Judy appeared gobsmacked at first then sagged. It was a long anxious moment for Victoria before she turned to her with a nod. "I guess I haven't noticed my daughter is a mature woman. You and I will have to sit down and have a long talk, Vic. I have no intention of alienating my only child, so if she wants you then that's fine with me."

"Of course. I'll come over one day this week if that suits. Now I guess I'd better be off home."

Abby rose and collected the coffee cups. "Wait a minute and I'll come with you. I'll just clean the kitchen first."

"Leave them, dear. I can manage. I'll see you in the morning," said Judy with a wave of her hand.

Abby pulled her mother into a hug. "You're going to like her, Mum, but she can be a bit bossy sometimes." She reached for Victoria's hand. "Let's go."

Victoria eased the car into the traffic and glanced at Abby. She was leaning to the side, gazing out the window. "Penny for your thoughts," whispered Vic.

Abby's eyes brightened. "Oh, I was just thinking how much I love you, Victoria Myers."

"Me too. I'm head over heels and can't wait to get you in my life forever." Vic squeezed her knee. "That was a brave thing you did in there, Abby."

Abby chuckled. "Oh, yes. I've never stood up for myself before. Quite liberating really."

"It's a pity I have to work tomorrow or we could stay in all day. What're your plans?"

"I'm going to start painting again and I'm ready to start the first canvas." Abby reached over to massage her thigh. "Can you take a few weeks off next month?"

"I intend to wind down a lot now that I've got you. Where are we going?"

"Japan. It's to the opening of the Nippon Steel building—I want you to see the panels I painted for Akio. Then we're off for a holiday in the snow fields."

"Sounds good," said Victoria as she turned the car into the expressway to the city.

Abby chuckled. "Ever made love in a hot spring?"

EPILOGUE

Abby was nervous. After a year and a half, her first exhibition was ready for the grand opening. Thirty-one paintings in total, mostly of people she'd photographed on the Orianis trip. Portraits of subjects in their own environs; buskers, dancers, fishermen, stockmen, miners, steel mill workers; they were all there, immortalized on canvas. Jan kindly lent her commission of Malcolm as an exhibition piece for the foyer. But the last was yet to be unveiled. Her huge centrepiece for the night.

Victoria was a tower of strength as she organized the food and drinks. Abby paused to sweep her eyes over her, and arousal tingled her skin like a blanket of goose bumps. Even after eighteen months, she couldn't get enough of her. Victoria was dressed in *the* tuxedo and looked fantastic. She caught Abby's eye and gave a wide smile. Abby grinned, blew a kiss and mouthed, "Love you."

Guests began to trickle in. The canvases were arranged to be viewed individually, so they filled the walls of two rooms. The third, the smallest room, held the special painting. Abby supervised the hanging of it herself.

Fiona arrived on the arm of a tall bearded man and Abby nearly dropped her glass. "Meet Angus Campbell, Abby. He's a friend of that cousin of mine from Melbourne I found on the ancestry site." And to Abby's astonishment, she actually simpered. "Abby is a very dear friend of mine, Angus."

Victoria appeared at her side and whispered, "There goes my toaster, Fiona."

When Angus asked her with a broad Scottish brogue what she meant, Fiona huffed and dragged him away to look at the art. As the night wore on, Abby's face flushed with excitement as more red dots signifying sales were added to the title cards next to each painting.

And then it was time. The grand finale.

Abby led everybody into the third room and waited until they formed a semicircle to view her masterpiece. She slowly pulled away the drape. Her Archibald entry came into view, though the picture had been altered. No longer was it Victoria Myers, Ms Devil Incarnate,—no—the woman in the painting was Victoria Myers, Ms Sex Goddess. Abby had captured her in a moment of total intimacy, a portrait created out of passion and love. Vic sat there enriched in vibrant colours; her full lips pouted with desire, her eyes hooded in ecstasy and her face flushed with a delicate shade of erotic pink as she gazed out from the canvas.

Her mother took her arm while Fiona ushered the guests from the room and quietly closed the door. Abby looked at her in confusion. "Don't you like it, Mum?"

Judy patted her hand. "It's wonderful, dear, but I think you can keep that one for your bedroom."

Abby turned to look at Victoria. She was gazing at Abby with adoration, her face filled with love. She winked.

Bella Books, Inc.

Women. Books. Even Better Together.

P.O. Box 10543
Tallahassee, FL 32302

Phone: 800-729-4992
www.bellabooks.com